A MODERN DAY PLAGUE . . .
COULD IT EVER COME?

OR IS IT ALREADY HERE?

The Adjustment
A Novel

by Drew Rubin

Printed in the United States of America

PINE HILL PRESS, INC.
Freeman, S. Dak. 57029

Dedication

To my beautiful wife, Lisa. Ten years ago, I fell in love with you. This book represents the culmination of everything I have learned from you, with you, and because of you. You are my inspiration. You taught me what true unconditional love is. You gave me strength and hope when I had none. You have joyously celebrated my victories. Most of all, you love me the way I love you. I am so blessed to have found my soul mate. Without you, Lisa, I could never have written this book. I truly love you.

To my handsome son, Palmer. You have taught me more than I have taught you—love, patience, and trusting the process. It has been your smile that has set this book in motion. My dream, Palmer, is that some day you take up the work I have done and raise it to the next level. You will be a great leader. It has been pre-destined. Your greatness is exuded in your charisma. The world is yours—grab it and run with it, my bestest buddy. I love you.

Acknowledgments

There have been three people who have unconditionally supported me throughout the whole process of writing this book—my wife, my father, and Dr. Jim Dubel.

My wife is the best thing that has ever happened to me. From our magical first date to this very moment, I have grown more in love with her each day. Thank you, Lisa, for standing by me in this long and sometimes difficult journey.

My father has surprised me in the last 3-1/2 years since my son was born. He has been transformed before my eyes since Palmer's birth. And to witness this has been a special beauty in my life. But more than that, when my father said, "I can't believe this book was inside of you. It's the most amazing thing I've ever read." He did more for me in those two sentences than any praise he had ever given me in my life. Thank you, Dad. I never expected this kind of encouragement from you.

Dr. Jim Dubel, you've changed my life. You took a chance on me when nobody else would. You believed in me when I needed someone from outside my family to believe in me. Your neverending encouragement for this book has kept me going on this project in which I have taken tremendous criticism. When I was about to throw the manuscript into the fire only this past winter, you told me to keep on going and let innate lead the way. Your chiropractic weekend, New Beginnings, has renewed my faith in chiropractic and my faith in humanity, because it is the few who can change the many. "I love you because you love the things I love," as our mentor, B.J. Palmer, once said.

My special thanks to many important people in my life. To my great teachers and mentors, Dr. Sid Williams, Dr. Jim Sigafoose, and Dr. Dick Santo, your vision gave me my life's mission.

To all the readers of the original manuscript, thanks for your time and comments, Stanley and Charlotte Rubin (my mom and dad); Dr. Ken and Gloria Friedberg (my wife's mom and dad). My wonderful patients, Libby Anne Ripans, Debbie and Howie Altschuler, Patty Hassett and Jake Funicelli. To my great chiropractic assistants, Susan Evanella and Karen Jesson. To inspirational chiropractors, Dr. Dick Santo (whose tapes gave me the idea for this book), Dr. Jim Dubel, Dr. Bill Henry, Dr. Barbara Sanoudis, Dr. Bob Tarantino, Dr. D.D. Humber, Dr. Dave Schwartz and his wife, Marina. And to my bestest buddy in chiropractic, Dr. Brian Casey. Thanks, Brian, for forcing me to go to the Dynamic Essentials seminar. That got me back to why I became a chiropractor in the first place. And thanks to special readers, Neil Amdur, Brian Schiffler, Robert Cohen and Shelley O'Connor.

A grateful thank you to Captain Foreman Dowling, who gave me permission to use a picture of B.J. Palmer's hands as a prototype for the front cover. And a hearty thank you to Betty Hunt, who typed the manuscript, and braved my almost totally illegible handwriting.

To all my patients—I thank you, for there is a little bit of each of you in this book. To my first chiropractors, Dr. Ed Zawacki and Dr. Jeff Cantor—thanks for sharing chiropractic with me and for helping me to breathe again. I owe an asthma and allergy free life to you both.

And a final thank you to Tony Robbins, whose seminars and audio tapes have taught me the power of commitment, follow-through and living with passion.

Foreword

To have the privilege of contributing to Drew Rubin's book, *The Adjustment*, is one I truly cherish. In 1989 Drew and I graduated chiropractic school. We set off individually sharing a vision. A vision of a world free from suffering; a world of unlimited possibilities. We knew that we had a very special gift to offer our global community. The gift that we offered was one of health, vitality and truth. Our unique gift: Chiropractic. We knew that the recipients of this awesome gift could benefit in ways that would astound them. Every day, the members of our individual practices would prove us correct. People that were once skeptics, became ardent and loyal followers of the chiropractic lifestyle. For many of them, the results that they achieved via chiropractic were nothing short of miraculous.

And yet, in spite of the growing number of people that accepted this awesome gift as a natural part of their life, far too many still have not. The chains of fear coupled with blind adherence to antiquated ideas regarding health care have enslaved many to a life of pills, potions and unnecessary surgeries.

This is a book about the near-term and long-term future of health care. It is a book about history and the direction of the future, about the qualities and frames of mind that will sustain us as race of humans "being." It is a book about taking the blinders off, about seeing things whole and in the light of truth. But most of all, this is a book about change, change so rapid and so massive that it will have swept away nearly the entire foundation of modern medicine.

The plague of the future will be ignorance. The antidote, knowledge. Intuitively, most people understand the need for the change that is taking place in health care. Most of us know that we are straddling worlds between what has been and what will be. We know that the old rules no longer apply. Attitudes and behaviors have become unhinged from the "way we've always done things."

This novel is just that: "Novel." You are about to embark upon a journey. One that is firmly rooted in reality. An all too honest reality of what can happen when and if we choose to remain powerless and yield responsibility for our health.

Dr. Rubin and I have both had gifted lives. Maybe the greatest gift of all has been this: We have been allowed to immerse ourselves into the lives of so many patients, been allowed to lead them from chaos to order, and because of this, we've been able to see hope shining as clear as the risen sun on the horizon.

I am proud to call Drew Rubin my friend and I am honored to be on the same side as him. Like this book—he's the best.

—Tony Palermo, D.C.
President and Founder of
"Back to Basics"
Bethlehem, PA

Preface

I will never forget when I first got the idea. I was driving home from work one day in February of 1997, listening to an audio tape by Dr. Dick Santo, one of my chiropractic mentors. He was going on about how there are all these new antibiotic resistant bacteria and all these strange viruses cropping up around the world. And then he said, "One of these days there's going to be a plague in this country, and the only way it can be stopped is if everybody goes to a chiropractor and gets adjusted."

All of a sudden, my eyes bulged out and I slammed on the brakes and came screeching to a halt. I rewound the tape and listened to it again. " . . . the only thing that will stop the plague is if everybody gets adjusted." Ding, ding, ding, ding, ding. Oh, my God! Oh, my God! Oh, my God! I started babbling to myself as I scrambled for a pen and paper.

An entire book flashed before my eyes, everything in a matter of seconds. An entire story based on chiropractic saving the world from a plague as modern medicine experiences a total and complete collapse. I sat there stunned for a moment, the emergency flashers going, "Click, click. Click, click. Click, click," in an otherwise silent night. I started writing feverishly. After a few minutes I had the first ideas for the book scribbled across several sheets of paper.

From that night on, every time I sat down to write, I would put my pen down to the paper, it would start to move, and the next thing I knew, it was two hours later and the pen would stop. In December of 1997, the pen stopped moving and I had this book.

I looked at the almost 400 pages of manuscript and asked, what am I supposed to do with this? "Give it to the world," was the answer.

But I am not a writer, I'm a chiropractor. I don't know the first thing about writing a novel. I know about adjusting.

"Find a way," said the voice.

Prologue

May 4, 1997, 9:10 AM

The room started to shake.

While reaching for the keys, his hand shook so badly that he dropped them to the floor with a loud clunk.

Trying to pick up the keys, which, a few minutes before, would have been a simple task, now took several tries.

The shaking came to a halt as quickly as it had begun.

A wave of heat overtook him. In a split second, sweat formed around his scalp and his hair became instantly moistened. Looking down at the table, he saw the sweat dripping from his forehead and making a row of salt water beads along the wooden surface.

Looking up again and out the window, he sensed all the buildings beginning to shiver as his focus of the city was lost in a shimmering fog.

He tried to stand up and fell crashing to the floor like a lump of jello.

The shaking stopped again. The stained wooden floor had crumbs all over it and the bottom of the stove and the refrigerator needed some desperate cleaning.

He noticed that his legs weren't working, but his fever was so high that he didn't even think about panicking. He thought about water, about a tremendous thirst that had overtaken him. So he pulled himself, with his once strong arms, towards the kitchen sink.

He saw himself in a reflection in the stove, covered in sweat, his hair matted down, eyes bloodshot and puffy as the shakes started again.

He watched for a moment as his image blurred. The weight of his head became so heavy that his arms could not support himself. His head crashed to the wooden floor.

A searing pain emanated from his nose as the shaking stopped. He heard an ambulance outside and wondered if it was for him. He knew they knew all about this.

1

He strained to pull himself up toward the sink, using the kitchen cabinets. All he could think about was water.

He thrashed at the one piece faucet, and cool, clean water flowed out. Slowly, yearning to taste a sip of that cool, calm water, he lowered his face with open mouth toward the stream, the clear, filtered oasis.

As the cool water touched his lips, he felt his whole body calm down for a moment. He opened his mouth for the next sip, but before he could swallow, the sink was splashed in bright red as blood poured out of his mouth.

As he slid down the sink, down the cabinets, and onto the floor, he heard the door burst open.

"He's over there. Oh, my God!" yelled a burly man in a black suit and mirrored sunglasses.

Behind the man in the black suit, he saw two men dressed in white paramedic uniforms pulling a stretcher. The man in black pulled out his cell phone, speed dialed a number, and began talking rapidly with his back turned. The men in white picked him up, now covered in red, and placed him on the stretcher.

"Am I going to die?" he asked the men in white. "I don't want to die."

The two men looked at each other, looked at him, and then pulled the stretcher out of the apartment.

May 5, 1997, 7:25 PM

A small man with black horn-rimmed glasses stared at the computer monitor. An army of people stood behind him in total silence. Through the view cam in Clone #5's left eye, the men surrounding the monitor could see a kitchen cabinet. A circle of blood grew wider and wider as it cascaded from their experiment's mouth.

The little scientist sat there looking at the scene in utter disbelief. This was the seventh time this had happened in the last two days, and already an alarm was coming from Clone #2 in San Francisco.

An older gentleman broke the silence. He was a tall thin man with a mix of jet black and grey hair barely noticeable under the camouflage cap with the three red stars. "Should we just deactivate the other two remaining clones and call it a wash, doctor?"

"No, general," the little man retorted. He had spent so much government money and invested so much of his lifetime in this experiment that he wasn't about to quit now. "We have to glean all the information we can from this. Even though this is unpleasant, it is giving us vital data that can be helpful in the next phase."

"But they are suffering, aren't they? They do feel, just like we do?" asked another tall man in a highly decorated white uniform complete with white cap.

"It is for the better good of all mankind that we have come this far. This is acceptable, considering the importance of this matter. Besides, these are isolated incidents. They are only clones. They are expendable."

Chapter 1

July 23, 1997, 8:30 PM

I hadn't watched TV, let alone a speech by a President, in years. But as Jim Bouchard or Thomas Flemings, or whoever it was, analyzed the President's speech, I sat there pondering the strange deaths that my patients had been telling me about in the last few months. A number of my patients' friends and relatives who lived in New York City had contracted a disease and died within 48 hours.

The President had just declared a state of national urgency. He said that it was one step below emergency, which would cause the military to be brought into action. I guess Governor Alfonso's death the previous day had made the matter more critical. Prior to that time, deaths were being pooh-poohed as an hysterical reaction.

The phone rang.

Should I answer it? I asked myself.

The phone rang a third time. Something told me I had to get it and I picked it up.

"Dr. Adio?"

"Yes."

"This is Senator Bart Gallo's office. Please hold for Senator Gallo."

Hold for him? He wants to talk to me personally? Can't be . . .

"Dr. Adio?"

"Yes?"

"This is Bart Gallo, Senator from the great state of New Jersey."

"Yes sir," I said, excitedly. It was Senator Gallo! What do I say? "Ah, good evening, sir. Sorry about the Governor's passing."

"Yes, thank you. Did you watch the President's message tonight?" the Senator asked.

"Yes," I answered after a moment's hesitation. "Very sad that this could happen."

"Yes it is. You know Dr. Arthur Rifkin, don't you?"

"Yes, of course. My father-in-law's partner." Where is he going with this? I was introduced to the Senator at a function a long time ago but he couldn't possibly remember who I am.

"He recommended I call you. He says you are one of the few chiropractors he knows in New Jersey and one who seems to get good results."

"Well, I'm flattered. I love chiropractic and what it's done for me, my family and my patients."

"That's exactly why I'm calling. With the Governor's passing, this disease has taken on a whole new meaning. Let me ask you, have any of your patients contracted the disease that the President described?"

"No, sir. Not one."

"Do you find that odd?"

"No, sir. I expect that chiropractic patients should have a stronger immune system than the general population."

"Yes, I understand that. But this disease kills everybody it comes in contact with within 48 hours."

"Ah, what are you getting at, sir?"

"It seems, since the start of this epidemic, every person who has come in contact with the disease has died, with one exception. The ones under chiropractic care did not contract the disease."

"Really?"

"Yes, really. The Center for Disease Investigation and the National Medical Association are flatly denying that these facts are related, or that chiropractic has anything to do with their survival. But when I read the report with Arthur today after Governor Alfonso's funeral, he asked me to call you since you have no political affiliation and, hence, are, shall we say, 'safe' to talk to. Can I trust you on this, Dr. Adio?"

"Yes, of course, sir. What do you need me for?"

"Dr. Adio, the NMA is a very powerful organization. They don't particularly like chiropractors. Just do this, Dr. Adio, keep doing whatever it is you do to your people and get as many new patients as you can right now. Do not, under any circumstances, tell them what we discussed. I will keep in contact with you since I trust you and your position, or should I say, lack of position, in politics."

"Wait. You're telling me you finally figured out what chiropractic is and you don't want me to tell anybody?"

"That's not the point, Dr. Adio, and you know that. We can't say something that broad until we know for sure. I must go now."

"But, but, Senator . . . "

"Thank you, Dr. Adio, we'll be in touch."

"Yes, wait . . . " Click.

The dial tone seemed much louder than usual. Ellen, my wife, was standing next to me. We were married seven years ago, and she is more beautiful today than the day I married her. About 5' 4", slender, athletic, untamed dirty blonde hair. The only thing being a mother has done to her physically is to create barely noticeable circles under her eyes. In every other way, she is identical to the woman I met ten years ago when I was at Southern Chiropractic College in Atlanta and she was a junior at Georgia University.

Ellen was holding our son, B.J. Her mouth was wide open and her beautiful blue eyes were even wider. "Was that about what I think it was about?"

"Yeah. That was Senator Gallo. He got our number from Arthur Rifkin. He says chiropractic patients don't die from this disease."

"Senator Gallo? He called you? Chiropractic patients don't die from this disease? How did he come up with that?" asked Ellen.

"Well, he said everyone who has come in contact with a person who had this disease has died with one exception, those under chiropractic care. That's great news, but there's a problem."

"I can see lots of problems with this, Gary. What one problem are you thinking about?"

As she asked this, B.J., my precious little two year old (named after the developer of chiropractic, B.J. Palmer), squirmed out of Ellen's arms and jumped down to the floor. Everybody says B.J. and I look alike. I don't see how, with the exception of his curly brown hair and his hazel eyes. That's where it stops. He's got Ellen's facial coloration, her small nose and her beautifully shaped mouth. B.J. smiled and yelled, "Da, da, da, da, da," and ran away. His typical method of travel.

"The problem is that the Senator doesn't want me to tell anybody about this," I said, shaking my head. "He said we have to wait until they investigate this more."

"What? If this disease is as deadly as the Senator says, then there isn't much time to dilly-dally and do research."

"I'm not very good at math, but statistically speaking, it doesn't take the power of ten too long to get from hundreds to hundreds of millions," I said.

"If this thing spreads like wildfire, then we don't have much time at all."

7

"How long do you think?" I asked.

"It depends on how many chiropractic patients there are in this country," Ellen said.

"Well, studies show that the 55,000 chiropractors are taking care of 10% of the population. That makes 30 million or so patients. That ain't gonna do it."

Ellen and I looked at each other for a while. B.J. was running around us, oblivious to what was happening in the world. Probably better that way.

"Gary? Go on-line to the *Times Herald* website and see if we can find the latest headlines from the last few months. When did this start? Where did this come from? That's what I want to know."

I gestured that we all go into the den where our computer lay hidden beneath mounds of junk mail.

We put all the junk mail on the floor. "Let's recycle all of this," said Ellen. "We're never going to read it anyway."

I agreed as I typed in our password and sailed away into cyber space. A few moments later, we were at the *Times Herald* website, searching for the right topic to click onto.

"They have a huge list to select from," I said as I scrolled down.

"There, Gary. 'Top Stories of '97.'"

"Thanks," I said, and clicked in. From there I clicked onto "Top Health Related Stories" and pulled up today's headline:

NEW JERSEY GOVERNOR DIES SUDDENLY
FROM STRANGE NEW DISEASE
WHITE HOUSE RESPONSE TONIGHT AT 8 PM
NEW JERSEY POLITICIANS IN AN UPROAR

It even had tomorrow's headline:

PRESIDENT DECLARES STATE OF NATIONAL URGENCY
INVESTIGATION OF NEW DISEASE IS HEIGHTENED
AS NATION MOURNS DEATH OF NEW JERSEY GOVERNOR
RICHARD ALFONSO

I decided to go back a few months and went through April and May with nothing catching my eye. Then, I found this one on June 1st:

**NEW TYPE OF AIDS VIRUS FOUND IN NEW YORK CITY
RASH OF UNEXPLAINED DEATHS OF HOSPITAL
PERSONNEL IN MANHATTAN GENERAL,
INCLUDING SEVERAL DOCTORS**

A few days later, was this: June 6th

**TEN CITIES IN THE UNITED STATES REPORT POSSIBLE
NEW VIRULENT AIDS' SUPER VIRUS:
MAJOR HOSPITALS IN COUNTRY REPORT MULTIPLE
UNEXPLAINED DEATHS OF HOSPITAL PERSONNEL.**

"Think this is related, Ellen?" I asked.

"Could be. Keep on following the trend," she replied while feeding B.J. some applesauce and trying to pay attention.

There was nothing else like it as I scrolled quickly through the top headlines of each day. Then, on June 25th, came this one:

**PENTAGON SAYS SUPER-AIDS MAY BE GERM WARFARE.
WITH OVER 100 DEATHS IN ONE MONTH, MILITARY
TAKES OVER SEVERAL OF THE COUNTRY'S FINEST
HOSPITALS, CREATING QUARANTINE SECTIONS**

I turned to tell this to Ellen, but she was on the floor reading a book to B.J.

June 30th:

**"NO CAUSE FOR ALARM" SAYS SURGEON GENERAL.
"SUPER-AIDS HAS BEEN CONTAINED IN
THE HOSPITALS." OR HAS IT?**

I remember reading somewhere that when someone in a high place says, "There is no cause for alarm," there *is* cause for alarm. But the papers were quiet again until the middle of July.

"Look at this one, Ellen," I loudly said. She looked up from B.J.'s book.

July 14th:

**RETIRED MAJOR AND NOW NEW JERSEY GOVERNOR
RICHARD ALFONSO HEADS COMMITTEE ON SUPER-AIDS
AFTER HUNDREDS DIE AND MORE SUSPECTED ILL.**

Then on July 19th:

**THOUSANDS PROTEST AROUND MANHATTAN GENERAL,
HUNDREDS ARE ARRESTED, SCREAMING:
"WE WANT ANSWERS!"**

Then I knew why the Senator had called. Dr. Rifkin, my father-in-law's partner, was heavily entrenched in the politics of medicine. He had headed multiple fundraisers for Senator Gallo. But what do they want from me?

"What is this disease, anyway?" asked Ellen.

"It doesn't say," I answered. "But it certainly sounds like the next plague."

Chapter 2

One week later, I was sitting in the Senate Chambers in Washington, D.C. The Senator had called me again two nights before, personally, and asked me, or should I say, told me, to testify at a hearing conducted by the Senate Special Health Crisis Committee. What was I getting myself into? I should never have agreed to this. This double breasted, brown pin-striped suit is stiflingly hot, I thought. I've never liked wearing ties either—now I remember why.

The next comment snapped me out of my trance.

"Under the circumstances, considering national security, don't you think, Senator, that this should be a closed meeting?" asked Dr. Chapman, the assistant director of the CDI, a geeky looking guy in a very expensive suit.

Senator Gallo shook his head. "Dr. Chapman, chiropractic may be the link to saving the planet, and you want to close the meeting?"

"I know you are the Chairman of the Health and Human Welfare Committee, sir, but considering the strong implications regarding the welfare of our nation, I can assure you that we have everything under control and there will be no need for . . . "

"You have nothing under control!" yelled the Senator. "Millions of people's lives are at stake and you are still willing to hold on to your territorial complex. You are so ethnocentric, you can't even see the light shining in your face. Maybe you have to sit back on this one, Doctor, and let the chiropractors take control."

"But he's unqualified, sir! He's alternative."

"Who cares? If Jesus came down and laid his hands on people, would you call him a quack because he didn't have a medical degree? This is a national emergency. Get off your high horse and start this meeting."

Senator Gallo's voice resounded in the hall. There was dead silence after his words, except for the echoes that were heard repeatedly throughout the chamber.

"Yes, Senator. Dr. Block, would you begin please."

Dr. Chapman bit his lip. He was obviously not used to being treated that way.

"Good morning, Doctors, Chairman, Senators, Congressmen and women. Ladies and gentlemen, my name is Dr. Arnold Block." He was a broad shouldered, older gentleman, without a single hair on his head. "I'm the senior research officer at CDI in Atlanta, Georgia. The following information was an experiment performed in conjunction with the Pentagon and represents the highest national security."

He looked right at me when he said that, and paused. With no expression on his face, he went on. I knew what he meant.

"As you are aware, cloning became a reality in 1996 when, in Scotland, a scientist successfully cloned a sheep. Of course, immediately thereafter the CDI and the Pentagon stepped in to insure the safety of the free world, since the obvious implications of cloning human beings presented a major threat in the wrong hands.

"The Pentagon asked the CDI to begin research into cloning humans. Within a short time we had perfected the technique. The majority of these clones were deactivated shortly after their creation, but the most advanced clones were allowed to remain viable. Ten such clones existed. The next experiment was to put one clone in each of the following cities: New York, Boston, Philadelphia, Atlanta, Miami, Chicago, Dallas, Seattle, Los Angeles and San Francisco. Each one had multiple tracking devices implanted in him, including a video surveillance system that could be turned on and off at will by the CDI."

Dr. Block paused again. This time he took a deep breath and pursed his lips.

"Excuse me." He said, almost inaudibly. The doctor took a sip from the water glass, cleared his throat and continued. You could tell he was getting to the good part.

"So, the problem arose, when the clones were activated at their different sites in the different cities after exactly two days. Each one of them, without exception, broke out in a serious fever and shakes which we were able to detect with our equipment at the CDI. Within a twenty-four hour period, each clone was taken by special ambulance to the nearest military hospital under extremely guarded and secure conditions. Unfortunately, each clone was deactivated within 48 hours of arriving at the military hospital."

"Dr. Block, excuse me. What do you mean by 'activated' and 'deactivated'? And what time frame are we talking about?" asked

12

the senator seated next to Senator Gallo. I had been introduced to him earlier, but was so nervous I didn't remember his name.

"We had designed for national security to control the clones with a system for 'activating,' or turning them on and 'deactivating,' or turning them off, at the discretion of the CDI and the Pentagon. This way, if there were any problems that arose, such as this particular situation, we could deactivate the clones before the problems were heightened. The experiment began on May 1, 1997."

"Thank you, Dr. Block. Now, why did you have to deactivate the clones?" asked Senator Gallo.

"It seems, Senator, that the clones were not able to function in a regular crowded urban setting. We thought they were physically able to withstand the viral and bacterial environment of the urban population but instead they became susceptible to every virus and bacteria they came in contact with, much the way a full blown AIDS case will succumb to a simple cold."

He's beating around the bush, I thought to myself. I can't believe that he's not telling the whole story. I know there's something more.

"What did the clones die from that also killed the people who had come in contact with them? And the people in contact with those people, and so on?" asked the second senator.

"Uh, well, Senator, it seems that even upon deactivation, the clones were all carriers of all the viruses they had come in contact with. But it appears also that the combination of the viruses and the antibodies that the clones' immune systems created were so unexpectedly powerful that they actually mutated several diseases. That seems to be the cause of the unusual deaths associated with the clones' deactivation. The original name for the disease, Super AIDS, is actually inaccurate. Our researchers have concluded it is not in any way related to the AIDS virus."

"You're forgetting something, Dr. Block, aren't you?" asked Senator Gallo.

"Uh, sir?"

"The only survivors of the incidents were . . . "

"Oh, yes. The only people who survived were people whose spines were manipulated."

Manipulated. I hate that word. I wanted to speak up and say, "Chiropractors adjust spines. Used car salesmen manipulate." But I bit my tongue as the other senator, whose name I had forgotten, spoke.

"Yes, Doctor. And who are the physicians that performed the manipulation?"

"Well, it seems, Senator, that they were manipulated by various physicians across the country. It was not one doctor doing the manipulations, it was a multiple of different doctors in . . . "

"Dr. Block, what kind of doctor, please?" asked Senator Gallo, whose eyebrows were really creased now.

"Yes, of course. It was chiropractors, actually. It appears that of the 400 people involved, there were only 30 survivors, and the only thing that they had in common was that they each went to a chiropractor. We cannot figure out why this means anything, nevertheless, the medical community stands ready to study it at length to determine how spinal manipulation affected the survivors. For preliminary discussion, we have Dr. Lipke, a physical medicine specialist from Hamlett University."

What a nice looking guy. Really fit. Bet he's a runner.

"Thank you, Dr. Block. We at Hamlett Medical School believe that spinal manipulation could not be the only factor affecting all 30 survivors, which mandates that we study the survivors more carefully to determine other factors. There is no evidence that spinal manipulation would have any impact on the survivors with the exception of reducing lower back pain and other joint related problems. However, if, in fact, it becomes a necessity to administer spinal manipulation to the American public, we are prepared to set up a weekend class in every major city in the country, where we can discuss and disseminate the basics of spinal manipulation so that the medical community could, by Monday of the following week, be using this technique."

What? My eyes popped wide open, my heart pounded. I broke out in a cold sweat. These bastards! I used every ounce of control I had not to scream out at these CDI doctors. They think they can learn in a weekend what it takes four years to learn and years of practice to master? These damned . . . the Senator broke in on my mental gymnastics.

"Dr. Lipke. You mean to tell me that you think by training medical doctors you could mobilize an army of physicians prepared to do this work in a weekend?"

"Yes, Senator Gallo. Yes, of course. Manipulation is under the scope of our practice, even though it was never taught in any of our schools. But being that it involves relatively simple procedures, it

14

could be easily taught in a weekend. We feel that 12 hours training is sufficient to produce an effective mastery of . . . "

"Mastery?" yelled Senator Gallo.

"Well, relative mastery, of course. It would take a few weeks to perfect."

"Perfect? Mastery? You must be kidding. A chiropractor like Dr. Adio right here takes four years to learn this, and you want to teach it in a weekend?"

"Well, Senator Gallo, we have all had basic training. It's just a matter of learning the technique of manipulation, which cannot be that hard."

My eyes were crossing and I was gritting my teeth. Control yourself, Gary. Deep breaths, take deep breaths.

"So you feel confident you could do the same job as a chiropractor with only one weekend of training?" the Senator asked.

"Yes, absolutely, Senator. We are the primary caregivers in this country and it would be just another adjunct at our disposal."

"So," Senator Gallo interjected, "if you want a highly technical military operation performed with a high degree of national security, you wouldn't ask the Navy Seals, the most highly trained military unit in the United States to perform it. You would train a couple of security officers in a weekend and have them get involved. They both carry guns, but one is the most highly trained personnel in the country, the other is an average security officer. Who would you want to rescue hostages from Saddam Hussein?"

A hush fell over the chamber. The Senator turned to me.

"Dr. Adio. You've been asked here as a matter of national security. Can you tell me the answer to that question?" asked Senator Gallo.

"Yes, Senator Gallo, I can answer that question for you," I said, nervously at first. "You want the best, most highly trained individuals to perform your rescue mission. And that's what chiropractic is prepared to do for you."

I focused right at Dr. Block and Dr. Lipke as they unsuccessfully tried to hide their attention. They averted their eyes and the sweat beginning to bead upon their foreheads was clearly visible.

"Thank you," Senator Gallo loudly replied. "Why do you suppose those 30 people who were in contact with the clones survived? Can you give me the chiropractic explanation?"

"Yes, sir," I answered, gaining some composure. "Chiropractic works because it follows a natural law. One that has been operat-

15

ing since the beginning of time. There is an intelligence that runs the Universe and that same intelligence runs us. The master communication system of the body, which is the brain, spinal cord and nerves that come from the spine, allows that intelligence to communicate without interference. If the body has no interference, then the body runs at 100% of its potential.

"Simply put, if your arm was a hose," I said, looking right at Dr. Block, "and I stepped on it, what would happen to the water?" I asked.

Dr. Block regarded me silently.

"Dr. Block, what would happen to the water if I stepped on the hose?"

"It would stop, of course. What has that got to do with anything? You are an untrained, uneducated pseudo-doctor. You have a limited license to practice your own brand of witchcraft, and . . . "

"Enough!" Senator Gallo yelled in such a loud voice everyone jumped in their seats. "Keep your ego out of this, Dr. Block. Please continue, Dr. Adio."

"Thank you, Senator." I was so glad to have someone on my side. "So the water stops when the pressure is put on the hose. Well, if you put pressure on the body's communication system, the nerve flow is reduced. A chiropractor's job is to find that pressure, which we call a spinal subluxation, and remove it to allow the body to return to 100% of its potential. Once at 100%, the chiropractor helps keep the communication system at 100%, thereby building a stronger body."

"Has any of this been proven?" asked Dr. Block.

"Yes, is there any research substantiating your position, Dr. Adio?" asked Dr. Lipke.

"Oh, come on. You know as well as I the amount of research there is linking the immune system to the nervous system. There's a whole branch of science called neuro-immunology that has been studying this recently. The latest medical and chiropractic journals are filled with references to how the nervous system and immune system work hand in hand," I answered.

I took a breath in, and decided to throw a wrench into their line of reasoning.

"Don't you believe in chiropractic, doctors?" I asked. They seemed quite surprised by the question.

Dr. Block answered, "Well, honestly, no. I do not, Dr. Adio. I believe in the power of medicine."

16

"Do you believe in gravity?" I responded. He looked at me as if I had two heads and had just landed from Mars.

"What did you ask?" said Dr. Block.

"Do you believe in gravity?" I repeated.

"Well, of course. Gravity is a natural law of physics."

"If I dropped my pen, what would it do?" I asked.

"What are you getting at, Dr. Adio?" Dr. Block was getting annoyed.

"Please answer the question, Dr. Block, you'll see. What happens when I drop my pen, where does it go?"

"It drops down to the ground."

"And if I drop it again, it drops again. And if I drop it tomorrow, it still drops."

"What are you trying to say, Dr. Adio?"

"Chiropractic is a law, just like gravity. It works whether you believe it or not. If you decided you didn't like the law of gravity, it wouldn't matter. If you dropped a pen, it would fall, no matter what. The same with chiropractic—it works no matter what."

"And more importantly are the miracles. I have a large family practice back home, and whether you believe it or not, I've seen chiropractic work in cases that were deemed hopeless. And I'm not a little isolated island to myself. There are 55,000 of us in the United States alone who get spectacular results and have done so for over a hundred years. Chiropractic works because it does. No one can refute it under any circumstances.

"Now, there's a fundamental difference between the medical approach and the chiropractic approach. You treat symptoms, we don't. Chiropractic is not being asked to treat the victims of the virus, rather we are being asked to keep the country's immune system at its peak potential so Americans can fight off the disease naturally. That is how the hospital personnel who are chiropractic patients survived this virus. Their immune systems had no interference, so this crazy virus couldn't take hold in their bodies. Natural immunity by inner strength. Inner strength provided by chiropractic."

Dr. Block couldn't take it.

"I have personally taken care of many cases in which chiropractors have actually harmed or seriously disabled the patient. And I know I speak for my colleagues in saying that we have all seen chiropractic malpractice. Chiropractic is, in my opinion, unscientific and dangerous."

"Chiropractic failures? Your brand of health care kills hundreds of thousands of people each year. An average of 106,000 people died last year because of prescription drug reactions. That makes you one of the top six leading causes of death in the country, behind heart disease, cancer, and diabetes. That number is according to a recent article in your own *Journal of the National Medical Association*. Now, if chiropractic killed 106,000 people last year, where would we be? That's right, off the face of the earth. You tell me what's dangerous and what's not."

"Your simplistic explanations amuse me," said Dr. Block. "And that is precisely my issue with chiropractic. You make it sound so simple."

"Exactly. It is simple. Why is complex so good? Find the bone out of alignment that is affecting the nerve, which we call a subluxation, and put it back in alignment. Then stand back and watch the body do its own work. Why is that such a problem for you? Why do Doctors Bernie Segal, Deepak Chopra, Larry Dossey and Andrew Weil make sense, and chiropractic does not? What are you so afraid of?"

"First," Dr. Lipke answered, "those 'doctors' you mentioned are more best selling authors than practicing physicians. Second, what am I afraid of? I'm afraid for the general public which can easily be swayed by a smooth talker like you. People out there, even before all this happened, were searching for something, anything to hold on to. Along comes you with your lies and your charisma and they fall for it because you make it sound so easy. How many patients of chiropractors have suffered because of delayed medical treatment is impossible to say, but I know in my office I see it every day."

I interrupted, "Dr. Lipke, I don't want to keep bringing this up, but I see patients in my office every day and ask the same question. Why wouldn't the doctor just say, 'This approach isn't working. Why don't you try chiropractic for awhile and, if it doesn't work, then come back?' Why can't we be in this together in peace? We are all doing this for the better good of mankind. You know as well as I that chiropractic is safe and effective. You can't deny it anymore. Why can't we just cooperate and help the people instead of fighting ourselves in this one upmanship? Yes, there are chiropractic failures. Yes, there are medical failures. But so what? We've got to help the people and chiropractic is ready to do it right now, with no additional training needed. We are ready now. But if we keep on fighting, more people will keep on dying needlessly. You deal with the emergencies, we'll deal with the general population. Let's work together for a change."

There was silence again.

I knew the task before us was big, but I wasn't really prepared for how big.

Chapter 3

I also wasn't prepared for the press that flocked along the stairs of the Capitol. Nobody warned me a few days previously when Senator Gallo had asked me to come do this, that they would be like vultures just waiting for me to drop my defenses so they could attack. How did they know my name?

I saw them as I opened the huge, heavy doors of the Capitol Building. I probably should have stopped, closed the doors, and turned the other way, but I didn't. For whatever reason, I kept walking down the stairs toward them. They covered the bottom half of the long cement steps and came at me like dozens of amateur fencers practicing the *en garde* position.

"Dr. Adio! Dr. Adio! Dr. Adio! Dr. Adio! Dr. Adio! Dr. Adio!" everyone was saying my name at once trying to get my attention. They swarmed me, engulfed me while microphones were thrust in my face. Dozens of questions were asked of me but I only heard one in its entirety and I stopped to answer it.

"Did you have to sleep with anyone to get your position?"

You can see why I stopped. I looked at the young woman, wearing a typical long overcoat that basic reporters wear with very dark sunglasses that hid her eyes.

"Yes, I did," I replied loudly.

The crowd of reporters became suddenly silent. I paused and said, "I slept with my wife. Any other intelligent questions?"

"Dr. Adio, can chiropractic really save the world?" was the next question I heard completely. I couldn't tell where it came from, somewhere toward my left. I turned toward the questioner.

"Chiropractic has been trying to save the world since it began in 1895. When the discoverer of chiropractic, D.D. Palmer, and the developer of chiropractic, his son, B.J. Palmer, realized what they had in their hands, they knew it would change the world. There was one problem, though. D.D. and B.J. Palmer were reviving an almost extinct idea called vitalism—that man is a part of the bigger picture, that he is controlled by a force greater than ourselves. They believed that man the physical and man the spiritual must be united to create the healthiest possible person. You must look at the whole body when dealing with a man or woman, not just a part.

"Medicine has thought for too long that the whole is equal to the sum of its parts, but that's not true. The whole is equal to more than the sum of its parts, because the force that creates us—call it God, or Nature, or whatever—creates something much greater than a liver or a kidney or a heart. And if anything interferes with the brain's ability to keep the body connected, then the body's magnificence falters and the more it weakens the more problems we have. Chiropractic is the reconnection—reconnecting the parts to the whole. Yes, chiropractic can save the world."

"Save the world from what, Dr. Adio?" a reporter asked sarcastically.

"Save us from back pain?" asked another reporter.

"What was discussed in the chamber?" was another question. "Is this Super AIDS really a killer plague out there? And how can a 'back cracker' help stop the disease?"

"Okay, here's the deal," I replied. "This disease everybody's been talking about since May. . . . .it seems everyone who comes in contact with infected people contracted the disease. Only the people under chiropractic care survived, all others perished. Luckily the scientists noticed this about the survivors, and now it's my job to help get chiropractic to everybody, not just people with back pain.

"So you have two issues that you can all assist with. Are you ready to help?" I asked loudly. But the enthusiastic "Yes" I expected didn't happen. They all looked at me as if I were invisible.

"We don't understand the connection between chiropractic and saving the world." It was the same voice who had asked the good question moments before. The reporter was now right in front of me, wearing dark glasses and a long overcoat.

"Rick? Rick Lord? Oh my gosh! I haven't seen you since Tony's wedding. Weren't you a business major?" We hugged as old friends do. Rick and I graduated from New York State University together in 1985. He was Uncle Thomas' roommate in our senior year. His tight curly brown hair hadn't changed a bit, except for a touch of gray here and there.

"Yes, slight career change. But seriously, Gary, as old friends, will you tell me the connection? We'd all like to know."

"Okay, here's chiropractic in thirty seconds. Here's your brain, Rick, and your brain sends information down the spine and out the nerves. This is the master communication system of the body and as long as nothing blocks the system, everything works perfectly. But if a spinal bone goes out of alignment, which is a very common thing, then that creates a blockage to this communication system. The chiropractor's job is to unblock the blockage and return the system to a hundred percent. When it runs at less than a hundred percent, it affects everything, not just whether or not you're in pain. All the organs of the body, especially the immune system, are tied into the spine. So if there is less than a hundred percent communication, then there will be less than one hundred percent immune function. Only a chiropractor is trained to locate and correct this problem, called a vertebral subluxation. And here's the key, subluxations do not always cause symptoms, just like a cavity which takes years to build before you feel any pain. Dentists find cavities before they cause massive problems. Chiropractors find subluxations."

"Do you see now how important it is that every spine in America be checked for this blockage?" I heard dozens of reporters respond, "Yes."

Rick asked, "So how can we help you?"

"Number one, I need the press to promote what I just said, with no opinions. I don't care whether or not you believe what I said, this is a national emergency. So leave your opinions for when this is over. I need you, the press, to get the people into chiropractic offices now.

"Number two, I need you to reach the chiropractors too, and tell them that this is the moment we've been waiting for. Time to put over 100 years of chiropractic to the test. We'll all have to open early and close late and miss lunches and work weekends until this blows over. But I need you to reach them and say, 'Drop our differences, and let's work for one thing, the welfare of our country.' Tell all the chiropractors that we'll be on WBC News special edition Saturday night at seven o'clock to explain specifically to the chiropractors themselves what the next step is, although the public is encouraged to watch it also. Instead of trying to organize a seminar, we're going to go into each and every chiropractor's house via the TV."

The questions came roaring in. I heard ones like, "Isn't there a drug that we can take? Isn't there a vaccine? How can chiropractic help this? Isn't chiropractic for back aches?" But the one I answered was: "I'm not going to a chiropractor. Aren't they just back crackers?"

"Chiropractic doesn't cure disease. It doesn't cure anything. Chiropractic's goal is not to cure people with this disease, but to prevent them from getting it in the first place by boosting their own natural immune defense system. We work with getting the body operating so efficiently that a disease can't take root in your system. The basic premise . . . "

"Excuse me, Doctor, but I think you are full of you-know-what. I think I'd rather hear the final word from the senators themselves, or from the M.D.'s that were in there," another reporter said.

Unfortunately, I heard a lot of "Yes's" and "Me too's" from the crowd of reporters.

"Fine. They will confirm what I said to be true. Please, I beg of you, this country needs you to do the right thing. For once, stop your negativity and sensationalism and just do what is right for the country."

"Is this some ploy by the chiropractors to build up your businesses?" I heard.

"That's enough. No further questions, please. For those who took me seriously, I thank you and so does your country."

I put my arm around Rick, who was still writing feverishly, and whispered to him, "Do you want to go for lunch? I'll tell you everything."

His pencil stopped moving and he looked up at me and said, with a smile crossing his face, "Not lunch, dinner. I've got to get this into the paper first."

"Will you be done by three o'clock? I'm catching the six o'clock back to Newark."

"I'll be done. Where do we meet."

"Oh, you'll love this place." I wrote down the address on the back of my card and gave it to Rick. "See you at three."

Chapter 4

"I cannot believe you have taken me to a place called 'Eat Your Vegetables'!" said Rick as we sat down in a very plain, rustic restaurant. "If you'd told me this, I would have said, 'No.'"

"Yeah, yeah. Suffer. For a change you'll have to eat vegetarian food," I laughed. "You won't die from such healthy stuff."

"Yes, but I may gag," answered Rick. "I'm a meat and potatoes and more meat kind of man."

"I'm sure your heart really appreciates that," I said sarcastically.

"Listen, I didn't go to dinner with you so you could tell me all the downfalls of my carnivorous behavior. How the hell did you get involved in all this?" asked Rick.

"You mean, being a vegetarian? Or being here in Washington?"

"To be honest, Gary, your being a vegetarian is not exactly front page news. We can do a whole article on you and how much you've changed since your college days after you and your chiro buddies save the world. Now tell me exactly why you're here and why you're telling me."

"Rick, I trust you. You and I hung out a lot during our student years. I don't know if you believe in chiropractic or not, but I know you will print the truth, and I'm sure you will go to a chiropractor once you've heard all that I have to say."

"How do you know I'll print the truth? You haven't seen me in years and I wasn't Mr. Goody Two Shoes back then either," exclaimed Rick.

"I know you will print the truth because I know you know what's right in your heart. We don't have the luxury of time on our side. There's not a year to dilly dally and banter and then come out with an apology headline like, 'Chiropractors Were Right, M.D.'s Were Wrong. Six Million Died Because of Killer Disease. Go To Chiropractors Now.' Millions will be dead, Rick, because they weren't told the truth. Unless you tell it, it will be too late."

"Do you know what kind of fiasco it's going to be in tomorrow's paper or tonight's news? Do you know what you have created?" asked Rick.

"What I have created! Hold on, this is a government mess up, not mine. Chiropractic is in a position to help change that which was messed up by the government, and it's the journalists and newscasters choice as to how they want to position themselves."

"Yes, that may be true, but you are now the national poster child for chiropractic. You've got to assume some responsibility. Now tell me how you got involved, anyway." Rick took out his pen and pad and suddenly his face changed to a much more business like look.

"Well, I'm not politically connected in chiropractic, but my father-in-law's partner is. He knows Senator Gallo and is working with him. Senator Gallo is the head of the Health and Human Resource Committee and, while talking to my father-in-law's partner, Dr. Rifkin, my name was mentioned. The next thing I knew, the phone rang and it was Senator Gallo. He wanted someone with no affiliation so he could get an unbiased opinion. I didn't expect this or anticipate it, or know really what I was getting myself into. But now I'm into it, and I will take the bull by the horns and run with it."

Rick stared at me for a while. The silence, though, was not uncomfortable. It was calm. It was as if he was reading my mind. He lifted his eyes, put his right hand on his chin and said, "I believe you, Gary. For some reason I believe you and believe in you. I'm going to take a leap of faith here that I don't usually do, but this time I'm going to follow my instincts."

He paused for a moment, his hand still under his chin, took a deep breath and sighed. "Can chiropractic really save the world, Gary? Is it as bad as they say?"

"Yes, Rick, chiropractic will save the world. And yes, it is as bad as they say. Worse. It's our worst nightmare and it's the fault of a few crazy doctors and scientists. And what's even more scary is that they would rather have thousands die than admit that chiropractic can help. That blows me away."

"What do you mean? What went on inside those Senate chambers today?" asked Rick.

"Well, to make a long story short, the facts are that the government made some human clones and placed one each in ten major cities. They were highly monitored with video and audio surveillance and some sort of apparatus that measured their heart rate, blood pressure, temperature, etc. But they all malfunctioned, somehow, within a few days and came down with some weird disease that killed them and everybody who came in contact with them. All the ambulance crews, nurses, doctors, etc. Everybody. Except those people who were under regular chiropractic care. That's the whole mess, in thirty seconds."

Rick was face down, writing like crazy. He looked up at me with his eyes popping out wildly and said, "You mean to tell me that this all came about because of some clones?"

I sighed. "Yes, Rick, yes. I'm sorry to say that our tax dollars caused this disease. Some day people will learn that we can't fool with God's perfection."

"But, but, but . . . how could the clones malfunction and catch a disease that's so deadly? Aren't they exact duplicates of a person? I mean, where did this disease come from?"

I noticed a little commotion at the front door. It sounded like a large group of people were coming in so I turned towards my right to see what was happening. I saw about 20 people in overcoats carrying pads of paper and holding tape recorders.

"Damn, they found us," Rick said quietly. "Answer the question and we'll get out of here."

"That's the big problem, Rick. They didn't say where the disease came from. That makes me very suspicious. It's your job as an investigative reporter to find that answer."

By now the group had spotted us and was coming our way.

Rick said softly, "I will print everything you said on the steps of the Capitol, Gary. I will run an exclusive on what we just talked about, and I'll try to get everybody I know to work on it if you will talk to only me about the inside stuff, okay Gary?"

"You have my word, Rick."

"Fancy meeting you here," said one reporter.

"What have you been discussing?" asked another. "Dr. Adio, is there any statement you'd like to make right now?"

"Yes, there is." Everyone was silent. "Number one, you just interrupted a meal with my old friend Rick. We went to college together. Number two, who wants to get a chiropractic adjustment?"

"What? Here? Where?"

"Yes, why not? There's no better time than the present. Who's first?"

Rick stood up and said, "I am, Gary. Will you please adjust me?"

"It will be my pleasure, Rick, thank you. Sit down here." I pointed out a chair next to our booth. Rick sat down and I stood to his left as I felt his neck with my right hand. A crowd gathered around us.

"Chiropractic works like this." There were about 60 people standing around us by then, including waiters, waitresses, the maitre d', and people who were dining in the restaurant.

"The brain is here inside the head."

"Not in Rick's case!" someone yelled out. Everyone laughed.

"Well, imagine it was here anyway. The brain sends the message down the spine and out the nerves. That is the master communication system of the body. As long as this system works perfectly, you work perfectly. If there is a blockage in the system, then the communication system is down. If that happens, the body malfunctions. A chiropractor's job is to remove the blockage, which we call a subluxation, and allow the system to work at a hundred percent. Got it?"

"It's that simple?" someone asked from behind me.

I turned around, "Yes, it's that simple. Chiropractors take nothing from the body and put nothing into the body. We work with the body's own healing powers to allow it to repair itself naturally with no interference."

"Why is this communication system so important?" a reporter asked to my left.

"Well, imagine you tried to call work and said, 'Hi, it's Joe. Have I got a story for you,' and all they heard on the other side of the phone was mumbled, garbled voices. So you hung up and called back, and that's all they hear again. So you call again and again and all they hear is mumbling. Can you tell your story to your boss that way?"

"No," he answered, and he looked genuinely intrigued.

"That's what happens when a spinal bone is out of alignment, or subluxated. Your body asks the brain about something, but it can't understand the brain's answer. The body is saying, 'What do we do down here?' and all it hears from the brain is, 'Mmmm ummm phhhf.' Do you see how this can cause a malfunction in your body?"

"Yes sir, but how do you fix it?" asked the reporter with the intrigued look. He even took his sunglasses off and ran his hand through his thinning hair.

"By gently adjusting or moving that spinal bone back into alignment with my hands, a closed nerve channel reopens. If you step on a garden hose, what happens to the water?"

28

"It stops," Rick said.

"Exactly. And if you take your foot off the hose, what happens?"

"It flows again," said Rick. He continued, "So, Gary, the adjustment takes the pressure off your nerves and allows them to flow normally again."

"I think you've got it," I smiled, with a little Cockney accent. "So are you ready for your first adjustment, Rick?"

"Yes, but will it hurt?" he asked.

"No, it will not hurt. As a matter of fact, it will feel really good. You may or may not hear any noise, like a popping or clicking as the bones move back into alignment. Whether you hear a noise or not doesn't matter, the key is the direction. My goal is to get the bone moving in the right direction. Not to make a lot of noise. Okay, Rick?"

"Yes, Gary, I trust you."

"Okay. Let me feel your neck first and see if I find a bone out of alignment. " I felt an obvious muscle spasm in the top right part of his neck.

"Do you feel how the left side is much softer than the right, Rick?"

"Yes, I do. Is that it?" asked Rick.

"Yep. Here is a bone out of alignment, or subluxation. Now I will give you a gentle, specific, loving adjustment." And ever so gently, I cradled his neck in my hand and gently turned his head. There was a muffled popping sound as the bone went back into the proper alignment.

"Wow! That felt good. What was I so scared about?" exclaimed Rick.

"The unknown. Everyone tends to have fear of the unknown to some extent. Plus all the negative propaganda that's been written about chiropractic over the years doesn't help. But now you know the truth."

"Can I have an adjustment, please?" asked the reporter with the thinning hair.

"Absolutely," I said. "Thank you, Rick. Thank you for helping me get this message out."

I put my hand on his shoulder. "It's not going to be easy, but in the end the rewards will greatly out weigh the cost."

Rick got up from his chair, turned towards me with a knowing smile and a brightness in his eyes. The brightness was the loving side of him that was released by the adjustment. I see it hundreds of times each week in the eyes of my patients. Rick and I embraced tightly as long lost friends getting back together for a higher purpose.

"Rick, everything you've ever done has led you up to this point. You have chosen the right path. The path of truth, the path of love."

"Yes, I know you are right, Gary," he said as we parted from our embrace. "Go adjust everybody you meet, and I'll talk to you tomorrow."

I turned to the man seated now in front of me. "Have you ever been adjusted before?" I asked him.

"No," he said, "but I trust you after what I saw you did to Rick."

And so from there I adjusted practically everybody in that restaurant. All the reporters, the waiters, the waitresses, the maitre' d, the customers, the cashier, the cooks and the bus boys. I adjusted a delivery man, a mail woman and someone who walked in to pick up a take out order. No one knew what importance that adjustment would have on their lives in the next few weeks. They just lined up, one by one, sitting down and asking for a gentle, specific, loving adjustment. They didn't tell me about their neck aches or back aches or much of anything, actually. They didn't think about it. They all sat down kind of silently and I felt their necks, asked them if they felt that bone out of alignment, and adjusted them.

Each person, when we were done, got up and hugged me and the next person would sit down. And so it went for an hour. It was a magical moment that I'll always cherish because, during the next few days, the magic was replaced by desperation as the effects of the disease began to snowball.

Chapter 5

I felt very evangelical after that 'Eat Your Vegetables' adjustment marathon, as if I then had to bring the adjustment to everybody I came in contact with. So I adjusted the taxi driver and the bellhops at the airport. My plane was scheduled to take off in a few minutes as I ran through the airport and made my way to the gate as they were announcing the final boarding call.

After I adjusted the three ticketing agents and was running up the jetway to the plane, I realized that nobody refused an adjustment. It was as if I was so on purpose that every person felt the energy and wanted to get adjusted.

I sat down and actually felt upset that there was no one sitting next to me. I wanted to tell everybody about getting adjusted but realized I would have to wait until we took off. Meanwhile, I just sat there reflecting on my life and how it had led me in this direction. I had never asked to be here in this position, but somehow or other it was meant to be. I thought about my wife, Ellen, and son, B.J., about how supportive they have always been. I knew that they would help me in the monumental task yet ahead. In the few hours since the meeting in the Senate Chambers, a lot had happened.

As I sat there on the plane, I leaned my head against the back of the chair, closed my eyes and continued to think about my life. I had always been on sort of a mission, as a chiropractor. I was one of those miracle cases that you see as the patient of the month on the wall of a chiropractic waiting room. "Asthma and Allergies Disappear After Going to a Chiropractor," would have been the headline.

God, that was 15 years ago, I thought. For the 15 years before that, before I found chiropractic, I popped asthma medication like Theophylline and Slo-bid, and puffed on inhalers like Proventil. Took all kinds of allergy medication, like Actifed and Sudafed and Tavist. I used to need bottles and bottles of Neosynephrine. I was a sick kid, from age five to age 20. Man, was I sick. Nothing seemed to help me.

I remember being 20 years old and in college with Rick living across the hall from me. I was pre-med, since I had spent so much

31

time in and out of doctors' offices, and I figured I knew most of the stuff already. Then fortune rang my bell in the form of a serendipitous event—my mother began going to a chiropractor.

She had experienced back pain for years on and off and finally it was so bad that one of her friends in her office told her to stop complaining and go see her chiropractor.

"He's right down the road from the office, so you've got no excuse," she said to her.

Dr. Ned starting talking to my mom about chiropractic and telling her that it was more than just about back pain.

"Yes, it works wonders for back pain, headaches and neck pain, but that's just a little example of what chiropractic can do. That's just the tip of the iceberg. The nerves in your spine go everywhere, to every organ, muscle and tissue in your body, including the heart, the liver, the lungs, everything."

My mom said, "Stop. Did you say lungs?"

Dr. Ned told her, "Of course. Everywhere. Every organ, including the lungs."

So guess who got a phone call that night. My mom told me, "You have to see this chiropractor."

I told her, "But mom, I don't have back pain."

She told me that the spine does a lot more than just take care of your back.

"You're my son. Make an appointment."

Fine. I did so, just to satisfy my mother. Little did I know that would be the day that changed my life. We sat down in Dr. Ned's reception area, my mom and I and another new patient. Dr. Ned proceeded to talk for about a half hour or so about how amazing chiropractic was. He read many of his patients' testimonials, each one seeming to be a miracle healing.

I was impressed. Then he pointed his finger at me and said, "And if you have asthma and allergies and there's a bone in your spine blocking the energy going from your brain down to your lungs, you won't be able to breathe right. Remove the blockage, and you will breathe better."

Up until that point, the best news I had ever heard about my asthma was, "We have a new medication for you. It's stronger and better." It seemed I was destined for a life of daily drug taking and inhaler puffing. This was not what I wanted for my life. I didn't have any dreams or visions of my future because I was so afraid of what it might look like. And then some wacko was telling me I might be able to breathe better.

But . . . he gave me hope. For the first time in my life, someone gave me hope. Hope that I could breathe like everybody else.

He asked me, "If everybody breathes the same air, how come you have allergies and asthma and I don't?"

Good question. I had never thought of it that way. The problem wasn't out there somewhere, it was in me. In my spine. Something he called a subluxation. It made sense to me and gave me hope.

I gave it a shot (no pun intended). And in three months my asthma and allergies were completely gone! I had suffered for 15 years and in three months they were history. Gone! Bing! Instant career change! I was now pre-chiropractic and, as they say, the rest is history.

I opened my eyes with a jolt as we were taking off. The sudden acceleration did it to me every time. In a few minutes we were leveled off and the pilot announced that we could walk around the cabin. An attractive flight attendant with brown hair asked me if I would like a bountiful meal of peanuts, pretzels and soda.

"Soda? That stuff could take the paint off a car! How about some bottled water?" I replied.

"What are you, a health nut?" she laughed.

"No, I'm a chiropractor. Would you like to get adjusted?"

"Sure. Thanks," she said, a little surprised.

So she sat down and I adjusted her neck. I then asked, "Would any other crew members or the pilots like to be adjusted?"

She ran up to first class and went to the cockpit. The next thing I know, I was being motioned to come up. I adjusted three other flight attendants on my way to the cockpit.

"Thank you so much, that felt great," said one flight attendant.

"Thank you, it's been a while since my last adjustment," said another.

"I never was adjusted before. That was so gentle, so relaxing. Thank you," said a third.

"Where do you practice?" said the first attendant.

I handed her a business card and said, "Well, thank you for allowing me to adjust you. I'm in Freelake, New Jersey, about a half hour north of Newark Airport. You are more than welcome to come to my office on your time off." I shook their hands and went into the cockpit. The captain and copilot looked like identical twins, both good looking older gentlemen with crisp uniforms and those cool pilot caps.

"Hi, I'm Captain Green. This is Captain Philip, my copilot. I understand you're the chiropractor who adjusted our crew?"

"Yes sir. I'm here to adjust you both. Who's first?" I asked.

"I am," said the copilot. "I love getting adjusted. I started when I was a little kid in Iowa. Ever hear of the Palmer School of Chiropractic?"

"Sure. I named my son after the developer of chiropractic, B.J. Palmer. You used to go there?"

"Yes, my dad used to take us to the clinic. He would tell us stories of how his mother was adjusted by Dr. Palmer himself!"

"Wow, that's awesome," I said as I moved into position and adjusted him.

"Ah, that felt good. I haven't been adjusted in awhile with my schedule, and all. Where did you say you practiced?" he asked.

As I was getting my card out, Captain Green said, "I've never been adjusted before. It looks easy and gentle, but I'm nervous about it."

"Sure, many people are nervous about the unknown, but I promise you it's gentle and very relaxing."

"Okay, give it a whirl. If you adjusted Captain Philip then you can adjust me."

I adjusted the pilot and he was amazed. "That's it? My wife has been going for years and I've always been afraid. Wow! I can't believe what I've been missing."

"Captain, I would like to offer to adjust everyone on the plane. Would you make an announcement to that effect?"

"Oh, sure." He picked up his microphone and spoke with that clear and deep voice that every captain seems to have. "This is Captain Green, your pilot. We have a special treat for all on board. Our friend, chiropractor Dr. Gary Adio, would like to donate his services today and give any passenger who wishes a gentle chiropractic adjustment. He adjusted me for the first time a few minutes ago and it was a wonderful experience. Please take advantage of this special offer that Innate Airways has provided for you at no extra charge. Thank you and have a pleasant flight."

"How's that?" Captain Green asked me.

"Near perfect," I replied with a smile. "I thank you for your kindness and it was an honor to give you your first chiropractic adjustment. Please come visit me at my office in New Jersey any time you are in the area, guys. Thanks." I shook both their hands, gave them the last of my cards and walked out of the cockpit.

"Are you Dr. Adio? I'd like an adjustment. Especially if Innate Airways is paying for it," a passenger in first class laughed.

"With pleasure."

And so it began. Out of the 230 men, women and children on the plane, I adjusted about 200 of them. Those that didn't want an adjustment perplexed me. At first I asked them why, and they usually would tell some long story about how their mother's sister-in-law's brother's girlfriend didn't have a good experience. But I realized, after going through this a few times, that I had many more people to adjust and I only had an hour or so to do it.

It reminded me of a story that a chiropractor once told me. Imagine you were in a burning building and you were knocking on the doors and yelling, 'Fire! Get out of the building!' Many people would open their doors and run out of the building, but if you were to come to one door and one person said, 'I don't believe the building is burning.' And you replied, 'But it is, you have to get out!' and they answered, 'Why should I trust you?' or 'Prove it to me.' Would you keep on talking to them, wasting precious time? Wouldn't the time be better spent saving the many and not trying to convince the few disbelievers? It's called it the "Next" philosophy. 'You want to stay in the burning building? Okay. Next!'

So that's what I did on the airplane. I knew how important the adjustment was going to be, especially in the next few days. I wanted to give as many people as I could the satisfaction of knowing they had been adjusted before the media began to hype this whole thing up. I had no idea of what was about to happen, but maybe anybody who was adjusted would have a little sense of calm.

As soon as I finished, the Captain announced it was time to get back in our seats as we approached Newark Airport. I was almost at my seat when the first flight attendant that I adjusted came over and thanked me again.

"I live in Oaktree, not far from you. I'll be stopping by soon for my next adjustment," she said.

"Great! See you soon," I answered.

"My name is Jackie, so you don't forget."

But suddenly, as I walked back to my seat, I felt a heaviness in my heart. I looked at all the faces, some young, some old. Parents with their kids, professionals in their suits, a few senior citizens—

I knew in a few days the anxiety that would be throughout the country. I hoped that this adjustment would make a little difference in these people.

I plopped myself back into my seat as the pilot said, "Please make sure your seats are in an upright position and your seat belts are securely fastened."

"Chiropractic has never faced a challenge like this before," I said to myself. The plane started its bumpy descent—"Turbulence, that's what we're in for, turbulence."

Chapter 6

"My God, what have I got myself into?" I thought as I pulled out of a deep sleep into a seated position. I strained my eyes to see what time it was on the alarm clock across the room—5:02 AM. Wow. When I had finally gotten home, Ellen was giving B.J. a bath upstairs and I had run up and rehashed the day's activities.

After the bath, we continued the account in our bed, and Ellen and B.J. just listened to me babble on for an hour or two. We must have fallen asleep together in the bed. I hadn't even put on my PJ's.

What a bizarre dream I was having. People dressed in white robes, almost like monks' robes, were chasing me in a big castle that had many, many rooms. I ran down a long winding stone staircase, and at the bottom of the stairs was an old bicycle. Not a ten speed, but one like we used to ride when we were young children. The upright kind with the big long handlebars and the banana-shaped seat. I jumped on the bicycle as the characters pursued me downstairs. I peddled my way outside, crossed a drawbridge over a moat, and it began flashing lightning and thundering and pouring like crazy. I peddled and peddled as fast as I could, and got soaked in the teaming rain. Lightning was crackling all around me, and the thunder claps rocked my bicycle.

Then I was back in my old neighborhood, riding toward my house, when suddenly there was a huge thunder clap. Everything around me went bright and lit up like a ball of fire. Wham! I was struck by lightning. My body arched backward as the shock hit me and instantly I woke up.

Should I wake up Ellen, I pondered in the dark, or let her sleep? It was 5:10 A.M., earlier than I usually got up. Today will be quite a bit more unusual than the average day, I thought. So I slipped myself out of bed, careful not to wake up my precious family, and went slowly downstairs.

Every morning upon arising, I follow a morning ritual. First, I read a "Green Book" for a half an hour. The developer of chiropractic, B.J. Palmer, wrote 39 volumes on chiropractic called the "Green Books." I then meditate for 20 minutes, pray for 10 minutes, and do breathing exercises for 5 minutes. This gets me mentally prepared for the day. And I was sure I would need lots of preparation in the days to come.

I wrote a note for my wife and my son who usually got up later. By 7:00 A.M., I was on my way to the office. That would give me a good two hours to do work before I start to see patients at 9:00 A.M.

It is a ten minute drive from the house to my office, but that early in the morning it would take even less time. My practice is on one of the main roads in northern Bergen County and gets quite a lot of drive-by traffic. Plus, I'm one block away from a large traffic circle, so during rush hour people are moving very slowly past my office. That was a good marketing advantage.

Several blocks away from my office, traffic slowed down almost to a halt. As I inched my way up toward my office, I saw a lot of cars turning left in front of my office. I guessed there was an accident at the traffic circle. There were two police cars with their lights blinking at the corner.

Then it hit me. As I crept closer, past the trees and other houses that blocked the direct view of my office, there was a WBC News van parked on the grass in front of my office with a tall transmitting antenna on its roof. There were wall to wall cars on the little side street of Circle Place, but here's the thing that blew me away—the people.

There was a line of people beginning at my office's front door and wrapping around the side of the building and down the street to the corner of Circle Place and 21st Street. As I made the turn, I saw one of the police officers who was a patient.

"Andy, what's going on here?" He pulled off his sunglasses and his blue eyes looked tired.

"You tell me, Doc. You're the one on TV. We got a call from a neighbor about an hour ago that the news truck was here, and then people started piling in. Are all these your patients?"

"Well, they are now. Sorry about this. I never expected it."

"No problem, Doc. I'll pop in later for my adjustment."

I pulled into the driveway and the WBC News crew was on me. I opened the Jeep's door and battled a barrage of questions.

"Dr. Adio, can you give a statement?"

"Dr. Adio, how can chiropractic do what you claim it's going to do?"

"How is chiropractic going to save us from this disease?"

I pushed my way past my Jeep and said, "I'm sorry, but right now I honestly don't have the time for a statement. Tomorrow night everybody in the country should watch WBC at 7:00 P.M, because we have a satellite TV conference sponsored by the UCA and the NACA, the two major chiropractic associations. Until then, I've got to get busy. Thank you, and tell everybody to start going to a chiropractor if they don't already go."

"Well, what about . . ."

"Dr. Adio, can you comment on the . . ."

"Dr. Adio, how do you know Rick . . ."

Their questions kept on coming and coming as I walked to the office. I made it a point to shake every person's hand who was on the line from my Jeep to my front door. Some of them were my patients already. A lot of my patients had brought family and friends. Even one of the flight attendants from the plane was on the line, Jackie. Her hair was down and she was dressed in T-shirt and jeans.

"Hi, Jackie. Good to see you. Are you busy today?" I asked.

"No. Why, do you need a little help?" she laughingly replied.

"Yes, it seems that I'm not prepared for this. It will be easy. Just give people forms to fill out and help me get them in and out as quickly as I can."

"Sure, no problem, Doc," she answered enthusiastically.

We got to the front door, and the first in line was a patient, Terry. One couldn't tell that she was in her sixties. She had a full head of red hair, coupled with the vim and vigor of a 20-year-old. She said, "Do you remember when I told you about the dream I had? About a line of people outside your office, and I came to help?"

"Yes, Terry, I do," I answered.

"Well, here I am," she smiled, "this is the dream I had."

"Wow," I said, "you should have prepared me better for this. Come on in, Terry. This is Jackie, she'll be helping out also. Can you call Martha and get her here? We need our office manager's help big time."

"Sure thing," Terry said, and she got on the phone as I turned on the lights.

"Jackie, here's a stack of new patient forms and some pens. Go down the line asking everybody, 'When was the last time you were here?' Give each new person a form to fill out. Any established

39

patients, send them to the front of the line, we can adjust them much more quickly. Got it, Jackie?"

I can't believe I didn't say "please" or "thank you."

"No problem," said Jackie. "This looks like it's going to be a fun day."

What a great attitude she has, I thought as I was tapped on the shoulder by one of my very favorite patients, Carl. Carl is a tall strapping man who had many injuries from his years in Sanitation. Chiropractic has kept him very stable, strong, and healthy.

"Dr. Gary, this is some situation," Carl said as I turned around and shook his hand.

"Yes, it is, but somehow we'll get through it."

"You're absolutely right, Doc. Now explain to me how you're going to adjust all these people?" asked Carl.

"One person at a time," I answered, "No other way I can think of, but I'll have to go fast."

"Yes you will, Doc. If the disease is out there as they said on the news last night and chiropractic is the answer, you can't be adjusting and talking and massaging. You've got to really move," Carl commented.

"Hmmm, you're right. I'll have to do it like I did on the plane and in the restaurant—only work on the neck. That's the most important part of the spine. It's like 'Mission Control.' All the nerve information from the brain begins its journey in the neck, so if there is a blockage in the neck, the whole body suffers, especially the immune system."

"Get busy, Doc. And me first!"

By this time there were so many people in the waiting room, it was beyond standing room only. The phones were ringing off the hook and Terry couldn't keep up with them. I spotted Elena, another one of my favorites, in the crowd. Her straight brown hair had become slightly streaked with gray since having four kids in six years, but it suited her well. I taught her oldest son Luke how to look at X-rays and he told me last week that he wanted to be a chiropractor when he grows up.

I asked Elena, "Could you please use this portable phone and answer the calls along with Terry? I'd really appreciate it."

"Sure, Doc, I can help you till twelve when I have to go pick up the kids. Is everything going to be okay?" she asked.

I heard the fear in her voice and tried to calm her. "Yes, Elena, your family has been adjusted for years. Everything will be okay."

40

"But what about everybody else?" she said as I grabbed the phone out of its wall jack.

"It won't be easy, but chiropractic will get everybody adjusted. You'll see. If you're adjusted, you're going to be okay."

She smiled and said, "Thanks, Gary. I feel in my heart that you're right." She answered the phone as I brought Carl into the first adjusting room.

"Lie on your back, Carl." He laid down on the adjusting table, and I felt his neck and gave him a gentle neck adjustment on both sides.

"You got the magic hands," said Carl, "and that's what you have to do all day long until the crisis is over."

"You're so right, Carl. Thanks for your insight. I can always count on you," I said.

He got up off the table as Terry came into the room. "Gary, the President of the Universal Chiropractic Association is on the line. He wants to talk to you."

"I knew I wanted to get to the office early for something. How am I going to handle all this?"

"I don't know. I don't even work here," Terry quipped. She gave me the phone.

"Dr. Adio?" asked Dr. John McCroy, a long time favorite in the UCA. "Where did you get the idea for a TV press conference?"

"Dr. John, the thought popped into my head and I figured it was easy and cost free to us," I hesitantly answered.

"Brilliant idea! I wish I'd thought of it," said Dr. John.

"I've got a line out the door and I don't even know how to handle all this," I said.

"I'm getting reports of lines all over the country at almost every office. News travels very quickly on TV. I'll call you tonight at 11:00 PM and we'll figure this out. Get to it, son."

"Thanks, Dr. John. We'll all be busy for a while," I said.

"You're not kidding. See ya'." And with that, he hung up.

I took a breath and yelled, "Next!" and my day began to roar. I don't even know how many people I adjusted in the following hour or so. It was astonishing how quickly I could adjust and then move on.

Martha suddenly walked in. "When did you get here?" I asked.

"About an hour ago, after I dropped my kids off at school. You're way too slow, Gary, with new patients. Isn't it more important to get them adjusted than to explain chiropractic to them?"

She's been working for me almost since day one. She reminds me of an older version of Goldie Hawn.

"What shall I do, just lie them down and adjust them?" I asked Martha.

"What do you think, silly?"

"You're right. That's why you're my office manager, Martha. I love and appreciate you," I answered.

So I told the new patient I was with, "Did you hear that? How about an adjustment?"

"She's right," said Jane, "that's what I'm here for."

I adjusted Jane. She got up off the table, hugged me and said, "Thanks, I'll bring my husband and kids later. And by the way, do that the rest of the day with all your new patients and you will satisfy everybody. Stop talking and start doing."

"Thanks. This is all so new to me," I said as Jane ran out and another new patient came in. In the plane and restaurant I was doing that, but I guess in my office I felt I had to do more. But what needed to be done was adjust more and do less—what a concept.

Next thing I knew it was noon. I came out of the room I had been in since 7:30 A.M.. I said to Martha, Terry and Ellen, "I'm hungry. How about you guys?"

They agreed. "Let's order some pizza from Uncle George's. Make mine a Vegetarian pizza without cheese, okay?"

"Sure thing," said Terry. "There's no end in sight. The line keeps on getting longer the more people you see."

Unbelievable how many people I didn't touch before all this happened! I used to stand by the front door and look at all the cars driving by and wonder why so many of them weren't chiropractic patients. "How many more I have to reach," I would say to myself. Well, here they are. The office is packed with people. Their friends and families, their coworkers and neighbors and all kinds of people who had heard about us or even just drove past the office were swarming in. It was scary to look around me and see the commotion. No, it was overwhelming. How can I do this better and quicker? I thought, but there was no time for an answer.

Two of my patients, John and Roger, walked in with a person on a stretcher. They are both members of the local volunteer ambulance corps.

"You've got to take a look at my buddy Steve, right now," said Roger.

"Yes, come on in the back guys. What happened to him?" I asked, even though I already knew the answer.

"We'll tell you in the back," said Roger, and he and John walked past me into the last room. They put the stretcher with Steve still on it down on the adjusting table. John closed the door. Steve was writhing in pain and having tremendous difficulty breathing.

"He's got it," said Roger in a low voice. "You said on TV last night that chiropractic could prevent it, well can it save someone too? He's my best friend, but he's always been too stubborn or busy to come see you. Can you do something?"

These two big framed men were clearly broken up. Roger's bottom lip was quivering as he asked me this.

"I move the bones, God does the healing, Roger. That's the best I can offer him."

John spoke up very softly, "Aren't you afraid of—of . . ."

"Of what, John?" I asked.

"Of—of—uh, getting it too? I mean, I'm an ambulance person, that's part of my job, it comes with the territory. But you and your patients . . . Roger, maybe we shouldn't have brought Steve here."

"No, you guys did the right thing. We've got nothing to lose by adjusting him and seeing if he can build up a resistance to this disease. And as for me and my patients, as long as you're adjusted, your immune system is strong enough so you should not get the disease. You both have been under my care for a long time, so your resistance is strong."

"Well, yes, that's true," said Roger, "but what about the new people?"

That one hit me. "Hmmm, I don't know. Would one adjustment today do it? I don't know. It's in God's hands. Let me adjust this guy and then get him out of here. We'll only use this room for cases like him."

Wow, that was a question from right field. What about the people out there who had never been adjusted before? Is such a casual encounter with a contagious man walking by them or passing them on a stretcher enough to infect them? I sat on a stool behind Steve's head. He was gasping for air, shaking like a leaf and in tremendous pain. He was sweating so much I could barely get a solid hold on his neck. As I adjusted his neck there was a loud sound on both sides, showing how out of alignment he was.

"Ohhh," said Steve, barely audible, "oh, the shaking has finally stopped."

43

"Great," I said. "I move bones and God does the healing."

"Thank you. Thank you. Thank you," he kept repeating.

"You're welcome. Now guys, get him back home and get back here for your adjustment."

They picked him up and, as they walked out, Roger said, "Thank you, I knew you wouldn't turn us down."

They left and I raised my head up to the ceiling and asked God, "I guess this is the service you want me to perform for you. Has it all been leading up to this? Am I ready for this? Is chiropractic ready for this? Are we too late?"

As I sat there, looking upwards, asking God the questions, Terry appeared in the door.

"Oh, Doc, sorry. You've got to be like the Energizer Bunny," she laughed.

"Sorry, Terry, God and I were having a little chat," I answered.

"What did he say," asked Terry with a smile.

"Nothing yet. In the end it will be revealed." I didn't know where that came from, but it sounded right.

I washed my hands well and scrubbed them with alcohol, took a deep breath and plunged into the chaos like you plunge into a pool the day after it rains and you know it's going to be ice cold.

Chapter 7

It was 9:00 P.M. the next time I stopped. The office had been churning for hours non-stop and there were still people coming in. The line had dwindled down to just a packed waiting room by 7:30, but now there were just a few stragglers wandering in. Jackie was asleep in the chair in my office, and Martha and Terry looked completely pooped.

"Let me adjust you guys and then you can get home," I said.

"Okay, Doc. You know I didn't even bother scheduling appointments. I couldn't write them in even if I wanted to. I just told everyone to come next week on Monday or Tuesday. I think, by the way, we'll have to open all day Tuesday and all day Thursday to keep up with this," Martha said as I rolled my eyes.

"Yeah, I figured that. I guess we'll have to do this as long as it takes," I said.

"But you are forgetting one thing," added Terry. "This is not going to change once the disease is wiped out. Once people experience the feeling they receive by getting regularly adjusted, they're not going to stop."

"You've got a point," I said. "I hadn't thought of it that way. By the time this whole thing blows over, 'Please let it be soon,'" I muttered—"the whole country will be under chiropractic care. I guess it was what chiropractic needed to get us beyond the stigma of backache fixers. Although this isn't the way I would have predicted chiropractic would come into the limelight."

Jackie must have woken up, because she came over to us and asked, "Do you really think this disease will ever go away?"

I pondered a moment, "All diseases have a bell curve life line. They rise up rapidly and then fall just as rapidly. So yes, Jackie, I do think that with God's help and some chiropractic adjustments, the life span of this disease will shorten. The more people get adjusted, the fewer people will get the disease. It's not about symptoms, it's about prevention. About building strength from within."

"But why can't medicine help? What about a vaccine?" asked Jackie.

"You see, that's called outside-in thinking. True health comes from above-down, inside-out. Chiropractic is inside-out, medicine is outside-in. Get it?"

"Well, no," answered Jackie.

"First off, you don't get sick because of a lack of medicine, so you can't get well by taking medicine either. Second of all, you don't need a vaccine. Look at the bubonic plague, as an example. It came and went on its own with nobody's help and no vaccine. Third, and most importantly, chiropractic opens a direct and strong nerve channel right to the immune system. If you get adjusted, you should be strong enough to fend off the disease," I said.

"Yeah, but . . . . .Will everybody who gets adjusted stay well, or will there be people who get adjusted and get sick anyway?" asked Jackie.

"Well, honestly," I thought for a moment, putting my hand to my chin and scratching my five o'clock shadow. "I don't know how to answer that question. I can only say that, if your body is working at a hundred percent, you have the best chance of fighting off an invasion. However, there are limitations of matter."

"Limitations of matter?" asked Terry.

"Yes. In other words, if the physical body, otherwise known as 'matter,' is that seriously damaged before getting adjusted, then by turning the power to a hundred percent, it may be too little, too late. However, the severely weakened body will have a better chance with an adjustment than it would without one. That I know for sure. But if you are already battling cancer or something, you may be too weak physically, even with a hundred percent nerve flow."

"So getting adjusted is not a hundred percent proof you're not going to get this disease?" Jackie said with a hint of fear in her voice.

"Getting adjusted is a hundred percent way of guaranteeing you the best possible chance of defending against it, Jackie. You are infinitely better off without a subluxation in your nerve flow than you are with one. But nothing is a hundred percent. That's all in God's hands," I replied.

"Hmmm," thought Jackie. "Okay. Hey, can I get adjusted, please?"

"Sure," I said, "let's all go into adjusting room one."

"Are there enough chiropractors to physically adjust everybody in this country?" Martha interjected.

I took a deep breath and blew it out as we all walked silently into adjusting room one.

"Well, once again, I can't say I know for sure. After tomorrow night we'll have a better idea. Almost 55,000 chiropractors and 4,000 students for 255 million people. Quick, Martha, do some math."

"Well, 255 million divided by 55,000 is 4,000 and something. So every chiropractor needs to reach 4,000 people regularly. I guess it can be done," exclaimed Martha.

"Thank you, my math whiz." I gave Martha a hug and hugged Terry and Jackie as well. "Thank you guys, too. I can't do this without you."

"One other thing I've been thinking about, Gary, although I think I know your answer," said Martha.

"Yes?" I asked her, puzzled by her expression.

"The, uh—the money thing—insurance and all that. How are we handling this?" she asked, hesitantly.

"Hmmm, well, like usual I guess. If they have insurance, bill their insurance. If not, we'll come up with a payment plan and reduce our fee, so that everybody can afford this, not just people with insurance. We will do all right," I answered, as if I had solved that problem.

"That may have been true last week, but you're not going to have time to sit down and explain this to everybody and meet everyone's personal needs like you usually do," Martha said.

"Damn, she's right again." I shook my head. "That's why we've been together for so many years, Martha."

"If and when the insurance runs out, or if they have no insurance, we'll charge them half off for cash and, if they can't afford that, ask them to pay whatever they can afford. We'll do all the financial stuff, you're not going to have time for that," Martha commented.

"Thanks, you guys, for handling all this. This is going to be crazy," I smiled.

"What do you mean, 'you guys'? I thought I was volunteering for today," asked Terry.

"Nope, sorry, you've been hired. I pay well and you'll get free adjustments for you and your family. That goes for you too, Jackie, whenever you're around."

"I'll be here when I can, Doc, whenever I'm not flying," said Jackie.

"You've got yourself a new employee, Gary," added Terry, "but I think you'll need more staff."

"More chiropractors, too." Jackie said.

"Yes, you're probably right. Too much to think about. Okay, before I pass out completely, let me adjust you guys. Thanks again for everything," I said as Martha laid down on the table first. I adjusted them lovingly, quickly and in silence. The moment I finished adjusting Jackie the phone rang, breaking the quiet.

"It's your wife," said Martha.

"Oh my God, I haven't called her all day. Damn," I cursed myself and shook my head as I walked out of the adjusting room and picked up the phone.

"Hey, babe, I'm so sorry I didn't call. I didn't have a moment to think today."

"I know, and I love you anyway. I saw Mary today and she said she drove by your office and there was a line around the block. She said there were TV men there too. Were you interviewed?"

"No, not really. I told them they could follow me around if they wanted to but I didn't have time for an interview. I never saw them again. I guess they packed up and left after awhile. Let me ask the girls what happened." I walked toward the front desk and noticed that Jackie and Terry had already left. Martha was closing up the computer.

"Martha," I asked, "when did the TV guys leave? Did you notice?"

"Yes, they left around nine or ten o'clock. I forgot to tell you. But they were interviewing people on the line outside. Jackie said they asked her some questions too. Then they skedaddled out of here."

"Thanks, Martha," I said. "Did you hear that, Ellen?"

"Yes, Gary, but I have to tell you that Mary scared the you know what out of me today," Ellen said. "She is still watching the news. She says that no medicine on the planet can fight this, and people out there are dying left and right. All walks of life, no socioeconomic barriers, just everybody. All except the chiropractic patients. So where there are no chiropractors, the towns are going crazy and trying to get the government to send them some. It's amazing but it really looks like chiropractic could save the world. What a shame it took something like this to get the message across."

"I agree, and trust me, I'm scared too. I mean, how many adjustments does it take to give someone a strong immune system? Is a new patient who has only one or two adjustments under their belt strong enough? Only time will tell. Nobody expected this, I can tell you that. You know what?" I asked.

"No, what?" Ellen responded, surprised.

"I need a hug," I said.

"No problem. Got a bunch of them right here waiting for you. I'm proud of you, Gary, you are handling this so well."

She always says the right thing when I need her to.

"Listen, El, it's nine-thirty, let me close up and I'll be right home. Dr. John from UCA is calling me at eleven and I'll need to talk to him for God knows how long. See you in a few minutes. You're my rock and my inspiration. I love you," I said.

"I love you too."

"See you soon."

I turned off the portable phone and hung it back in its charger.

"Martha, this is going to be a long, tough road ahead, so I ask you to please stick by me during this craziness. I will be forever grateful to you if you do."

"No problem," Martha said, "I'm in this for the long haul. I won't leave you till the cows come home."

"Well, this is such a weird time that seeing cows come home wouldn't surprise me right now."

Chapter 8

I rushed home and after a fast dinner with Ellen and B.J., I rapidly told the story of my day. It almost sounded surreal, like a Dali painting or, as Ellen said, like Escher's Waterfall, full of people instead of water. It was a nonstop day in which time ceased to exist at a normal pace. There was no beginning and no end, just the constant hum of the now, and moving, moving, moving.

"Where do we go from here?" I asked Ellen, finishing my third helping of vegetarian chili and rice with a spinach salad. "How am I going to pull this TV thing off tomorrow? What do I say? What do I do? It's going to be a two-minute program. 'Okay, chiropractors, adjust as many people as you can. Only do neck adjustments because there's no time for anything else—no machines, no exams, just adjustments. Don't charge crazy fees.' I'm done."

"Well, one thing you've got to talk about is the areas that don't have any chiropractors in them. I was thinking, why don't you have the senior students at the chiropractic colleges fly to those areas?"

My eyes bulged out. "That's brilliant! I can't wait to tell that to Dr. John. Perfect! You're a genius!" I jumped over and gave Ellen a big hug and kiss. "That's why I married you, you're so smart and so beautiful."

"Just let your innate flow, Gary," Ellen said. "That's how you are going to handle this. How did you handle today? One patient at a time. How will you handle your TV debut? One moment at a time. You know what to do, Gary. Everything you've ever done has prepared you for this."

"Wow," I stammered, "that was good. Will you tape that for me so I can play that back?"

"I believe in you, Gary. I know you can do it," Ellen said. "You're just a hard working, principled, loving chiropractor, and that's who they need to lead them."

"What happened to the scared girl you were a few days ago? You seem very self-assured all of a sudden?"

"Well, I've done a lot of thinking. You don't know it, but I drove past the office several times today," Ellen said.

"You did! Why didn't you stop in?" I asked.

"Because there was a line out the door, around the front of the office and down the road a bit. I thought there would have been a riot if I went to the front of the line and just walked in. Besides there was no place to park anywhere. People were parking on the grass and across the street in the parking lot. And it wasn't just your office, Gary," Ellen said.

"What do you mean? There were lines everywhere?" I asked.

"Yes, Gary, everywhere. Every chiropractor had a tremendous line. Which is what you always wanted, isn't it?" she said, laughing.

"True. But this is not how I anticipated it to be," I replied.

"You always get what you really want, just maybe not the way you expected to get it," Ellen returned.

"You are full of great quotes today, aren't you?" I gave her another kiss. "Hey, what time is it anyway?"

"It's almost eleven o'clock. What time did you say Dr. John was going to call?" asked Ellen.

"Some time around now. How am I going to tell the President of the Universal Chiropractic Association about this when I've never done anything like this before?" I asked.

"Do you think he's done anything like this before?" Ellen replied.

"Well, no, but, ah, I . . . my intelligence is so outstanding sometimes," I smiled.

Ellen laughed at me. "You were chosen by a United States Senator to do this. Why? Was it luck, coincidence, or was it meant to be? This is God's plan for you, Gary, and what we have been in training for all this time. Why do you think we've become so narrow in our focus? To hone our skills. We let nothing interfere with our objectives. The reason we don't do anything the way everybody else does is why you are where you are right now. You've trained for this for years."

"Ellen, I think you should take the phone call and do all of the talking tonight," I replied.

"Gary!" Ellen laughed.

"Ellen," I chuckled, "I know you're right, but I'm scared. Not scared that I'll mess up, because how can I mess up something that's never been done before? But I'm scared because of how big this is. I'm scared because this is not a little office thing, this is a national emergency. Are we going to be inspiring enough to get the whole chiropractic community together to focus on one thing? That's never happened in our 100-year history. But then again, the only people who have ever tried to lead chiropractors before have been chiropractic politicians, and often their focus is off purpose.

"I guess that is why I somehow got chosen for this, because I'm not a politician. And I've been tested and tested in my life to make sure that I stay on purpose no matter what comes my way. Maybe. . ." The phone rang, ". . . Maybe, I've got no time to think any more," I said as I ran for the phone.

"Dr. Adio, please," said the voice on the phone.

"This is he. Dr. John?" I asked. It really didn't sound like him.

"No. Don't do what you think you are going to do. I'm telling you now, you are making a grave mistake."

"Uh—and who is this please?" I motioned for Ellen to get the cordless phone and listen in.

"It doesn't matter. Not one of your colleagues, I can tell you that. You made a lot of enemies yesterday and I suggest you go on TV tomorrow night and retract everything you said."

By now Ellen was listening in.

"I should, huh? And watch the whole country die because you don't want chiropractic to work? I don't think so."

"Listen, you don't know what you're getting yourself into," said the voice.

"You know, all I have to do is hang up the phone and dial *69 and trace this call."

"Go ahead. Make my day," the voice growled back.

"So, this is Clint Eastwood, huh? I didn't know you were so against chiropractors."

"I had nothing against chiropractic until you came along. You'd best do as I say."

"And you'd best do as I say. Call me again, or threaten me, or have any more contact with me, and I will not budge from my position. Thanks for the wonderful conversation." At that I hung up and dialed *69. He obviously was at a pay phone.

"What the heck was that?" I asked Ellen.

"Your stepping on a lot of toes, Gary. Like Dr. Lenappe always says, 'If you're not getting hate mail then you're not being outrageous enough.'"

"Yes, but I'm worried about you guys and your safety."

"Me, too," Ellen said with a grimace. "But chiropractic has got to get it together. Why don't you check the voice mail and see if Dr. John called during this lovely phone conversation."

I dialed our voice mail number and Dr. John had left a typical message, saying, "Who the hell were you on the phone with when I was supposed to be talking to you? Call me back. It's your dime now."

Ellen and B.J. sat down to read some books as I picked up the cordless phone.

B.J.'s latest trick was counting from one to ten, "One, two, tee, foh, pie, sih, seven, eight, nine, ten!" and he clapped his hands.

"That a' boy, handsome!" I proudly said and kissed him on his forehead and then made my way to the basement. It was the safest place for me to talk without interruptions. I sat down in the basement's big comfy chair and dialed Dr. John's number. He answered on one ring.

"Who the hell have you been talking to, boy?"

"Hi, Dr. John. I just received my first threatening phone call."

"Well, now you're a real chiropractor," laughed Dr. John. "You're pissing people off. So what did he say?"

"He said I better not go on with this TV program thing. He must have been working for the NMA or a pharmaceutical company."

"Or the government," said Dr. John, "don't forget them. They have their fingers in everybody's pie. But that's beside the point. So what's your plan for this TV thing?"

"My plan?" I asked, "I, uh . . . "

"Here's my idea. Me, you and Larry of the stinking NACA— don't tell him I said that—each present a segment of ten minutes in length or so, then we take calls on an 800 number to answer questions for the next half hour. One hour and no commercials—we're done."

"Sounds great. The key is telling everybody to adjust as many people as they can, forgetting exams, or protocols, or machines, or massage. I figure just do upper cervical adjustments unless there is a special need. Plus, listen to this, my beautiful wife had this idea. Have senior chiropractic students flown into rural areas or inner cities where there aren't enough chiropractors to go around."

"Great idea!" said Dr. John. "I've gotten reports from all across the country that every chiropractor is overwhelmed with patients. You know what, Gary? I bet this is going to change things a lot. I bet this is going to change chiropractic back to when B.J. Palmer was around, when the only thing that chiropractors did was adjust subluxations and miracles were the norm. I bet it's going to change from this lame back ache, neck ache, headache bullshit back to the real thing. This is God's plan, do you realize that?"

"Yes, Dr. John, I most certainly do. God always has a way of cleansing things when they need cleansing. We have fooled too much with antibiotics and needless surgeries and countless pain killers, and now the universe is fighting back. If you push too hard, you will create a super virus or a super bacteria and nothing will stop it. The experimentation that the pharmaceutical companies have been doing with the American public for years has weakened our immune systems so much that now most people can't fight back, unless . . ."

"Unless," Dr. John butted in, "unless they are under regular chiropractic care. But here's a puzzler, Gary, what about all those people who've never been adjusted before or come here for a few weeks and then are exposed to the disease? Will they be strong enough?"

"Over all, if we can get to enough people quickly enough and often enough, I know chiropractic can do it."

"I agree, but can we do that? Can we see enough people quickly enough and often enough?"

"I don't know. What do your UCA statisticians say?"

"Well, our knuckleheads over here say each chiropractor in the country needs to see a whole lot more people each week. That's hard enough, but the real question is, will they or can they?"

"What do you mean?"

"Gary, it's a question of intent and ability. Will they—or do they want to do this? And can they—are they really able to? Or will they block themselves and their patients? Money has to be secondary, and machines have to be thrown out the window. Exams, X-rays, everything. Chiropractors have to just adjust, and adjust and adjust."

"Hey, Dr. John, I have another question that I'm wondering about. If your, what did you call them, 'eggheads' figure it out . . ."

"Knuckleheads. But it's the same thing. I thought you were a vegetarian?"

"I am," I laughed, "Anyway, my question is, how long do you think this will last?"

Dr. John paused for a moment and I heard him take a deep breath and sigh loudly.

"Gary, I haven't a clue. It could be a few months, it could be a few years. Let's hope that we can reach enough people quickly, so we can keep losses to a minimum. Or else the NMA will call us failures and rush in with a vaccine that will probably be more dangerous than the disease itself." He stopped for a moment to let that sink in. "I do have some interesting news for you, though."

"What's that?"

"My guys say that this is the quickest, most virulent and fatal disease than anything ever before. We don't have much time. It's killing people fast. But the good news is, my guys say statistically, if chiropractors intervene with rapid speed, the disease can be halted just as quickly as it's now spreading."

"Not to sound pessimistic, but isn't that like throwing sand bags at a tidal wave, Dr. John?"

"Yes, Gary, I understand what you mean, but if you think like these guys think, you'll see what they see. They say this disease is moving at such a rate that, like in physics, if you hit it with an equal but opposite force, you can stop it dead in its tracks. You remember physics, don't you? You had to take it for your pre-reqs."

"Yes, Newton was one of my favorites."

"Yes, mine too, loved his hair," he giggled at himself. "Anyway, tomorrow night you've got to blow these people away. You've got to take the chiropractic profession and everybody who's watching by storm. You only get one chance at a first impression. Or is it that you never get a second chance to make a first impression? Something like that."

"Anyway, chiropractors look at me and Larry from NACA and think . . . 'windbags,' but they've never heard of you. You can have a very powerful effect as a captivating stranger. Tell them about the threat you had tonight. Let people know that others want to stop us and we won't back down."

"A scary thought, Dr. John, but even though I'm frightened out of my wits, I feel that we're ready for this. Somehow or other, in a crazy way, I think chiropractic is ready for this, too."

"Remember not just the whole profession will be watching, but also the whole country. This will be bigger than the Super Bowl and the World Series put together. I hope you've got a pretty spiffy suit."

"Oh, come on, not a suit, Dr. John?"

"No choice, Gary. I'll be wearing one and you can count on stuffy Larry wearing one, too."

"So what else am I supposed to do anyway?"

"Just tell them what you told me. A few great lines followed by telling everybody to get out there and adjust as many people as they can for a fair price so we can meet this head on. Tell them the quicker we get this whole country under care, the quicker we can get out of this mess. And say it in such a way that John Q. Public will want to run out and get adjusted first thing Sunday morning."

"Sunday morning? Did you say Sunday?"

"Yeah, what do you think? When we were in 'Nam did the North Vietnamese take Sundays off? This is a national emergency. Open later, like at noon or something, but you've got to open. And you can say that I've told you to say that."

"Oh, yes, that will win them over."

"Look, how come you never got involved in UCA politics if you've got such a sharp wit? I could use a few good men like you around me."

"No thanks. When this blows over, I just want a vacation and some family time."

"Yeah, well, in the meantime, nobody has a choice as to where they can open up a new practice. All new graduates and seniors will be sent wherever they are needed. I'll talk about that tomorrow. Don't worry your head over it. Also they'll be no buying or selling practices and no associates leaving practices or moving. No changes until this is over. And anyone caught overcharging or violating any other moral or ethical rule of conduct will have their license revoked for one year after this mess is over."

"You say, 'when this mess is over,' very confidently."

"Look, Gary, I know it's going to be over if we smash it head on. And that's your job tomorrow. 'Inspire the bastards' as General Patton would say."

"Did he say that? Exact quote?"

"Well, look, I don't know. I was in 'Nam, remember? How old do you think I am anyway?"

"Sorry, no offense. Well, I've got to get some rest. I'm not used to seeing so many people in one day and I better sleep when I can."

"Hey, don't go anywhere right now, there's one more kink."

"Well, of course, our work is never done."

"That's right. Do you remember B.J. Palmer's famous quote, 'We'll empty the jails, empty the hospitals and fill the churches and temples?'"

"Sure I do. I see what you're getting at."

"That's right, Gary. We've got a moral responsibility to get into the hospitals and prisons. Has your wife thought of one for that?"

57

"No she hadn't mentioned that one. Let me think. Hmmm." I heard a scratching sound from the other end. It sounded like Dr. John was pensively playing with his goatee.

"I've got it, Gary, the faculty! The faculty of the chiropractic colleges can go into the hospitals and prisons. Ah ha! Brilliant! See, I've still got it!"

"How will the faculty be able to teach and go to the hospitals and prisons?"

"Teach! What are you in a bubble or something? The President declared a 'national urgency' today. We'll close the chiropractic schools temporarily. Don't you guys own a TV, Gary?"

"Yeah, but the only time we watch it is for videos, especially for B.J. I know Cookie Monster just got more cookies from his Uncle Fred."

"Well ain't that helpful. I'll call you the next time I need to talk to Ernie or Bert. Listen, you sound delirious. Get some sleep and I'll see you for a test run via satellite at 6:00 PM. Make sure you're out of the office by four to give yourself a chance to eat and relax. I've been on TV many times before, but it was never this important. I'm even a tad nervous. But I know this in my heart—chiropractic has now reached a point where it can save the world. How we respond to this crisis can make us or break us. I think chiropractic can do it. I know you think that way too. Good night, Gary."

Chapter 9

I was inside an old castle, going room to room, searching for something. I didn't know what. A huge structure made of tremendous stones had a wet, funky, moldy odor to them. As I walked down a long wide corridor, I look to my right and there are giant pillars from floor to ceiling and a wall that extends down to the first floor below.

People were walking behind me as if I wasn't even there. Minstrels, knights, princesses, and everything else one could imagine. Suddenly, the castle started shaking and the pillars to my right started breaking into pieces. I ran toward the long stairway, and as I ran each pillar I passed burst into a thousand little pieces. I sprinted down the stairs as the entire second floor crumbled and dust flew over my head. I finally reached the bottom of the stairway and continued to run my fastest down another corridor that kept going, and going, and going.

I was running nonstop and could still hear the sounds of the castle destroying itself behind me, until at last I ran into . . . a cafeteria. A modern cafeteria with tables, chairs, a winding counter and those metal bar surfaces that you put your tray on as you walk by the food selections. I walked through the cafeteria a little confused, brushing the dust off my shirt and wiping sweat from my forehead. I then walked smack into Dr. Frankie Silver, one of my chiropractic mentors.

"There's no need to search anymore. You've got it all right here in your hands," Frankie said to me.

I woke up to the sound of my alarm clock playing a Genesis tape, "Whoa! What was that?" I whispered as I practically fell out of bed to get to the alarm before Ellen and B.J. woke up. Within a few seconds I has pressed the alarm button and the music stopped. Ellen and B.J. could tolerate about 20 seconds of music time before they stirred, and that day, I was a little slower than usual.

I plopped onto our glider rocker we had bought for Ellen to nurse B.J. to sleep at night. I was catatonic for a moment or two, my hands covering my eyes as I rocked effortlessly back and forth. Another crazy dream. Everything was falling down around me as I searched for something, and Frankie told me I already had what I was looking for. Slowly the weight of the day's importance came into focus as the rocking woke me from my slumber.

Reality check. Hmmm, sleep is so peaceful when you wake up to a day like this. "Now what?" I asked. I seemed to be asking myself that a lot these days.

"When you are scared, do what you are trained to do." I heard another chiropractic mentor, Dr. Charles, say these words as he had said many times before at seminars.

"Do what you are trained to do." It made sense to me.

"How am I going to adjust all these people?" I asked Dr. Charles in my mind.

He answered, "One at a time. You can do it, boy."

I can, I will, and I must. I made a mental note to call him the following week and thank him.

So by 7:00 A.M. I was on the road again. I listened to the sounds of the Jeep rather than my usual ten-minute "helping" of motivational or chiropractic philosophy tapes. I needed to be in the zone because I knew it would be a whirlwind day. Between adjusting God knows how many people during the day and the satellite conference tonight, the day will zip by in a blink, I thought.

I approached my office, noting a line significantly smaller than the previous day's. But then I remembered I hadn't pulled up as early the day before. The line stretched only around the front of the office rather than down the block. Martha must have gotten here early, I reasoned, because the door was already open. Another mental note—get more keys made up for my extra support staff.

I pull into the driveway and a patient came running up to me with a newspaper in her hands. Shara had been my first receptionist way back when. She was a senior in high school and was of typical Swedish descent; blond hair, blue eyes, and very smart. She was in her late twenties and a junior executive at a rental company. She plastered the newspaper's front page on my driver's side window.

NATIONAL MEDICAL ASSOCIATION PROMISES VACCINE FOR KILLER DISEASE

read the headline. Underneath it said:

WITHIN ONE MONTH, THE VACCINE WILL BE AVAILABLE

"Wow," I said to Shara as I opened the door, "what a crock."

"Yes, but how many people feel that way?" Shara asked. "And look at this. They named the disease: HADES; Hybrid Advanced Disease in Entire System."

"HADES! What a fitting name! I guess coming right out and saying 'Hell' just wasn't conservative enough for them." I shook my head as I closed the door to my Jeep.

"Now you've got your work really cut out for you, Doc. It's chiropractic versus the NMA. You chiropractors had better do something fast. And if you think that makes you sick, look at this, on page five, no less."

There, on the bottom of the page, was a column by Rick. The headline read:

Can Chiropractors Save the World From HADES?
Watch the first ever chiropractic video conference tonight.

I knew it was strange how this had been the lead topic on Thursday, but hadn't made it in any other newspapers on Friday. Obviously the NMA had their hand in controlling the papers too. Well, after tonight's satellite TV conference, people will see the other side, I thought to myself. We'll tell them they can either wait a month for a vaccine and stand a chance of getting infected, or get adjusted to boost their immune system and give themselves a fighting head start.

I started walking toward the office. "This is pretty wild, Shara. All these people."

"Do you need any help? My mother-in-law can watch the kids at least until their nap time at one."

"Sure, Shara, we need all the help we can get. Go inside and ask Martha for some new patient forms, clip boards and pens and ask any new patient to fill one out."

"Great," she said, "just like old times," and ran ahead of me into the office.

"Not quite," I thought.

I shook the hands of everyone standing in line and decided to make this a tradition. It only took a few extra minutes and it helped calm me down. For me? Waiting for me to adjust them? God, I never imagined anything like this, I thought.

As I continued shaking the hands of patients new and old, I suddenly remembered a dream I had had years before when Ellen and I were in Sedona, Arizona on vacation. I had awakened with a start one morning and jumped up out of bed and drawn an image of what I had seen. It was the exact image that I had seen when pulling up to the office yesterday morning . . .

Oh my God! I wondered, did I have this premonition years ago? I had visualized its happening but hadn't known why. The entire thought process occurred in a matter of seconds, and there I stood in my office waiting room, still shaking hands and exchanging pleasantries as my mind came back to focus. It's amazing how we can be doing two things at once.

Martha came running over to me, "There's somebody you have to call before you get started."

"No, it will have to wait 'till later. Look at everybody waiting."

"I think you'll have to keep them waiting," Martha said. "There's an important phone call from . . ."

"Look, I don't care if it's the President of the United States, I've got to adjust these . . ."

"It *is* the President of the United States!"

She stopped me dead in my tracks and folded her arms, daring me to stick to my word.

"Really?"

"No, but your wife said to tell you it was the President of the United States so you would definitely call her. Plus you got a weird message you should listen to. Don't know who it is from, but he says you'll know who it is."

"Okay, Martha, thanks."

I closed the door to my office, or should I say, Adjusting Room 1, which just happens to have a telephone and a small wooden desk in it. Other than that it's just like the other three adjusting rooms. I picked up the phone and said, "Hey, El, what's up?"

"Did you get a funny phone call today, yet?" Ellen asked, and did not seem amused.

"Ah, no. What do you mean by, 'funny'?"

"I mean like the threatening sort of funny."

"No. Was it the guy from last night?"

"I'm not sure, but it could have been. He didn't say much, just said, 'Tell your husband a friend called and hopes he does the right thing tonight,' and then hung up."

"Damn. Martha said there was a funny message here on the machine too. Didn't have time to listen to it because she told me the President called."

"As long as you realize who wears the pants in the family, Gary. I love you."

"Okay, Ellen. I love you too. Got to go, another line out the door today."

"It'll be like that for awhile, get used to it."

With that, my day raced on. I don't even know who else besides Martha and Shara were working with me that day. I didn't see anything but the three rooms until 3:45 or so when Martha stopped me in the hallway.

"You haven't eaten lunch yet, and you said you have to leave by four. Well, it's almost four and there's still a line out the door. What do you want to do?"

I thought for a moment and said, "Keep on adjusting. I can't stop now. We'll stop by five when everybody begins to eat dinner."

"How do you know it will slow down by then, Gary?"

"I can't turn anybody away. It would be wrong for someone to say, 'Sorry, got to go,' to a line of people. But the Conscience of the Universe knows the importance of tonight and will cause this to slow down so I can leave by five. This is about life and death. It's more important than anything else I know."

"Okay, get busy then."

It was 5:30 when I adjusted the last person, a newborn baby, born the day before into this crazy world. Will this baby grow up in a world decimated by this disease, this HADES? Or will he know a completely different one, one filled with health and love and peace?

That's what this was all about, I thought, as I ran out of my office to my Cherokee after calling Ellen. Tonight is about the next generation. If chiropractors can rally now and the people of the United States can open up their minds quickly and believe that the power that made the body can heal the body, we can wipe out this disease and change the destiny of the world. If the NMA takes over, if they get their vaccine out and start poisoning everybody, the world will take a turn that I think we can never come back from.

"God, so much rests on this," I said to myself out loud as I pulled out of the driveway of my office and onto the street. "How am I going to pull this off?" The hum of the engine didn't answer me, but made me think of when I was in chiropractic school and I was driving back home from Ellen's dormitory. She attended Georgia University and I was at Southern Chiropractic College, an hour north. It was early in our relationship, maybe a few months, and we had just come back from Amilola Falls in northern Georgia. I dropped her off and headed for home because I had an early class that Monday morning.

I was on I-75 buzzing along at midnight in the fast lane, when suddenly the car lurched forward. All of the warning lights went on at once and then I heard a loud grinding sound. I swerved to the right, the power steering gone, and crossed four lanes and somehow didn't hit anybody or anything. The car came to a dead stop on the right shoulder without me even putting on the brake. I looked around me to make sure that it had really happened. "Thank you, God," I said out loud, looking up to the sky. Obviously, I had not been responsible for steering the car to safety.

It was the pre-car phone or cellular phone era, so I got out of the car and decided to walk to the next exit. As I started walking, I thought walking was a bit slow, so I started to jog, then to run, then to sprint. It was during this half-hour sprint that my entire life changed. I realized that more than anything else, I wanted to be with Ellen. All I could see and think and feel and hear was Ellen. My body was in pain, not from the long run, but because I yearned to be with her, and realized how deeply in love I was. As I came sprinting to the top of the crest of a hill, I saw the gas stations that surrounded the exit ramp.

At that moment I said to myself, "This is what love is. Love is wanting to be with somebody so bad that it hurts." But more importantly, it transformed my whole life. I had been hurt before by women and had sworn up and down that I would never love again. I would never let that happen to me. But there and then I decided that love *was* my path. As I approached that gas station with tears in my eyes, I vowed something that I had never even thought of before. And that was to love unconditionally. Love without expectations. Love for the sake of loving.

I had heard that philosophy before from the President of the Southern Chiropractic College, Dr. Charles. The motto of the school is to "To serve for the sake of serving. To give for the sake of giving. To love for the sake of loving." But I had had no idea what it meant until I was running, sweating and crying on Martin Parkway at 12:30 at night. I was "Running from Safety," as Richard Bach says. I was running into the unknown and it felt good, even though it hurt.

It was a life changing thought. Click! My mind refocused on the road and there I was, turning into the driveway of our house.

Amazed at how we can do two things at once again, I thought about the day's newspaper headline, the NMA, and their vaccine 'cure,' and how maybe chiropractic finally had them shaking in their pants.

"Maybe those chiropractors are really right," I imagined the NMA thinking. "Maybe those chiropractors do have the answer to health and better immunity and not using drugs or surgery as a first but a last resort. Maybe they can save the world."

But then I sadly know what their next thought would not be. It would not be, "So let's encourage them and help them save this planet." Their next dominating idea would be, "We must stop them. We can't let them take control away from us. We've had this planet under our control since Louis Pasteur. We can't let it go now."

How unfortunate but true. The NMA thought process is, "If it ain't us, it ain't good," and that's it. No happy medium. No sharing in the creation of the health of the nation. It's either us or them.

I don't know how long I was sitting out there, parked in my Jeep in the driveway, the garage door open, my wife and son peering out the window wondering what I must be thinking. I waved sheepishly at them and opened the car door.

"B.J.!" I yelled, my traditional homecoming for my son. He smiled expectantly as I ran towards him.

"Dah-dee, Dah-dee, Dah-dee, Dah-dee. Hi!" B.J. yelled back as I opened the inside garage door and kissed B.J. and Ellen hello.

"What were you doing out there, Gary? We were watching you for at least two or three minutes. You didn't even move."

"Sorry. This TV thing has got me thinking about all kinds of stuff."

I gave Ellen another hug and kiss and held her as I looked at her. "Do you remember that night at school when my car broke down and I ran a few miles to get to the phone to call you?"

"Of course. And you took a taxi all the way back to my dorm. You could have walked home from that gas station. How could I forget?"

"Well, that's what it's all about, Ellen. It's about 'Running from Safety.' It's about running from something I know, that I'm comfortable with, that is familiar and easy and a no-brainer, towards something I know nothing about for sure, but have enough faith in to be true.

"That night I ran from my car, away from the old me, the me who wouldn't love again, to you, to love, to real love, unconditional love. The same with tonight. I'm running from being just me and my practice and not really getting involved to probably the most crucial event in chiropractic history since its birth. I know nothing about TV, nothing about what I should say. I have no notes, no preparation, but I'm running at full force and in full faith and with a made up mind. I will let my passion and my faith be the driving force."

As I finished my sentence, three big WBC TV News vans pulled up into the driveway. One of them had that big tall TV transmission antenna on it, sticking straight up into the air, 30 or 40 feet. We've all seen them before here or there, broadcasting about some important event or about some meaningless tidbit of information that no one will ever remember. Now they were here at my home, at my house. Oh my God . . .

"So, just another ordinary night with some company over," Ellen said.

"Yeah, just like every night. Come home from work, eat dinner and go on national TV. Ho hum. We need to become more spontaneous." Ellen laughed as I said this. "We've always been able to keep smiles on our faces, even when the whole world seems to be crashing around us."

"Yes, Gary, and we always are able to take each other's humor and go with it. We should be on TV."

"Well, here's our chance tonight. To hell with the serious stuff, how about 'The Gary & Ellen Show,' the new comedy team that's sweeping the nation? And . . ." ding dong. Silence. We looked at each other, ". . . and ringing the doorbells of America with our wondrous witticisms."

"You go get it."

"No, you go get it," I said.

"No, it's your hour tonight. They're not looking for me, they're looking for you."

Ding dong. Ding dong. So I let this small crowd of TV people in. No Jim Bouchards or Thomas Flemings, these were the behind the scenes people; the camera, sound people and lighting directors. After introducing themselves, I showed them to the den where I keep my B.J. Palmer chiropractic book collection. They busied themselves, flitting in and out of the house like ants building a nest, at a breakneck pace. They didn't talk, ask questions, or anything. They just ran in and out of the house until the den was transformed

66

into a mini-studio. They even put a makeshift desk up, complete with a folding desk chair.

We had just finished the last bites of dinner when somebody official sat down at our table, explaining to us the whole procedure. How the anchorperson (somebody he expected me to know, but I told him we don't watch TV so the name was unfamiliar) was in the studio and would "direct traffic," as he put it. He would ask questions of me, Dr. John (who hasn't called yet—hmmm?) and Dr. Larry from the NACA. Each of us would have ten minutes in the beginning and then a phone-in question time and then five minutes each to close. I would be the first and last speaker. He asked to see my prepared notes and was surprised when I told him I didn't have any. He asked me how I would know what to say? I told him that what I would say would come from inside out. His response to that was, "Oh," and then he dropped the subject.

At 6:45 P.M. Dr. John still hadn't called. The official-looking guy asked me to go "sit in my spot," as he called it.

"Am I ready for this?" I asked Ellen as we embraced tightly, my head on her shoulder.

"You are, Gary. You've got the mouth and the heart and the passion. Now you've got the time and chance. Make a difference. Say it like there's no tomorrow, because without chiropractic there may not be."

"You're right, El, thanks for always being there for me."

I looked around to give B.J. a kiss and noticed that he wasn't sitting in his chair.

Ellen and I walked from the kitchen towards the den where all the TV commotion was going on, and there he was, sitting at the desk with TV lights glaring down on him, performing a little skit for the TV crew. He was talking in his half gibberish, half English concoction of a language.

"Abuh, uppa dah, dah dah, cow moo, cat meow, horse neigh, wow, wow, wow, wow, wow."

"He's going to be a great performer, Doc, when he gets older. He's quite unafraid of this set up," said the tall cameraman with a big smile. "By the way, can you give me an adjustment when we're done? I haven't seen my chiropractor in months and while we're here, with you being a chiropractor and all . . ."

"Sure. It would be my pleasure, as long as my son can help," I replied.

B.J. kept up his conversation and must have noticed the letters on the camera, because he started saying, "W, B, C, T, V." Ellen and I and the camera crew were hysterical. He was so cute. It was nice to have such levity at a time when I was so nervous.

"He's taking after you, my dear," said Ellen. "You're both hams."

"I hope they taped this," I chuckled as Ellen picked B.J. up from center stage.

"We love you. Break a leg," Ellen smiled.

"Dah-dee, Dah-dee, Dah-dee," B.J. chanted, and they walked out of the room.

"It's show time, Doc, are you ready?"

Gulp. Am I ready? Are we all ready? Is chiropractic ready? Are chiropractors ready? I took a deep breath in and released it with a long sweeping sigh. "Ready," I said. And I was, and we were, and chiropractic is and chiropractors are.

Chapter 10

"My name is Gary Adio and I'm a chiropractor. As Dave Davidson explained, we are gathered here today because of an unprecedented event in the United States affecting its great people. This disease, appropriately named HADES, seems to destroy everything in its path. Everybody except people under chiropractic care.

"And that is why, as chiropractors, we've been called to perform a duty beyond anything ever done before. This is our moment to show the world what we've known for over 100 years. That chiropractic is far beyond back pain, neck pain, headaches and whiplash. Chiropractic is about restoring the body to a hundred percent of its possible potential and about revitalizing the immune system by insuring a hundred percent connection between the immune system and the nervous system.

"This HADES can and will be dethroned by chiropractic, but only under one condition. We chiropractors must act fast, swiftly and decisively. HADES is the most rapidly transmitted and most lethal disease ever seen. But it can be stopped, provided we hit it head on with the full force of 55,000 chiropractors.

"What does that mean? That means we must throw our differences out. Straight, mixer, machines, no machines, rehab, AK—I don't care who you are or what you do, we must adjust every man, woman and child in this country within one month's time in order to stop this disease in its tracks.

"Today's front page headline tells us that the drug companies are working on a vaccine that could be ready within a month. I have several questions about that. What should we do during that one month period of time? Just wait? Sit and wait and pray the disease doesn't find its way to us? No. We have to be proactive. Instead of waiting, we will adjust everybody we can get our hands on and boost each person's immune system. Create an all powerful defense mechanism that won't let the virus take hold.

"And who is going to do this? Who is now responsible for the welfare and health of our people? The chiropractors. We finally have the opportunity to show the world what we can do, what chiropractors have been put on earth to do. Look what we have before us. We have one month to make a stand. When D.D. Palmer discovered chiropractic in 1895, he said he had found the answer for uniting man the physical with man the spiritual. We have become a disconnected society with tons of crime, lots of anger and hatred, incredible physical and verbal abuse. And most of all, we are one of the sickest countries in the world. We rank number 64 in the world's top one hundred countries in terms of our health, and we are ranked number 25 in infant mortality, or infants dying before age one. We have seen more cancer and heart disease occurring each year even though billions of dollars are being poured into research by the American Cancer and Heart Societies.

"All that money has come up with nothing. And for our children, our poor sick children, between Sudden Infant Death Syndrome, ear infections, asthma, allergies and the rise in childhood cancers like leukemia, our innocent children are sicker and dying more in this country than in 24 other industrialized countries. That's crazy! And if that's not enough, AIDS makes its entry in the eighties. Well here we are in the nineties and now we have HADES. It doesn't matter where it came from, there is no medical technology that can stop it. Vaccines won't work. You can't tell me that taking a healthy body and injecting the most deadly virus ever seen into it is a good idea, whether or not the virus is inactivated or killed or whatever.

"Plus, how are they going to come up with a vaccine in one month's time if AIDS has been here since the eighties and they still haven't found a safe vaccine?

"Here's the answer. It's chiropractic. Chiropractors, please get ready. Be in your offices tomorrow at noon, because as has already been seen, there have been lines outside most chiropractic offices. But now, now is the test. The NMA has been fighting us for years, telling everybody that we are no good and trying to destroy us since day one. They have pushed us into a corner so that now they tolerate us, call us "lower back pain specialists," and even there they fight us tooth and nail. But now we have the answer and they are defenseless for one month. Here is our opportunity. Carpe diem! Sieze the moment! Take it in our hands and work the miracles our forefathers saw every day. The miracles will be the millions of lives saved. The miracles will be all the people who did not catch HADES.

"Chiropractors, I know we are not used to being in the catbird seat. We are used to being the underdog, the ones behind, the ones below. Well, now we have the opportunity to become number one, and it's not because we forced it or politically paid someone off, it's because the medical community has nothing more to offer. Their system has failed and its time for a new system of healthcare to take over. Imagine, in the next few weeks we will adjust every man, woman and child in the country. No time for talk, massage, machines, analysis, X-rays, anything. Just adjust. I will even recommend cervical or neck only adjustments unless there is a special need. But you can do what you want, providing you adjust, adjust, adjust, and adjust.

"Who am I? Why was I chosen to deliver this message along with the leaders of the UCA and the NACA? Because I am like you, I am a chiropractor out in the field with no political affiliation, only the deepest love for our profession. I am like you. I go to work, a sole practitioner, and I do my duty to my people, and when I'm done I come home to my wife and son. Chiropractors, our lives just got bigger. All of us, all together, have to go beyond our office and beyond our families and beyond our wildest dreams of how many people we can possibly adjust in one day, or one week, or in our lifetime. We must go beyond, and go deeper, and work harder and longer than ever before. We must charge reasonable fees. We must reach all of the people. We can't let any spine go untouched because of finances. We must rock our foundations to the core, chiropractors, to do what must be done. We must give beyond all expectations, realizing that the true reward is not our financial gain but the gain of our country's being saved by chiropractic.

"Without us this country may not make it. With our initial effort, we can, we will, and we must do it. We must perform the impossible to bring chiropractic to its new position. Our reward will be knowing that we saved our country from this crazy disease, and that by doing so, we have become the chiropractors that our ancestors dreamed we would become. No one could ever have predicted this. No one could ever have prepared us for this. But here we are, and now we are ready.

"B.J. Palmer once said, 'You never know how far reaching what you think, say, or do will affect the lives of millions tomorrow.' Well, tomorrow is now. We can make a stand. Change the world. Save the world, one spine at a time. One adjustment at a time. Or we can drop the ball and watch the world spin out of control, saying to ourselves, 'If I had only tried, maybe I could have made a difference. Now look what I have done.'

"Yes, Chiropractors, it is as big as that. We are all equally important now. You are now responsible for the health of your community. Of every person in your community. By being a chiropractor, whether you are still in school or have been out in practice for a year or 50 years, you have put yourself into a special position. We have been given a sacred trust, as B.J. Palmer said.

"My friends, my fellow Chiropractors, I love you because you love the things that I love. But to ensure that we are all here to enjoy these things that we love one year from now, we must go where no man has gone before. Watch as the world changes before your eyes. A whole new world. It's up to you."

My lower lip started to quiver, my eyes filled with tears. "Thank you."

The next 15 minutes went by in a flash. Dr. John spoke so eloquently that I cried when he was done, too. Even Dr. Larry from NACA spoke well, for him. He even said to give up the machinery, the diagnostic equipment, and just get the people adjusted. There was a brief question and answer period, but honestly, I don't remember it. I wasn't even all there. I was in a dreamlike state, sort of floating around after awhile. When I was asked questions, I answered them. I was being innately directed, inner driven.

Everything I said during the question and answer period was being spoken through me as if somehow B.J. Palmer was whispering in my ear. My answers were pure, unadulterated, one hundred percent principled chiropractic, nothing else.

There were so many questions coming in that the little microphone in my ear said, "We're going to skip the final comments and just continue with the questions for the last fifteen minutes, okay? So make your answers your final comments."

I nodded my head to this little voice from wherever (the studio, I guess), and that was that. Of course, the most popular questions were by far, "How can we possibly adjust that many people in one day?" and "How do we charge them?"

My answer to those questions was, "You accept all cases, regardless of condition or financial ability. Be fair and do what's right. Remember, this isn't about you, it's about saving the world, one spine at a time."

And then it was over. The lights went off and there it went. Ellen came running in with B.J. in her arms, hugged me and kissed me and told me how incredible it was and, "If that doesn't motivate them, I don't know what will."

I smiled at my beautiful wife and my handsome son, took them deeply into my arms. The TV crew dismantled everything and was about to take off before I even had a chance to adjust them. As the head TV guy was leaving, I asked them if he and his crew wanted adjustments. I didn't realize there were so many people outside; operating the controls, the antennas and stuff, but I adjusted each and every one with B.J.'s help, as he gently pushed on their backs, trying to imitate me.

Chapter 11

"We just called your home. We got here as fast as we could," said an out of breath Benny, a long time patient and Chief of the Fire Department. He could have been a defensive end for any major league football team.

"Luckily an older neighbor of yours saw someone strange snooping around the house and she was watching him very carefully. The next thing she saw was smoke coming from the back of your office and this guy running to his car. I'm sorry, Doc, I'm so sorry. He must have poured gasoline and you know how quickly that ignites."

My heart had stopped the moment I saw the fire trucks. With tears swelling up in my eyes, I turned onto my corner as Benny had motioned me over. He kept on talking and apologizing but I didn't hear what he was saying. I just saw the smoke rising from the far corner of the building, yellow and red angry flames leaping, the large picture window broken, and about 30 yellow coated firemen scrambling around to keep the flames down.

"And there was a note," was the next thing I heard as I was studying the three fire trucks on the street and two on the front lawn. And then I shook my head as I realized this, there were the people, my beautiful patients, standing behind police barricades. They looked stunned, disheartened, trying not to look at me in the Jeep as it idled quietly amidst the chaos in front of us.

"The guy left this note dangling off your wooden sign at the corner. Open it, Doc. What does it say?"

Crash! Another window broken by a fireman's ax. All these years. All those files. My computers. My tables.

"My tables! Oh my God, my tables! Benny! Benny! Get your men to bring out my adjusting tables. There are three of them in there. I can still work outside, it's summer, I can rent a tent. Please tell them now!" I shouted.

Benny ran off and I saw him and two others sprint into my building. I just sat there in my Jeep, transfixed by the scene, my mind taking mental photographs of this image and comparing them with the fleeting memories in my mind of the first few weeks of practice years ago. Signing the lease, my hand shaking and sweating since I had graduated less than a year before and had no money and no experience. My first patient came when I was having my X-ray unit installed. She asked if I was open. I said "Absolutely," even though there were corrugated cardboard boxes everywhere, from my walkway throughout the waiting room into the X-ray room.

I also remember the painting party when four of my college buddies helped me paint the office before my first open house. My first lecture at the office, which had attracted more people than I had ever dreamed possible. I'll never forget how every chair was filled and people were even standing. God, now it's all up in smoke. All the burning . . .

"Doc, we did it! We saved the tables!" Benny was panting and smelled heavily of smoke. "Well, two of them at least. The one in the front room was, ah, well, not usable, uh, melted, sort of. But we did it, Doc! We did it!"

"Thank you, Benny." I looked in his eyes with sincere gratitude. He was one of my first patients. "God bless you and your crew, Benny. How is it in there?"

"Well, honestly, it's not bad, Doc. Obviously this guy never did this before, because he only poured gasoline on the outside and didn't do anything on the inside, so only the front half of the office is badly affected. Unfortunately, that's where all your files are. The rest will be damp and smoky, but okay. Within a half an hour we will have it under control. Hey, did you read the note?"

"No, actually I didn't. I'm so wrapped up in watching my office smolder. I know who this note is from. I was warned by telephone not to go on TV last night with my chiropractic message."

"Yeah, you were great, Doc. Really inspiring!"

"Thanks, I sure hope so. But I've gotten calls from this guy who keeps on telling me that I'm making a big mistake by telling the world the chiropractic story and how it will stop this disease."

"Wow, arson! It hasn't happened in this town in years. We'll have to do a whole investigation. Make my job more interesting, you know."

He looked at me, realizing what he had said, "Well, I mean, I'm sorry about it's happening and everything, but this is intriguing to me in a weird fire chief kind of way."

"No reason to apologize, Benny. I understand. At least you saved my tables so I can still adjust my patients. I'll adjust the whole crew too, when they're done." I took in a deep breath, "So let's open this note."

I tore it open. Whoever did this went to the great trouble of cutting out individual letters and pasting them onto a page like you used to see in bad mystery movies. It read: "I told you not to do it, but you did. If you think this is bad, wait till you see the evening news."

Benny and I just stared at each other. I realized I was still sitting in my Jeep in the middle of the road. God, what does he mean by that? I didn't even want to say it out loud.

"Benny, could you guys please run in and pull out my cordless phone that's in the hallway? I've got to make some calls."

"You mean this one?" He handed me the black phone from his yellow fireman's jacket pocket. "I knew you'd need this. I called your home on it before, so it's still working."

"Thanks so much, Benny. Let me pull my car over and call my wife and the WBC News crew."

"Sure thing. By the way, I recommend you call Red to have the auxiliary police keep an eye on this place at night during your off hours."

"Good idea. Thanks." And with that, Benny smiled and turned to go back to supervise.

I realized that I should probably call Jack and ask him to protect my wife and son, too. He had always told me whenever I needed protection, to ask him. Well, the time has come. I jumped because just then the cordless phone rang. I answered it as chipper as I could, "Dr. Gary, speaking, chiropractic can help you."

"Gary, Gary, Gary! I heard the message from Benny! Oh, God, what's happening? Are you okay? Is everything ruined?" my wife said panicky, and I knew her lips were quivering and eyes watering.

"Ellen, I'm okay and the fire's almost out. It was set, obviously. Probably by the same person who made all the phone calls. Listen, I want the alarm system on all the time now in the house. As a matter of fact, I'm going to ask Jack to watch over you guys. To be your kind of bodyguard, okay?"

"Oh, God, Gary. B.J. and I will be right over. Don't let this stop you. Don't let them defeat you. You adjust people under the trees if you have to."

"I already thought of that, beautiful. Benny and his men saved two of my three tables. We'll adjust 'al fresco' until we can get back in. I'm going to call Fred DeGennaro and ask him to be our contractor and get the best men to fix us up ASAP. In the meantime, tomorrow, we'll rent tents so we can adjust whether it's raining or not. Good thing this is August."

"Gary, this is crazy. This is not what it's all about."

"Yes it is, Ellen. The National Medical Association and the drug companies can't take the fact that we are in control. They are going to fight this tooth and nail. They've got nothing left but arson now."

"You've got to call Rick."

"You're right. Good idea. Plus, I'm going to call Dave Davidson at WBC News and get a crew out here. I'm going to make this into a positive by getting more press and telling the story again and again on the news. Gotta go, El. Come over soon."

I clicked off the phone and put my head back on the headrest. "Oh, God," I said out loud, "what are you doing to me? I'm strong but not this strong. Are you sure I'm ready for this? Are you sure I'm the one?" I shook my head and got out of the Jeep. The walk to the front door was the longest it has ever been. Hoses everywhere, broken glass, the smell of smoke intensified as I got closer to the door. Adding to the sight of the smoke, the blackness around the door and window frames made a sharp contrast with the white of the once newly painted exterior. My shoes made a crunching sound against the broken glass on the sidewalk as I neared the open front door, or should I say, front opening, because the door was nowhere to be seen. I looked in. What remained of my waiting room was a really scary sight. The ten chairs were destroyed, the TV/VCR was melted beyond use. The front desk was now a pile of rubble on the floor, including my computer. Thank God for my daily back-up discs. Every picture, poster and brochure that used to be hanging on the walls was either gone or charbroiled. Most of my files were still smoking and hissing with the water and the fire. But amazingly enough, by the grace of God, the huge corkboard with all the kids pictures was intact and perfectly untouched. The center piece of my waiting room was unharmed. "Glory, glory hallelujah," I yelled like an evangelist, "The kids I adjust every week somehow had enough power in their pictures to save themselves. That's what chiropractic is all about. That's why I do what I do. It's about making the world a better place for them. A healthier place for my son and all the sons and daughters." I turned around and noticed I was talking to no one but the kids in the pictures.

I thought of my son, B.J., and how he loves to come to the office and play with all the other kids who come here. "God! B.J., I hope this is a sign that it's all going to work out. I feel like a man on a mission," I told my chiro-kid pictures. I plucked the corkboard off the wall and brought it outside to where Benny had left my tables.

"Hey, Doc, can you adjust me now or are you too busy?"

"This is a good enough time as any," I said, as I turned around and saw one of the WBC camera guys from last night. "Just the man I wanted to see! I was going to call you guys to get this on the news tonight, and here you are. But where's your truck?" I asked.

"Oh, I live around the corner. After I heard your message last night and felt the power you talked about after that adjustment, I said to myself, 'I'm going to make it a point to stop here tomorrow morning.' What the hell's going on here?"

"Well, I guess I made a few enemies. They've been calling me and today they even left me this dandy note." I pulled it out of my pocket and showed him.

"Jeez. This is crazy," said the camera guy. (I still didn't know his name.) "Do you have a phone, or did that go up in smoke too?"

"No, actually, a few things were spared. Luckily someone was watching the arsonist and called the fire department as soon as it happened."

"Man, I feel so sorry for you. I mean, how can you work out here with nothing? No walls and stuff?"

"Well, don't feel sorry for me. I'm lucky that it's as minor as it is. The main thing is that my tables were saved and my phone works and I'm still in business. Get a few tents, a few folding chairs and tables, a few lights for nighttime stuff, and I'm set. By the way, what's your name?" I asked.

"Brad. Brad Dunstreet." He was a good looking young man, with long curly brown hair, tied with a 'tail' in the back. "How can you be so positive when your office is burnt down the day after you made such a profound and monumental speech on TV?" He looked at me with his head cocked to one side.

"Because he's a man on a mission," Jackie said as she ran up behind us. We both turned to face her. "He adjusted me last Thursday on an airplane as he was coming back home from a speech in Washington. As a matter of fact, he adjusted the whole plane, passengers, crew, even the pilot and copilot. And now I'm working for him part time, in between flights."

"Hey, Jackie! That's right. We're all on a mission! Sure, things in my office are smouldering, but what should I do? Give in to this guy's demands? Stop adjusting people, stop telling people the chiropractic story? If chiropractic is going to save the world, we cannot stop now. This morning I hope there are chiropractors all over the country absolutely flooded with patients. As a matter of fact, I'm sure there are."

"Well, I can tell you one thing, Doc," said Brad the cameraman, "the ratings last night were higher than a Super Bowl, that's how many people were tuning in. You guys certainly had a lot of attention. But do you really think chiropractic is it? You almost sound religious, the way you talk, as if you were some kind of evangelist."

"I am an evangelist. I'm a chiropractic evangelist. Chiropractic is not a religion, but as chiropractors, we have a moral and religious duty to serve mankind, as the founder of chiropractic said. And now, in this crisis, more than ever, it is our moral responsibility to bring chiropractic to the masses. I mean, for years the greats of chiropractic have been predicting something just like this to happen. Some out of control virus to claim millions of lives, concocted in a laboratory by some mad scientists who are so narrow-minded that they didn't even realize that they are killing the world with every new drug, antibiotic, and surgery they came up with. And they all asked, who will be the survivors of this coming plague?"

"Chiropractic patients, just like what happened to the first people who came in contact with the disease," answered Jackie. "That's why I'm a chiropractic patient now. It makes so much sense, how the nerves control the immune system and all. I just never thought about it till now."

"This HADES disease gives us no choice. Before we were just biding our time, waiting for the straw that would break the camel's back." I hadn't noticed, but Brad had pulled a camcorder out of his bag and was video taping this whole speech. "The super viruses, one by one, came up that were not effected by antibiotics. The Gulf War veterans who contracted bizarre diseases, or whose offspring were deformed because of untested vaccines. Hundreds of thousands of people dying each year because of nonprescription drug reactions. Did you know that over 106,000 people die each year due to drug side effects? Isn't that crazy? That's more people dying each year from drug reactions than from motor vehicle accidents. And what do they do about it? Nothing. To put it into perspective, I've heard it said that 106,000 people per year is equal to something like one 747 airplane dropping out of the sky and killing all of the people on board, each day, every day, each year.

"Now if that really happened, if a new 747 crashed every day, after a few days or so, what would the government do?" I asked. Patients had started coming over and there was a crowd facing me, Jackie, Brad, my two adjusting tables and my chiro-kids corkboard. "The government would close all the airports, wouldn't they?"

"Of course," said Jackie emphatically.

"Well what happens when 106,000 people die each year due to drug side effects?" I asked.

"Nothing. Nothing at all," several people in the ever-growing crowd said in unison.

"Exactly, and that's not even counting deaths from unnecessary surgeries. Medical negligence is one of the top killers in this country (heart disease and cancer being numbers one and two). So what am I getting at? We did not have a healthy country to start with, even before this virus made its appearance. We have a failed medical system that is killing thousands of people each year and creating drug addicts of still more thousands. Instead of giving nutritional advice for a patient with high blood pressure, they say, 'Take a pill.' Instead of saying, 'Take magnesium,' to a migraine headache sufferer, they say, 'Take this pill or this injection.' Instead of saying, 'Exercise and eat right,' to an overweight patient, they say, 'Take a pill, or let's do a liposuction.' Instead of saying, 'Go to a psychologist and talk out your problems,' they say, 'Take Prozac or Valium.' How is that going to solve any problems? Or is it just perpetuating them? Just patching up the symptoms before they appear again. It's like putting a finger in a dam about to burst, or trying to patch up the Titanic as it was sinking.

"And who do they prey on the most? The elderly and the kids, the most helpless ones. We have one of the most unhealthy countries in the industrialized world and that is even more painfully so for our children. Why are ear infections so rampant in our children? It's because we poison our tiniest, most perfect little babies with heavy duty powerful poisons called vaccines that weaken an already immature immune system. Did you also know that the number one way to get a second ear infection is to give the child antibiotics for the first one?"

By now there was a sizable throng of people there, all listening to me babble on. "So what has been created here in one of the greatest countries in the world? A society dependent upon doctors to tell you what pills to take or what organs to remove. Dependent upon TV commercials to tell you what over the counter remedies you should take, or now, even what prescription drugs to take. All this is a substitute for taking personal responsibility for your own health. You, each one of you, control your health. You don't need anyone to tell you the Latin name for your problem. What you need is to assume full responsibility for your lives and your health. You can chose health without pills, without surgery, but you need one thing to assure that. And that is to be sure that your body knows exactly what to do at exactly the right time, that all the information from your brain is getting to all the parts of your body at a hundred percent so that each part knows what to do and when to do it and how much or for how long. What controls this master communication system? This pipeline of life?"

"The brain," I heard a familiar voice say.

"Exactly," I said, realizing who it was who said it. "Rick! Wow!" I said as I turned around, "I'm so glad you're here."

"Hiya, Doc. Never miss a big story," answered Rick.

I winked at him as I continued. "So the brain controls all this orchestration the way a conductor leads the philharmonic. The body depends on the brain to tell it what to do, so imagine your lungs, or your heart, or your liver, or your kidneys, or your back, or, most importantly, your immune system, not getting the complete messages from the brain. That part of the body will do its best at 90% or 80% or 70% or whatever percent less than normal, but here's the kicker. If the lungs, for instance, are working at 80% efficiency, what happens to the rest of the body?"

"It gets weaker," said another very familiar voice. There was no mistaking that voice.

"That's right, my darling wife," I answered. She had B.J. in a backpack so he was above the crowd and could see all the action. I smiled at them as I went on, "I have adjusted my beautiful son since the day he was born so that his perfect little body would stay perfect. Why wait until his body shows symptoms before rushing in to fix them? Why not keep his perfection as near to perfect as we can? We don't wait for our teeth to rot before we brush them. Why do we brush them every day, sometimes three or four times a day, and floss them too? To keep them healthy and clean. That's called dental hygiene. Well, I'm suggesting spinal hygiene. Now more than ever, you need to have your spines checked on a regular basis. Not just to avoid back pain or feel better, but to boost your entire functioning and especially your immune system, to the near perfect level it should be. How do you avoid contracting HADES disease?"

"You get adjusted," yelled several of my patients.

"That's right. That's the only way the initial survivors made it who came in contact with this horrible virus. All the survivors were chiropractic patients. All of them. One hundred percent. Our profession has been predicting this plague to happen for years and have been saying that we chiropractors have to reach the masses to prepare them for this. Well, I've got to say, our profession got hung up in back pain, neck pain, headaches and whiplash. But now the truth is coming out. The truth that has been known all along but it took a catastrophe of this proportion for our position to be heard and understood. You, you out there. It's too late for drugs. Too late for a vaccine. Their failure has lead us to this. Their failure has created this. Chiropractic and only chiropractic can lead us out. Out of the path of this darkness and into the light of a happier and healthier country and a new millennium. Yes! Thank you."

The crowd erupted with applause. My wife, with our son on her back, came up to me and kissed me. I held her tight. Well, as tight as I could with my son in a backpack on her back.

"So, about that adjustment?" asked Brad. "By the way, I got most of what you said on video. This will make the news tonight. At least some pieces of it."

"Great, Brad. Thanks." And he laid down. "When you help spread the message of chiropractic, then you're helping others."

Brad was on the table and said, "I videotaped the firemen and fire before I talked to you. It will make for some great footage."

"Chiropractic is bigger than this. Chiropractic is bigger than some petty arsonist. Chiropractic cannot be stopped by fire, by mudslinging, by propaganda, by anything."

"Can I quote you on that?" asked Brad.

"Sure, why not." And Brad's adjustment was done.

From there the day went. Ellen and B.J. had gone back home and brought back ten folding chairs and a folding table, and Jackie had salvaged some paper and was writing down who came in on blank sheets of copy paper. Our new patient forms were blank index cards with names, addresses and phone numbers and insurance information. If they didn't have insurance, we asked them to pay whatever they could. Jackie thought the idea to accept all cases regardless of condition or financial ability to be, "Amazingly cool and unlike any doctor I ever heard of." I told her many chiropractors practiced that way.

I adjusted one person after another, both tables always occupied, me going from one table to another and back again, over, and over, and over, and over. I thought I was hungry after a few hours but didn't stop and the hunger went away until around 3:00 P.M. when the crowd was down to a handful. Ellen had left awhile before to give B.J. a nap and told me not to forget to eat, but I guess I had. Just as I was thinking that, Lorenzo, the "Italian Stallion," as we call him because he looks just like "Rocky Balboa," showed up with two big plates of pasta with homemade sauce.

"You can cater my next party," I told him. He smiled and put a red and white checkered napkin around my neck.

"I can tell you're a slob when you eat spaghetti," Lorenzo laughed.

"How do you know that?" I asked, as Jackie and I ate plates of pasta in record time. The remaining dozen or so people courteously talked amongst themselves as we ate in hurried silence.

One of the older patients said, "Doc, take your time. You're not due on TV for another few days now."

I smiled at her and nodded because my mouth was full and I couldn't reply without looking like a complete slob. I looked down at my napkin and thanked Lorenzo because there were red tomato sauce spots all over the napkin. That would have been my shirt. I guzzled some water from a Poland Spring bottle that another patient had brought earlier, and was back in action for another hour or so.

At five o'clock I adjusted Jackie and gave her a big hug. She left saying, "Don't forget to see yourself on TV tonight."

Rick! Oh my God! What had happened to him? He'd been there in the crowd hours ago and I'd never had a chance to talk to him. I smiled and waved at Jackie as she made a left onto the main road. Just as I was about to kick my adjusting tables for not talking with Rick, the cordless phone rang.

"Gary, are you done yet? I've got a plane to catch."

"Rick, by golly! I was just thinking about you. How did you know to call now?" I asked.

"I've been calling Jackie all day. She's been giving me the inside scoop. Quite a resounding talk you gave this morning. Even better than your first TV appearance last night."

"Yeah, well, that's not why I'm doing this."

"Maybe you should give yourself more credit, old buddy," said Rick. "But anyway, you didn't answer my question. Can we meet before my plane leaves tonight at nine? Are you done?"

"Yes, come by now and we'll go back to my house and eat dinner and chat. You can meet Ellen and B.J."

"Okay. I'll pick up some take out food. Vegetarian, of course. I've got some bad news though," his tone suddenly changed.

"What, you're telling me some bad news? I don't want to know it."

"You don't?" asked Rick.

"Okay, tell me. Let me sit down, I don't know you well enough for bad news to be minor."

"Gary, you were not the only one affected," he hesitated for a moment, "the way you were today," said Rick very quickly.

"Uh, huh. Can you be a little more general, please?" I said, sarcastically.

"Well, ah, the fire thing? You're not the only chiropractor who had a . . . fire thing today," Rick mumbled.

I held my breath and bit the inside of my lip. "How quickly they organized," I mumbled, "those bastards."

"But the good news is, that most of your colleagues did exactly what you did. Very impressive. I don't think any other profession, or even any other business, would ever have done what you all did today. Remarkable!"

Rick sounded so genuinely enthusiastic, as if he were really getting into this. That made me excited. We really needed an ally in the press just then. Surreptitiously, fate made it that we should meet again at the right place at the right time. It was not a coincidence. Our old friendship had set the foundation for this.

"Well, I'll tell you, Rick, chiropractic is just about the only profession or business who could do this. All we need is our hands. They used to tell us in school that they could paratroop us anywhere in the world and we would be ready to work as soon as we hit the ground. One professor even said we could adjust in mid-air if we had to."

"So, I have two important questions for you, Gary. Number one, when do you think that this is going to stop? And number two, what else do you think will happen to chiropractic because of this?" asked Rick.

"I think I know where you're heading with this. First off, I cannot tell you an answer to number one, as to when I think this

HADES thing is going to be beaten. But honestly, I believe that if chiropractic really can mobilize and do what we were meant to do, and born to do, and trained to do, I believe that within six months to a year, HADES will be gone."

"Really!" exclaimed Rick, "That soon, six months! How do you figure that?"

"Well, if someone throws you a fast ball and you are an excellent batter and you connect with it, won't it fly out of the park faster than if someone lobbed a slow pitch to you?" I asked.

"Hmm," Rick mumbled, as he mulled this over in his head, "you know, you've got a point there, Gary. The faster it comes at you, the faster you strike back at it, the faster it will head out of the park. I think I've got it! That's why being on TV was so important last night, so that you can strike a chord and get everybody moving as quickly as possible.

"Now, answer the second question, Gary. Or are you avoiding it? Oh, by the way, I'm taping all this, okay?"

"Sure, no problem. What was the second question again? I was so into our conversation that I can't believe I've forgotten what the question was."

"Yeah, right. You don't want to answer my question about how else chiropractic is going to benefit from all this."

"My take on the whole situation is that after however long it takes to stop this thing, people will be so enamored with, number one, how chiropractic stopped HADES, and, number two, how much better they feel and how much healthier they are, that they're never going to stop getting adjusted. Getting chiropractic adjustments, I truly believe, will become a regular weekly routine, just like going to supermarkets. Plus, I'll tell you what else I think is going to happen. The price of the adjustments will go down. Do you know why?"

"Down? Are you kidding? Do you know I've heard reports of a few chiropractors charging outrageous fees already?"

"Sure, there will always be the crook who will take advantage. But no, Rick, the cost will go down so that everybody can afford to get adjusted, in every family, whether they have insurance or not. The insurance companies are going to realize that not only did chiropractic help this country, but it also saved them billions of dollars of unneeded drugs and unnecessary surgery, and will save money because people will be so much healthier they won't have much need for drugs and surgery like our society does now. Or should I say, 'used to?' That's besides all the money they are going to save because of people not dying from HADES, not having to use their insurance to pay for catastrophic life support."

"So, chiropractic will be a preventive measure, not just a stop gap measure?" asked Rick.

"Exactly. Precisely what chiropractors have been saying for over 100 years since D.D. Palmer discovered chiropractic in 1895. It's about how much sickness and suffering will be *avoided* and *prevented* simply because the nervous system in every man, woman and child in this country will be working at one hundred percent, one hundred percent of the time."

"Sounds great. Why don't you drive home and we'll meet there and talk some more. On the drive home, would you think of one more thing, though?"

"Sure, what's that?"

"What would B.J. Palmer be thinking right now?" asked Rick.

I was shocked. I didn't know what to say. "That caught me off guard, buddy. That's a bright question. Good thing I've got a few minutes to think about it."

"Okay, see you soon."

I immediately called Ellen. She sounded really excited. "Did you see today's newspaper? You made the front page, and Rick was the author!"

"It's nice to have an ally in the press. Plus, did you notice the cameraman from last night at the office this morning? He said he's going to get the fire and the speech on the news. Anything that can be done to promote getting people into chiropractic offices is great. The quicker the better."

"Come on home. You are doing an awesome job like usual. You're really making this happen."

"It's not me. It's chiropractic. God chose now, so here we are. Chiropractic has been waiting for this for years. I'll see you in a few minutes."

With that, I clicked off the cordless phone, adjusted a few more stragglers and gave a big hug to Red who was in charge of watching my office overnight until we got it repaired. Red was called Red for obvious reasons. Short but strapping, with red hair, red eyebrows and a red moustache.

I got into my Jeep, turned it on and realized I'd forgotten to take the cash box with me back home. I didn't want to leave it sitting outside. I left the car running, opened the door and went towards the makeshift office on the front lawn: two tables, a dozen folding chairs, a folding table, a cordless phone, a cash box and . . .

The next thing I remember was being face first on the ground and turning around, to see the fireball that a few seconds before had been my Jeep.

Chapter 12

The explosion had knocked me down so hard that I had to spit the grass out of my mouth. Red was by my side in an instant.

"Doc, are you okay?" he yelled, as he reached for me.

"Yes, I think so. Are you?"

"Yes. Oh, man, you're bleeding from your mouth. Jeez! Was that ever a close call. I hope you are a praying man."

"Yes, Red, and if I wasn't, I'd start right now. Oh, my God, Red, if I had stayed in my Jeep a few seconds more, that would have been me." By now the blood was filling my mouth, and as I sat up, I spat out a mouthful.

"Let me see your mouth, doc. Where is it coming from?"

"I think I bit my lower lip. That's where it hurts. I'm okay. Really." My head was spinning and my lower lip was throbbing, but I wasn't going to give in to all this.

By then the fire trucks had pulled up, for the second time that day. Benny came running up. "For Christ's sake, Doc! What happened now?" he cried as he looked at my bloody lip. "Gosh, are you all right?"

"Yeah, I'm fine. My Jeep exploded. Lucky for me I got out just after I started it. Otherwise, well, forget it. I can't let this frazzle me."

With that, two more fire trucks and three police cars pulled up. Even the volunteer ambulance came screeching to a halt. The paramedics ran toward me, holding two large crash cases. I sat there on the ground, blood dripping from my mouth, surrounded by two paramedics, a handful of police officers, and watched the firemen once again come to my service, using some kind of foam to put out the fiery wreck that used to be my beautiful red Grand Cherokee.

"Do I need stitches?" I asked dazed, breaking the awkward silence of the small crowd around me. We had all been staring at the firefighters racing around, watching the flames turn to smoke, then to hissing and smouldering. One of the paramedics told me I only needed a butterfly. As he cleaned off my lower lip, the police chief pulled up in his Bronco. He shook his head as he approached me. He made me aware that it would be awhile before I could leave since I would have to answer a litany of questions.

I called Ellen and told her I'd be late. When I told her why, she flipped out, understandably. She wanted to come over right away. I asked her to stay put since my next phone call, before answering questions, was to Jack. I asked him to come over and spend the night in our home, as our new official protector. Ellen calmed down, Jack agreed to be our bodyguard, the captain finished his investigation, and Red offered to take me home.

We drove to my house in silence, which I honestly appreciated. Red had had sense enough to know that I didn't want to talk, really couldn't talk, didn't even know what to say right now.

He pulled into my driveway and said, "I'm sorry, Doc, about what happened today. If it means anything, I support you a hundred percent."

"Thanks, Red, it means a lot. More than I can tell you. Hopefully that will be the end of this kind of stuff for awhile, so I can just go about my business."

"I hope so, but honestly, I'm glad I'm going to stay on guard at your office. Maybe you should have someone come to your home, too?"

"I thought of that, too, thanks. Another great patient like you, Jack will be my 'home bodyguard,' so to speak." I stopped for a moment, feeling very humbled by all this. "Red, thanks for being there," I said as I opened the door and shook his hand.

"See you in the morning, doc. No worries, right?"

"That's right, 'Crocodile Dundee', no worries. See you around six A.M."

As I stepped into my home, B.J. came running into my arms. "Dahdee! Dahdee! Dahdee!" I scooped him up and hugged him. "Noses!" I said, as we rubbed noses. "Kisses!" I said as we kissed each other. Tears started welling up. "Mwah! I love you, B.J."

I scarcely got out his name, before I broke down in hysterical tears. Ellen, who was watching our little welcome home ritual from a distance, came running over to me, held me tightly and said, "I love you, Gary." She looked at me and whispered, "It's okay, Gary. You're safe now."

I sank to the floor, tears running and my body quivering and shaking with fear, anger, frustration, plus the scene playing over, and over, and over again in my mind. I watched my Jeep turn into a fireball, imagining that somehow I hadn't gotten out. Hadn't gone for that cash box. The three of us were tightly together now, B.J. and Ellen holding me as I was slumped against the wall of our foyer. I was gasping and choking for air between sobs, my eyes soaked with tears.

"I love you, Ellen. Oh, God!" was all I could manage to say before I broke down even more and felt a thousand years of tears pouring from behind a dam with a million holes in it. The flood-gates strained to retain what force of power lay beyond the wall. I shook my head, sobbed and kissed them both. Wet and slobbery kisses as I looked up at God and yelled in a voice that neither B.J. nor Ellen could have ever understood, but I did.

"Me? You wanted me? Of all the people, you chose me? God, why? Am I who you want? Are you sure? Why me? Oh, God. Oh, God. Oh, God. Oh, Ellen, Ellen, Ellen, B.J."

The doorbell's ringing stopped my tears instantly. Ellen got up and looked through the peep hole. "It's Rick." The doorbell rang again.

"My Jeep. Oh, God, Ellen, my Jeep." I said as I was crying but gaining a small measure of control.

"This is about your Jeep? Who cares about your Jeep! This is about you!" demanded Ellen.

The doorbell rang and someone knocked on the door. "Go ahead, Ellen, open the door. It's okay."

Ellen opened the door. I was still sitting on the floor with B.J. Rick came in, holding packages, followed by Jack.

Rick and Jack looked at me with their eyes bulging out. I must have been an interesting sight. Bloody chin and mouth, blood stains all over my shirt, eyes still red and puffy with tears, sitting in my hallway in the dark, holding my son. They looked very puzzled by this whole situation.

"Hi, Gary. Everything okay?" asked Rick cautiously.

Jack said, "So you finally gave him one on the chin, huh, Ellen?" and smiled a sheepish smile behind his sunglasses. Black leather cap, black T-shirt, black jeans and black boots—Jack's trademark outfit.

"My Jeep. They blew up my Jeep!"

"What!" Even Jack took off his sunglasses.

"I'm lucky to be alive. I am so lucky. It must have been on a timer or something. I started the car, and then I ran out of the car to get something I had forgotten, and about 20 seconds later it was in flames. I, I could have pulled out and been, been . . . " I broke down in tears again. I was so embarrassed, but I couldn't hold them back. B.J. hugged me and Ellen sat next to me stroking my hair and kissing me. I regained composure again pretty quickly, not wanting to keep crying in front of Jack and Rick.

"Je-sus, Doc! Who did this?" asked Jack.

Now I knew why I wanted him to protect my family. He was huffing and puffing like a mad dog. "Jack, I'm so glad you are here. I really appreciate your loyalty. Unfortunately I haven't the foggiest idea who did this. I imagine it's the same one who set my office on fire."

"Your office on fire! What? Holy cow!" raved Jack.

"It's been one of those days, Jack, but I'm okay. That's what counts. They can't get me. They can burn my buildings and try to blow me up, but obviously God has other plans for me," I said, gaining some confidence back.

Rick was getting all of this down on his trusty pad and paper. He looked me up and down and said, "There were fires all across the country today, Gary. How is it possible to be that organized that quickly?"

"I can only think it's the power of the NMA and the pharmaceutical industry that doesn't want to see their little system overturned. They've had it really nice for a long time, and it's coming to an end and they're fighting back. Brad from WBC News taped my talk this morning and filmed the office fire, so hopefully he's got the pull to get this televised. We need to show people that if the National Medical Association was so confident, why would they resort to such violence? If they thought that chiropractic couldn't do what we claim it will do, why would they be so ready to commit arson a thousand times over. Obviously, they are concerned that what we are saying is right and are scared to death to lose their cozy little position."

"That's a good point," interjected Rick. "If they weren't afraid of you guys they wouldn't be reacting so violently and so swiftly and on such a massive scale. Hmmm." He wrote so fast I wondered if it was possible that he was writing in shorthand.

There was a long moment when none of us spoke. Four adults and one toddler just sat there, mesmerized by the intensity of the moment. We were in the midst of a metamorphosis that would change the world forever. It was a deep, cosmic, profound moment.

"Food! Yum, yum, yum," B.J. said, breaking us all out of the trance.

"Yes, Chinese tonight, okay? It's on me," said Rick, and we all retired to the dining room to wolf down some moo shu vegetables, vegetable lo mein, and other Chinese vegetarian entrées.

Rick left shortly after dinner, telling me I should look forward to his article in tomorrow's paper with a follow up story in Tuesday's science section. We asked Jack to stay over any night he could and sleep in the guest bedroom downstairs.

He said, "I'd take a bullet for you, Doc. It's my honor to serve you as you have served me over the past five years. It's my chance to give a little back to the man who saved me from the surgeon's knife."

We went to bed early that night, thankful for no phone calls, no doorbells ringing, no strange shadows lurking outside our windows. I slept pretty fitfully and woke up feeling very sore in my neck and shoulders, probably from adjusting so many people, and from falling face first after the explosion (which had created a whiplash-like effect in my neck).

So I called Dan, a chiropractor down the road from me, at around six A.M. Monday morning, expecting to hear a message, asking if I could pop by some time that day.

He answered the phone, "Hi, Dr. Dan speaking, can I help you?"

"Dan! What are you doing up?"

"Gary, why aren't you in your office yet? I just walked in and have a dozen people waiting. You probably have a line out the door, especially after that rousing little excerpt that was on TV last night."

"That's right! I forgot all about watching it. Well anyway, can I pop over for a quick adjustment in a few minutes?"

"Sure. We can trade adjustments. I can use one too. Sorry about your office. They didn't hit mine yet, but they sure hit plenty of others. It was all over the news last night, the news you forgot to watch."

"Yeah, I know," I replied. "I had a kind of crazy night last night. Not following the plans I designed."

"True, but sometimes God has other plans for you besides the ones *you* think are for you."

"It seems to me, Dan, I've been hearing that a lot lately. See you in a few minutes." I hung up the phone, dashed out the door, not ready to start the day until I got adjusted.

His office was packed, and so were the other two chiropractic offices I drove by. We adjusted each other quickly, exchanged hugs and off I went to see the scene I was to become very familiar with in the coming weeks, a line going around the office and down the block. Red, with his auxiliary police car was out front directing traffic.

"Whew. It's seven A.M.! When do I have to get here to beat the crowds?" I asked myself as I pulled up into the driveway.

Red called to me as I walked up, "I called you about a half hour ago, where were you? They started coming at six-thirty. Woke me up from a dead sleep."

"Sorry, Red. Thanks for watching this mess that used to be . . ."

"That is your office. Fred just called and said he'd fix up your office so you could be inside by the end of the week. He also said he's going to call a buddy of his to set up two tents for you so if it rains, you can still work. He told me that he's so thankful for not having to take painkillers for his arthritis since he started coming to you five years ago. He even said he hasn't had one cold since his first adjustment."

"I could barely walk myself before I met you, Doc. Thought I was destined for surgery. Been a hundred percent ever since, and no more sinus problems, to boot." His red hair was a bit disheveled after sleeping in his truck all night.

"There you go. This chiropractic is really something, isn't it?"

"Hey, doc. Are you scared by the NMA? They are going to do anything they can to fight you. Not just chiropractic, but you. You're the guy doing the talking."

"Well, that may be, but I'm also one guy just doing lots of adjusting. Yeah, I'm afraid. But, we have a mission to perform."

"You're right. Let me get some sleep. See you tonight."

"Thanks again," I said, as Red trotted off to his Bronco.

I shook the hands of everybody within reach and the day began as all the days had begun lately. I adjusted one person after another, after another, after another, not realizing when Martha had arrived, trying to keep my hands going as fast as I could, and making sure all the new patients had filled out a new patient index card. I didn't even notice when Fred DeGennaro, my favorite old time contractor, came over with his men and started ripping apart my burnt out office, until I heard a loud crash of a once useful filing cabinet being thrown into a small dump truck. Even then I just stopped for a split second to look up, nodded his way, yelled "thank you," and continued my non-stop adjusting marathon.

94

I took a quick lunch break at 1:30 when Ellen brought me over her delicious vegetarian roast and some salad. The three of us ate quickly and our conversation was even more rapid. By 2:00 P.M. I was back at it after kisses goodbye. By 9:30 P.M. the last patient was adjusted and I sat on a folding chair with sweat literally pouring off my forehead. Fred had gutted the burned part of my office, at least as far as I could see from my vantage point in the chair. I couldn't muster up enough courage or energy to actually walk into the office. Plus my lip was still throbbing from last night's fall.

This had begun only twelve days before, when Senator Gallo had called me to Washington, D.C. to give testimony to the Senate about the power and possibilities of chiropractic. I was to meet with him briefly tomorrow morning at the Route 4 Diner for breakfast to discuss the "new developments" as he had called them. I didn't know what he meant, but I told him 5:30 A.M. was fine as I gulped and shuddered to think how early I had been getting up and how little I was sleeping. I wondered out loud, "How long is this going to go on?"

For some crazy reason, after adjusting Red, I hopped into the rental car and tuned into the AM dial on the radio, something I rarely ever do except when it's snowing out and I want a quick weather report. And it was August, so I knew I would hear more than just a snow report today.

"Since the first outbreak of HADES in May, in about four months' time, it has claimed about 9,000 lives, approximately 100 a day. The scientists at the CDI expect another 30,000 lives claimed in the next thirty to sixty days. 'Can chiropractic really save us?' the NMA challenged today. Or can the anxiously awaited vaccine, which the NMA plans to make an announcement about tomorrow morning, save us? First reports in from across the country indicate people are going to chiropractors in record numbers. Lines around the block seem to be a commonplace occurence during the last few days at chiropractic offices."

"But the NMA asserts this HADES disease is too powerful to deal with by the chiropractic approach. 'It is exponential in its infection,' quoted Dr. Block from the CDI, 'if left unchecked, upwards of 800,000 people will die in the next six months. We plan on having a major vaccine breakthrough announcement tomorrow morning.'"

I turned off the radio. I didn't even listen to my motivational tapes. I yawned as the drive home seemed to take forever. I was a strong guy. I got adjusted once a week, worked out four days a week, played hockey once a week, ate vegetarian cuisine, slept well every night and had plenty of family time. Now I felt completely out of balance, out of sync. I was wiped out and it was only twelve days into this thing. Sure, lots had happened in twelve days, but how was I going to last six months, or even six weeks, for that matter? As a matter of fact, what if it took longer than six months? Or worse yet, what if all the chiropractors out there couldn't keep up this pace, myself included?

A bad thought popped into my head. "What if chiropractic isn't enough? What if it's too much, too little, too late—or however that saying goes? What if you need to have months or years of chiropractic care under your belt to be immunologically ready for this? How many people will die who do get adjusted because they didn't have enough adjustments? Or is one enough?

I never doubted chiropractic. I know my long standing wellness patients are not going to be affected by this at all. I know chiropractic will work for them. It's the new people I had just adjusted that day for their first time ever. Would it help them? Would they be ready?

Then my worst fear went through my mind. "What if we can't get to all the people quick enough because there aren't enough chiropractors to go around? God help us!" My mind was racing now and I was practically hyperventilating. Too many 'what if's.' I was relieved when I turned into my driveway which would give me time to talk to Ellen. She would calm me down.

B.J. came running up to me as I opened the door and he hugged my legs, saying "Kisses!"

I bent down to be kissed, and he kissed me making the "Mwah" sound.

Ellen came running over and said, "Hi, Gary!" with a big smile. When I looked up at her from kissing B.J., she said, "Uh oh, what's going on now?"

"Oh, Ellen, I'm just hyperventilating here. What happens if it doesn't work? If it can't work? If there are not enough of us to make it work? If we all can't keep up the pace? What do we do? We are not prepared for this, Ellen. What do we do?"

"You do what you're trained to do," said Ellen. But sensing that one sentence wasn't enough, she hugged me again and dragged me over to the couch while still wrapped in her arms. "I know that's not the answer you want, and it's too simple of an answer, but honestly, what choice do you have?"

"Oh, Ellen, I haven't had the time to work out or do yoga. I keep on getting up earlier and earlier and patients are already there. I need to sleep and eat right and exercise and meditate properly, and I can't."

"Gary, the reason you were in such good shape before this was to prepare you for this."

I took a deep breath as I looked into her deep blue eyes. "I know that, Ellen. I know that. But I'm scared. My whole body is sore, I'm tired, and it's only just begun. What will I do, what will we all do?"

The phone rang. I was right next to it, but Ellen said, "No way, I'll pick it up. Hello," said Ellen, "Oh, hi Thomas, how are you?" Pause. "Yes, I know you two keep on missing each other." Pause. "Yeah, it's been crazy for everybody, I guess." Pause. "Sure, hold on a second. It's Thomas, Gary."

My best friend, Thomas. We had met as freshmen at New York State University. I was the short, scrawny one. He was the tall, chunky one. We clicked when we found out we were both only children. "Hey there, old buddy, are you as exhausted as I am?" I asked Thomas, my bestest buddy in chiropractic.

"Je-sus H. Christ. F'in tired would be the proper terminology. And F'in sore, too," answered Thomas.

"Yes, I was just asking Ellen about how I was going to keep this up, and how were others going to keep this up. By the way, I'm sorry I haven't called. I can barely feed myself, shower, and go to sleep when I come home, let alone be social and make phone calls."

"Yes, between all your TV appearances, you mean?"

"Yeah, yeah, yeah. Like I planned all this?"

"I know, just joking. Honestly, Gary, I always knew you'd be the one for the job."

"Oh, thank you, Thomas, but what job did you ever think would match this one?"

"Oh, I don't know, but I really have thought of you as a sort of torch bearer. You just never had the chance to hold the torch until now, when it really counts."

"Thanks! If you didn't live so damn far away I'd come over and give you a hug."

"Don't come too close to me. I know how you smell after adjusting all day," Thomas chuckled.

"Yes, actually I'm surprised nobody dropped dead from the stench in the last few hours, although I must say I sense some odor coming from your side of the phone, too."

"Oh, that? That's my flatulence, darling. All those dead cow parts I've been eating. Yum, yum."

"You icky carnivore, you, Thomas. Get a life and go veggie. Maybe you'll live to be a hundred like me."

"No thanks. I'll die young eating my filet mignon and beef tartare, thank you."

"Fine, have it your way. Get it? A little Burger King humor."

"Very little."

"So, Thomas, did you call to make fun of my eating habits, after contacting me for the first time this century?"

"No, in reality I didn't want to call you at all. Anne Marie made me."

"Now don't you pull your beautiful wife into this. How is she doing? Getting bigger by the day? Do you feel the baby kicking?"

"Oh, it's awesome. You should see her, she's huge."

I heard her say, "Hey!" in the background.

"Well, she's perfect."

"That's better," I heard Anne Marie say.

"For a whale," Thomas whispered.

"Hey, I heard that," Anne Marie said.

Then Thomas said, "Ohh!" and I heard the phone clunk on the ground. "Chiropractor abuse! Chiropractor abuse! Help! Help! I'm being repressed!" Thomas laughed as he got back on the phone.

"You deserved that, you know."

"Yeah, and I love it."

"So am I talking to you in this conversation, or should I hold on?"

"No, no, I called you, Gary, and you are who I want to talk to. Oh, that rhymes, how pretty! That would make a good song: 'You are who I want to talk to . . . ' hold on, let me write that down."

"Wait a minute. You said, 'no,' when I asked you if you wanted me to hold on."

"No, I didn't."

"Yes, you did."

"No, I didn't." ·

"Yes, you did."

"No, I didn't."

"This isn't an argument. This is merely taking the contrary point of view."

"No, it isn't."

"Oh, God. Are we Monty Python heads, or what?"

"Oh, yes."

And we both laughed like old friends laugh, who know what each other is talking about without saying it.

"Yup, those were the good old days, Thomas. And we thought college was hard times."

"Yes, we were a little misled then," answered Thomas. "So anyway, I heard your office burned to the ground. Actually I saw it on TV. Very bold of you to adjust outside."

"Well, maybe, but I'm sure you would have done the same thing and pulled your tables outside, too."

"Yes, I have a much nicer view than you do. The mountains are much prettier to look at than main roads."

"Well, the nearest mountains I have are in B.J.'s diapers. Other than that, you've got me beat on high points."

"Oh, yeah, whatever you say, Gary. So, did I tell you we're having a baby?"

"Oh, is that what's going on with Anne Marie? I didn't want to say anything, you know how fragile she is."

"Oh, yes, fragile is a good description of her. That's why they call it the 'Pebble of Gibralter' too."

I chuckled. "Ah, yes. The wit and witticisms of Dr. Thomas. You've been swamped, I presume?"

"Gadzooks! Have we ever been. I didn't know this many people lived up here. Me and Andy have been packing them in. Hey, do you remember Doc James, the older chiro down the road from me?"

"Yes. Why, what happened? Did he renounce his membership in the NACA?"

"No, Gary, he quit. He said this isn't chiropractic the way he wants it. So he got up and quit. We were all begging him to adjust people at least until this is all over, but he said he's been looking for an out to retire and this was his chance.

"You know, you ought to take a look at this concept, Gary. You, me, Andy and chiro's like us, we love this stuff. The more the merrier. But there are lots of chiropractors out there who are probably mad as hell at being told they can't practice a certain way, even if it is temporary. And others who just don't want to keep up this kind of pace. I mean, I'm tired, but I can take it. I'm young and strong.

There might be a growing dissention in the ranks that you should look into."

"Good point, my chiro buddy. I'm meeting with Senator Gallo tomorrow morning, and I'll have to plan a meeting this week with Dr. John, too. I was just telling Ellen about how wiped out I was and this is only the beginning."

"Yeah, well, this is the vision that B.J. had, only not for this reason."

"Yes, maybe so, and also not this rapid transition. I mean, we're going from seeing 10% of the population to seeing maybe 50 to 70% in two week's time. Then, if this keeps up, we could probably get the whole country adjusted in a month."

Just then the call waiting beeped on my line. "Hold on, Thomas, I've got that annoying call waiting thing."

"Go for it."

"Hello, Adio residence."

"Yeah, yeah, yeah. Cut the fancities."

"Oh, hi, Dr. John, I was just . . . "

"Of course, you were. That's why I called. That's the cosmic AT&T in action."

"It certainly is. Karma, man. Could you hold on a second? I'm on the other line."

"Make it snappy, kiddo, this is my dime we're a-wastin'."

"Yes, sir." I clicked on the other line.

"Thomas, I've got to go, it's Dr. John."

"Sure, drop me, your bestest buddy, just for the president of the most important, influential, interesting, illustrious, innovative . . . "

"Yes, Thomas, I'm dumping you. Good bye, good night and good luck."

" . . . incredible, um ah, intolerable . . . "

"Um, ah, bye Thomas."

" . . . infamous, indelible?"

"Bye." I clicked off Thomas and back on with Dr. John.

"It took you too long. I'm billing your membership card an extra quarter this month."

"Fine. I'll pay with interest."

"So, I'm coming over to your house tomorrow night, okay?"

"When?!!"

"Tomorrow. I have to be up in New York City to meet with three board members, so I figured I'd pop bye and tell you some new developments. You don't mind that I've appointed you chairman of the HADES committee?"

"Ah, no. Thanks for asking. So, do you want dinner?" I asked.

"Yeah, well—wait, you're one of those veggie chiros aren't you?"

"Yes sir, and damn proud of it."

"You don't know how to curse. Okay. I'll eat your tofu and bean sprouts or whatever godforsaken plants and wheat grass and okra and wild oats you may have sprouting in your backyard garden."

"Oh, yes. In my spare time I manage to do a little organic farming as a side hobby," I retorted.

"Sarcasm! I hear sarcasm! Anyway, you don't happen to have a video conference call set up, do you, in your computer room?"

"In my computer room? You must have mistaken my house for a different mansion."

"Oh, you should see my house. It's the electric gizmo capital of the world. It comes in handy when you're the UCA president, you know."

"Yes, I'm sure, Dr. John."

"Dr. John, Dr. John, why do you call me, 'Dr. John?'"

I paused, not knowing what he meant exactly. "Because that's who you are?"

"No, I mean, just call me John. Do I call you Dr. Gary?"

"Whew, okay, John. So I'll see you when tomorrow?"

"Nineish. And don't forget about the tofu sandwiches."

"Absolutely, with extra soy cheese to boot."

"Dee-lish!"

Ellen and B.J. were waiting for me to eat dinner as they always did.

"El, honestly, between your pep talk, Thomas' and John's, I feel better."

"Of course you do. That's why you chiropractors are always networking and calling each other. Because it's so hard to stay focused on the truth when there are lies all around you."

I sat down at the dinner table next to B.J. "Let's say a prayer tonight before dinner, okay?"

"Okay. That's a nice idea. We should do that every night."

"Dear God, thank You for everything You have given us. Thank You for Your love, for our beautiful family, and for chiropractic. Thank You for keeping us happy, healthy, safe, and together. Thank You for helping spread chiropractic to the masses because chiropractic and only chiropractic can save us from this HADES disease. Thank You for giving us the strength to go on when we feel like we have no more strength. Thank You for giving us the courage to speak our minds, to speak the truth no matter who believes it, because we know it is right. Thank You for giving us the heart to love the philosophy You taught us, that is: God first, family second, chiropractic third. The 'GFC' principle is the centering force of our family. Thank You for leading the way, showing us the right path to take, even though the road has many forks. Thank You for always giving us the energy, determination, motivation, and perseverance when we need it the most. When we are tired, You soothe us. When we are out of breath, You breathe for us. When we are in pain, You heal us. Thank You for leading us out of the fear that is HADES into the truth that is chiropractic. Amen."

"Wow!" Ellen said with a sniffle. "That was really beautiful."

"Wow, wow, wow, wow. Dahdee, dahdee, wow. Kisses!" said B.J., and I leaned over and kissed B.J. and then Ellen.

"I love you, Ellen. You're my best friend in the whole world."

"Do you remember when we first heard Dr. Charles speak? Maybe seven years ago? He told a story of how there was a garbage dump near Southern Chiropractic College. Someone bought that land and built a multi-million dollar shopping mall on top of that dump. The lesson in that story, he said, was that you can build a castle on top of a garbage dump. You don't have to wait until you've removed all the garbage; you just go ahead and build your dreams on top of the garbage.

"That lesson changed our lives, Ellen. Thank you for taking the journey with me."

"It's been worth every minute of it," said Ellen, as she came over to me and sat on my lap.

"Oh, I forgot to tell you," I said. "Dr. John is coming here tomorrow night, and I've got to meet Senator Gallo tomorrow morning at the Route 4 Diner."

"Tomorrow morning, are you kidding?" asked Ellen.

"No, Ellen, I wish I was. I told him 5:30 AM so I could still be at work by seven. Crazy, I know. Masochistic really, but when else can I meet him?"

With that, Ellen sighed, "I love you, Gary, no matter what you do. Okay, everybody, let's eat, then it's bed time."

Chapter 13

I pulled up to the Route 4 Diner and realized instantly that this was not going to be an ordinary breakfast. Police were everywhere. Four black limos with U.S. flags on the front bumpers were parked by the front entrance, as well as a black van with several antennae and radio dishes sticking out.

"I guess I'm not dining alone with the Senator today," I said to myself, as I pulled my car into the parking lot. I noticed my car was the only non-government or non-police car in the lot. In my rear view mirror I saw a policeman turn a car away that was coming in right behind me.

Several men in black suits and mirrored sunglasses approached. I rolled down the window, since I had a feeling I shouldn't step out of the car.

"Dr. Adio?" said the suit closest to me.

"Yes sir? I suppose you need to see . . ."

"I.D., please, Sir."

I pulled out my wallet and I was about to pull out my driver's license when he said . . .

"We'll take the whole wallet, sir. Please wait here." The other suit stood next to my door. I figured out by now that I was officially waiting. A few minutes passed, and the first suit came back to the car and said, "Thank you for waiting. Please come with me."

I walked inside to the unfamiliar sight of a completely empty Route 4 Diner. Empty, that is, of customers. There must have been about 25 police officers, 15 Secret Service agents and a few other official looking people. The Senator was sitting with another gentleman at one of the round tables in the middle of the restaurant. I didn't recognize the other person from the back until my escorts and I got up close.

"Oh, my God! Mr. President! Senator! Good morning! It's an honor, Sir. I would have dressed more for the occasion if I had known you were going to be here, Mr. President, Sir," I said, kicking myself as I realized how stupid it had sounded.

"Oh, so you wouldn't dress up for me, would you, son?" laughed the Senator. He was such a grandfatherly type in the way he looked and the way he spoke.

"Oh, no, well, that's not what I meant, Senator, sir," I stumbled and stammered, not expecting the kind of breakfast that lay before us.

"Sit down, son, and don't be so nervous. I may be the President, but other than that, we're all the same."

The President's smile was even more disarming in person than it had always been on TV. Well, they say you never get a second chance to make a first impression, and his certainly was good. He looked like an older John F. Kennedy with FDR's glasses.

"Yes, Sir. Thank you, Sir. I guess I'm a little surprised meeting you here, Sir."

"Well, Bart and I didn't want to stir anything up. I wanted a chance to meet with you one-on-one, with no press involved, to talk to you about the current situation."

"I'm honored, Mr. President, and equally honored by the Senator's asking me to help out in any way that I can."

"Well, that's good, son, because frankly this whole HADES thing has me very worried. Everybody knows how close I was with Governor Alfonso. His passing really shook me up. Honestly, I don't know much about chiropractic, and what little I do know has nothing to do with helping people's immune systems. So my question to you, Dr. Adio, is this: Is this really going to work? How can I believe this when all I know about chiropractors is that they are good for back aches?"

"That's a good and very valid question, Mr. President, and I'm glad you brought it up. The Senator called me one month ago asking me why it was that all the ambulance and hospital personnel who had been in contact with the first victims died, except those under regular chiropractic care.

"Chiropractic is not about making pains go away or making someone feel better. It's about changing people's lives. It's about making sure the brain and the body are working in perfect harmony with each other, in perfect balance, by insuring perfect communication between the master communication system and the rest of the body. The brain controls everything and sends all this information down the spinal cord and out the nerves. The goal is to make the system stay intact and working at 100%, so the body can work at 100% and fight off anything adverse that comes its way. If there is a blockage anywhere in this system, instead of getting 100% information, a nerve is now interfered with, and is only transmitting 90 or 80 or 70% information. If that's happening, then you will have reduced function in that nerve and everything that nerve serves to 10 or 20 or 30%. So if something is supposed to be operating at 100% and is now operating at 70%, what would that do to that person?"

The President looked at me and the Senator and said, "I see what you're saying. That person would be less than he or she should be."

"Exactly. It's like, it's like . . ." I tried to think of a presidential analogy.

"But," the President interrupted, "what you are saying sounds nice to me and it may look good on paper, but you still haven't answered my first question, which is . . ." the President hesitated for a moment and I swear I saw a tear in his right eye. "Is this really going to work?"

"Mr. President, with all due respect, my answer has to be, what other choice do we have? The supposed miracle vaccine won't be available for a month. Shouldn't we do something between now and then? We can't just sit around and wait for the scientists to come up with something. They are the ones probably responsible for this crisis in the first place."

"Now what you're telling me, son, is that we should bank the entire welfare on this chiropractic profession that, up to a few weeks ago, was accepted only for back pain relief? I just don't get it, Dr. Adio." He shook his head with a clenched fist over his mouth. "If what you're saying is true . . . let me ask you this. Why has chiropractic been such a secret?" He said this so low, it was just above a deep whisper.

"Why has this been such a secret?" I repeated in a low whisper. "I don't know. Maybe it's because the National Medical Association and the drug industry has, for so many years, been feeding the American public negative propaganda about chiropractic. Many chiropractors felt that the only thing we had a right to talk about, without getting ostracized or criticized, was how chiropractic helped back pain. Just because we work on the back doesn't mean that chiropractic effectiveness is limited to the back and surrounding muscles. The spinal nerves go everywhere, not just to the muscles around the spine. The nerves go to every muscle, organ and tissue in the body. So when you effect one nerve, you effect the whole body.

"Okay, here's an analogy. Let's imagine that a tire on your limousine out there is slightly out of alignment. That's a small problem. But because that tire is out of alignment, the transmission of the car has to work a little harder than before to run the car smoothly. And if the transmission has to work harder, then the engine has to work harder to run the transmission to turn that tire. And if the engine has to work harder, then you will burn more oil to keep running the transmission to turn that tire. And if you burn more oil, one day your mechanic will check your oil and say, 'Hmmm, the oil is low. I better add more oil.' Now, is your mechanic solving the problem, or is he merely fixing the symptom by adding more oil?"

"Well, I see your train of thought," said the President. "He's fixing the symptom."

"Right. Now suppose he keeps on checking the oil every few weeks and keeps on finding the same situation, that the oil is low. In response, the mechanic, thinking he is being a good mechanic, keeps on adding quarts of oil every few weeks. Patching up the symptom instead of solving the problem. Until one day, you're driving in your limo, and the oil gets so low in the engine that the engine seizes up and the limousine goes out of control and an accident occurs and our country loses a president. Now that small problem became a big problem, because that small problem now affected the whole country, and what effects the whole country, affects the whole world.

"But you see, Mr. President, everybody is that important. When one person is affected, the whole country is affected. So when one person has a misalignment in their spine, it affects the whole country and, because of that, the world. That is the biggest problem I know of, as B.J. Palmer once said."

The President and the Senator sat speechless for a while. I continued.

"The answer, then, is to realign the tire. Why? Because when you realign the tire, the transmission works smoothly, the engine runs more effectively, and you don't burn oil as fast. The whole car works better simply by realigning the tire. The whole world works better simply by realigning the spine. The moral of the story is that HADES isn't the only problem. The real problem facing us is that the American public doesn't have a strong enough immune system

106

to fight it off. Using a vaccine to fight HADES is like trying to boost the oil's performance by adding an oil treatment to the oil to improve its viscosity. The HADES virus isn't as much the problem as is the susceptibility of the weakened immune system of each American."

"Okay," said the President with a completely straight face. "So chiropractic is the right choice to strengthen our country's immune system?"

"Yes, Sir. Chiropractic knows how to get to the source. That's what we've been doing for over 100 years. That's why the medical profession and the pharmaceutical industry hates us, because we do with our hands that which they can't bottle in a pill or cut out with a knife. Why has chiropractic been kept such a secret? Because we have been backed into a corner for years until now. The current medical system is crumbling under its own weight. HMO's and PPO's are making decisions on what chiropractic and even medical doctors can and cannot do. That's not how the system is supposed to work. Now the medical system that has been in place for years is crashing down. Which leads me to my next point, if I may be so bold."

"You've been bold enough already, young man, so you might as well keep on going," said the President, smirking.

"Well, the tire analogy illustrates the same problem with vaccines. You can't create health in a test tube and inject it into somebody. Health has to come from within. Health is a result of the body's working at 100%, something called homeostasis, which is the term physiologists use for perfect balance. You can't artificially create balance. The idea of a vaccine is a noble one, but a HADES vaccine will create catastrophic results."

"Why?" asked the Senator before the President could say anything.

"Because vaccines don't work. The whole idea of putting a weakened or killed version of a virus that has been chemically altered, stabilized, and preserved and then thinking that it will cause the body to produce the same antibodies needed when it sees the real thing is preposterous. The antibody system works like a lock and key. Do you think my car keys will work in your limousine?"

"I hope not," answered the President.

"Well, here I am being bold again, Sir. What makes you think that a vaccine will work if it is not the same as the real thing. One lock, one key."

The President answered, "Well, the vaccines have worked for over 50 years. That's all the proof I need."

"Marketing. Propaganda," I said. "This is a philosophical question about logic. If the antibody system works like a lock and key mechanism and the immune system creates an antibody for a disgusting mess called a vaccine, is that the same thing as a virus in the real world?"

"Well, I don't really know, son," shrugged the President.

"Exactly. Precisely. And that's what modern medicine calls science. They don't know either. Medicine is guess work and so are vaccines! And get this, you know as well as I do that viruses tend to mutate. As a for instance, we have new strains of viruses such as colds and flus every winter. So what will stop the HADES virus from mutating? What if everybody in America is vaccinated with the HADES virus and either HADES itself mutates or the vaccine mutates? Then you have either a useless vaccine or a vaccine that's a killer itself."

The President stared at me for awhile. It felt like ten minutes, although it was only about thirty seconds. I was sure I had blown it. I should have kept my mouth shut and spoken only about . . . oh, well, too late now. The cat is out of the bag.

"Okay, okay. So you're saying chiropractic is going to protect our citizens from getting this horrible disease and the vaccines won't. What's your time frame?" asked the President, for the first time sounding a little shook up.

"Give chiropractic six weeks. You will see the changes. Like I said before, with all due respect, Sir, the NMA has nothing to offer right now except to wait for the vaccine. What should millions of Americans do in the meantime? Chiropractic is being proactive. Chiropractic has taken the bull by the horns before it has a chance to start charging at us full force. Chiropractic will take HADES down provided one thing happens, and that is that everybody in America gets adjusted. They've got nothing to lose and everything to gain. And we're not doing this blindly, your people as well as mine are tracking HADES statistically and we will plainly see, by the time they are ready to introduce the vaccine, that the death rate will either have leveled off or decreased. As long as we can get everyone adjusted. What choice do we have, Mr. President?"

"You know, Gary . . ." that was the first time he used my name, ". . . the NMA has been pressuring me to write a cease and desist order against chiropractic. Now I think I know why they have been pressuring me so hard. If what you say is true, then they feel very vulnerable right now because they can't do anything until the vaccine is ready. But," the President stumbled, "but how many more will die from this horrible thing like my dear friend, Governor Alfonso?" He took a deep breath in to control himself.

"People will die, Mr. President. I wish I could say we can stop it in an instant, but we can't. No one can. Here's what I believe will happen. Once a certain number of people get adjusted, two things will occur. Number one, everybody will want to get adjusted. Number two, at that target point called critical mass, HADES will start to fall. Once enough people start getting adjusted regularly, the tide will definitely change, and there will be enough strength in the masses that, due to the sheer force of opposition, HADES will be stopped."

The President stood up suddenly and in response, so did the Senator and I. "Okay, Gary. You've got a total of six weeks to show me the changes. But, if in six weeks there are no changes, then the NMA gets what they want and you have to step aside."

"Thank you, Mr. President. You haven't made a mistake. We'll deliver what we promise. Chiropractic will do it."

"My next problem is how am I going to explain this to the NMA. They don't believe in chiropractic and don't think it can help. How can I explain this to a bunch of nonbelievers?"

"Chiropractic is not about belief, it just works. Look at the results we get with infants and toddlers. I cannot explain chiropractic to them, show them pictures of model spines or X-rays, or verbally in any way get them to understand chiropractic before I adjust them. I just get down to their level, look right in their eyes and adjust them. And they heal like wildfire. Why? Because it works. Belief has nothing to do with it. These babies aren't convinced by me, so there's no placebo involved. Chiropractic works just like gravity, whether you believe in it or not."

"You've got an answer for everything, don't you, Gary?" chuckled the Senator. "My heart led me to you and that's usually when I make my best decisions."

"You will keep in close contact with the Senator who will keep me informed. You have six weeks from today. Better tell your boys to get a move on and make a miracle happen."

"Yes, sir. Thank you, Mr. President, sir." I shook his hand and smiled at him. "You've made the right choice. I'll stake my life on it."

"I sure hope you're right, and somehow I believe you are. The Secret Service men will escort you out. Thank you for your time and for your service to our great country."

"Thank you, President. Oh, two last things. Number one, can I have your autograph, for my son, of course? And second, have you been adjusted yet?"

Chapter 14

I ended up adjusting the President, the Senator, and his entire entourage of Secret Service men and police officers. By the time I got back to the office it was about 7:30 A.M. A throng of people stood waiting for me. I don't even know how I did it. We were still outside, but now we had tents set up, one for the adjusting area, and the desk where staff sat, and one for people to wait with lots of metal folding chairs. I felt as if I were putting on a play and they were the audience. We started using the old fashioned ticket method so everybody got adjusted in the order they arrived. We had several two piece ticket rolls, and whoever sat at our desk called out the numbers in order. We even had an on deck area, a few feet from the adjusting tables, where the next five people could wait until their turn.

We were becoming more and more efficient and had even found some old filing shelves in the basement so every person had their own file. I had brought my laptop computer from home and downloaded my chiropractic program into it so that we could keep track of all the patients. Good thing our insurance filing was done electronically, because there was no way we could have kept up with the volume of paper claims that would have been involved.

Somehow from all the chaos, order was appearing. We were developing the systems and the speed to handle all this and the organization was taking place by itself out of necessity. However, I was missing lots of lunches, missing lots of time with my wife and son, and not knowing how, at 5 P.M. I was ever going to keep on moving. By 9 P.M., my muscles aching and wiped out with fatigue, I raced home after talking to my wife who told me that Dr. John had just called and said he would be a little late. I don't even know how many people I adjusted and, at that point, was just happy to hear that Fred would have my office rebuilt by Friday or Monday of next week. Not that I minded being outside. So far my luck had held and we were having beautiful August weather.

I pulled up onto the driveway a little more relaxed, B.J. pressed his face against the kitchen window and was probably saying, or should I say, yelling, his 'da-dee chant'. I came out of the car and

111

walked over to the window and we blew kisses through the window with a "Mwah" sound. It was so nice to come home to such excitement.

I want so desperately to give B.J. a better world. Now I'm getting that chance, I thought, as I looked at my beautiful son. I never thought it would be like this. I had had a patient a few weeks before this happened say to me, "A few years ago, I prayed constantly about losing weight, and do you know what happened? I got food poisoning and lost 14 pounds in two weeks. You have to be careful what you pray for, and you have to be specific, because you never know how God's going to answer you."

I had prayed for a better world for B.J. and for me to somehow play a part. It was blowing my mind to think that my patient had been right. God had answered my prayer, just not in the way I had thought He would. "Maybe God has different plans for you than you have for you," I had heard so many times recently. How right they were. We're doing this for my son and for all the sons and daughters in the world, to help give them a better place, a healthier place, a subluxation-free place.

My son started banging on the window to get my attention back. "Dah-dee, Dah-dee, Dah-dee," he chanted, so loud it was as if there were no window separating us.

"I'm coming, I'm coming. I love you, B.J." I said as I woke up from my trance. He slammed into me as I opened the door, hugging my knees, and we kissed each other and he went screeching through the kitchen yelling, "Dah-dee. Love you!"

Ellen came over, hugged me strongly and whispered, "I miss you so much, Gary, I never get a chance to see you any more."

"I know, baby, I know. When we're together we have to make the most of that time. Quality is the key now that quantity is very limited. Hang in there. It isn't going to be like this forever."

"I know, it just seems like forever when you're in it."

We all ate and for the first time in a long while, B.J. sat through the whole meal. Ellen and I talked and with B.J. so calm, I even pulled my chair next to her so I could hold her hand. It was a nice moment, then . . .

The front door bell started to ring and ring and ring. "That's Dr. John. He always has to make an entrance." I ran and opened the door.

"Yeah, yeah, yeah. What's all the small talk about? Let's get on with business, okay?" He burst past me and gave Ellen and B.J. a kiss and hug. I always loved the shirts he wore—loud, just like him. His bright Hawaiian shirt really made his light skin color and the red freckles around his nose stand out.

"What about me?" I asked.

"You want a kiss too? No way, you're too ugly."

"Whenever I'm with you or even talk to you on the phone, it's like being in a fun whirlwind," I said.

"Yeah, nice comment. What do you want? You're already famous, more famous than me, and that pisses me off."

"Sorry, I only asked to help to change the world for B.J. I didn't know it was this involved or would take this sort of path, either."

"Sure, I position myself perfectly as president of this organization, and you steal the spotlight. You're lucky I like you and that you named your son correctly."

"Didn't you just walk in and say, 'Let's get right down to business?'"

"Oh, wise guy, eh? Okay, no more small talk for you. Sorry, I guess trying that friendly thing didn't work. So, you got any food?" He walked into the dining room and sat down. "Yum, pasta primavera, I presume, you crazy veggies." He pulled his handkerchief out of his jacket pocket and tucked it neatly into his collar. "I'm ready."

"How does your wife stand you?" I asked.

"She doesn't. That's why I'm always on the road traveling so much. She says she can tolerate me only in small doses."

I served Dr. John a big heaping plateful and Ellen gave B.J. a fork and said, "Give this to Dr. John."

B.J. went over to John and said, "Fork, fork. Eat, eat. Yum, yum. Taste good."

John took the fork and said, with a big smile, "Thanks, little man. What's his name again?"

"B.J. I know, tough one to figure out."

"Hey, I'm older than you, Gary. Give my brain cells credit for following the directions and getting here. So sit down guys and allow me to be rude and eat and talk at the same time."

B.J. sat in my lap and Ellen pulled a chair up next to me as Dr. John ate and explained the reason for his visit.

"Okay, first the details. We are starting Operation F Troop. The hospitals and prisons will be hit in all the major cities by the teachers from the various chiropractic colleges. We can't reach them all, however, and that leads me to the next point. There are rural areas and inner cities where there are no chiropractors. The solution:

113

Send in the senior students, and there are a lot more of those to go around. We're trying to coordinate all this as much as we can, but we only know where to go based on phone calls we're getting from people telling us where there aren't enough chiropractors. We're also relying on the Medicare model of physician shortage areas, assuming that where there are few doctors, there will probably be few chiropractors.

"Anyhow, now the kicker—morale. We're having a huge morale problem. Understandably so. Chiropractors are adjusting more people in a day than they used to in a month. The good news is that we are already reaching such a huge percentage of the population that it's astonishing. We are reaching more than half of the U.S. population already with at least one adjustment. The bad news is that chiropractors are falling apart physically from exhaustion and mentally from the stress of seeing such huge volumes, and to reach another 40% or so they will need to see even more.

"The hospitals, prisons, inner city, rural areas only amount to about 10% or so, so that still leaves a 30% increase per chiropractor. That's not going to be easy to do, or to sustain their morale. So, now that I've spewed all that out, got any ideas?"

"Hmmm. Well, what are some motivating factors we can come up with to boost the morale? What motivates you, John?"

"What motivates me? Sex, money, chiropractic philosophy and giving a great adjustment."

"Okay, great. Well, we can eliminate the sex thing . . . That just won't work."

"I betcha I could make it work," said Dr. John.

"I'm sure, of all people John, you probably could."

"Flattery. That's also high on my list. Now what about money? I like money. So do most people."

"Did I tell you I met the President this morning?"

"The president of what?"

I hesitantly said, "Well, uh . . . the President of the United States."

John stood up, "What! How do you get all this good stuff? What am I, chopped liver? Why didn't you invite me?"

"I didn't even know about it. I thought I was just going to meet Senator Gallo, and then here's the President sitting next to him! Do you know what he wanted?"

"An adjustment?" John said, as he sat back down.

"Well, I did adjust him, but what he wanted was the answer to two questions. 'Is this really going to work?' And, 'Why has chiropractic been kept such a secret?'"

"Good questions," said Dr. John, "I can't believe you met him without me."

"Next time I meet the President, if he gives me advance warning, I'll let you know. So anyway, let me tell you the idea I just had about money. The President is very eager to get rid of this HADES thing and obviously doesn't know whom to believe. As a matter of fact, he's getting lots of pressure from the NMA to make us cease and desist."

"Those bastards!" John pounded the table and the plates and silverware shook on the table.

"Hello! There's a child in this house," I interrupted.

"Oh, yeah. Sorry. I get so hyped up," said Dr. John. "Anyway, I just had a meeting with one of those S.O.B.'s last week. He talked about cooperation, and—oooh, that doggone . . ."

"John, John, John. This is a game we're used to. Don't worry. He gave us six weeks to prove ourselves."

"Okay, okay, okay. I'm calm now. I'm calm now. Six weeks is good. Just enough time for the numbers to start changing, according to our knuckleheads. So I mentioned sex, money, philosophy, and a great adjustment—and flattery. What's that got to do with you meeting the President."

"We've got to talk to him. We've got to ask him to insure that all chiropractors get paid for every adjustment they deliver, even if the insurance companies don't pay us. Or get a blank amount of dollars per chiropractor. Something to get chiropractors to realize that they will be rewarded for this, for their hard labor."

"Okay, we can do that. No sex though, huh? I really have a good idea."

"John, I don't want to hear it. My two year old is running around here someplace so you've got to keep it clean."

"Damn. Okay, okay. But seriously, Gary, there is a lot of dissension in our ranks. People are getting overworked and they're tired, frustrated, and cranky. What can we do for them now? I'm telling you, I think sex is the idea."

The phone rang. Ellen picked it up and I saw a puzzled look on her face. I heard her say, "Oh, hi. You're talking so fast. Sure, hold on."

115

"Gary," Ellen called, "there's someone on the phone for you. He said he's got great news for you and he really needs to talk to you. I think it's one of your patients."

"Excuse me, John," I said as Ellen handed me the phone. "Hey, what's up?"

"Doc, it's Roger, and you're never going to believe this. It's a miracle! A true miracle! Chiropractic saved him! Chiropractic did it! It's a miracle! I can't believe it! I just had to call and tell you."

"Wait, wait, wait. Hold on a second. That's great news, but fill me in on the details. Chiropractic saved whom?"

"My friend, Steve, don't you remember? Me and John brought him in on a stretcher about a week ago. He had HADES, full blown, he was shaking and everything. You adjusted him. Once, only once, and today they let him out of the hospital. He's completely well. No sign of anything. It's a miracle, Doc! You've got to tell everybody!"

I sat there stunned and silent on the phone. I think even my breathing stopped.

"Doc, Doc? Are you there? Did you hear what I said?"

"Uh, yes, Roger, I did. Wow! Sorry, I'm a little blown away by what you're telling me. I mean, this is just one case, but the ramifications of this are incredible."

"Doc, you've got to get your people into hospitals. Not only can you prevent people from getting HADES, you may also be able to help the sick get well, too."

"Wow. Well, we are getting chiropractic into hospitals. It's a project we are working on right now, literally. But we didn't realize the potential importance of this factor until now. Thank you so much for calling me, Roger."

I became unusually softspoken as the emotions were running wild in my head. "This is the exact news we've been waiting for, hoping for, praying for. Thank you, thank you, thank you for this glimmer of hope."

"Hey, Doc, no problem."

I hung up the phone and turned to Dr. John who was staring at me, obviously trying to interpret my side of the phone conversation. "Did you hear that?" I asked.

"Not exactly. I got the highlights. By the look on your face it's tremendous news."

"John, remember we were just talking about needing something to hold on to, something that we can tell the chiropractors now to get them to press on?"

116

"Yes, well?" John asked.

"We just got it. We just got the sign. Even if someone is sick with HADES, chiropractic works. It's only one person but I'm sure, I believe in full faith, that there are others. John, do you know what this means?"

John sat there and the biggest smile I have ever seen came across his face. He didn't say a word. A grin on my face met his and suddenly a burst of confidence shot through my body.

"This," John began, broken up by tears of joy inside him, "is what we were looking for. This is what we need to tell them."

Yes! We were smiling and crying at the same time. I walked over to John, high fived him, and embraced him. I guess the loud popping sound of the high five attracted Ellen's and B.J.'s attention. B.J. came running in, noticed our hug, and as he always does, wanted to be a part of it, so he pushed his little body in between our legs and hugged my thighs. Ellen came in and hugged us and B.J. yelled, "Sandwich! Sandwich!" his way of identifying the 'hug sandwich' as Ellen and I call it.

"Wow, two grown men crying and smiling! This must be really good news," Ellen laughed.

John said, "You tell her."

"Okay. Umm, remember, Ellen, when I told you that one of my patients brought in his friend who had full blown HADES and I adjusted him?"

"Yes, about a week ago, right?" answered Ellen.

"Exactly. Well, Roger just called and . . ."

"It works on HADES too!" John interrupted happily. "Yes! Yes! Yes! I thought it would, I dreamed it would, but I didn't know. By the way, Gary, you were taking way too long to tell Ellen. Holy sh . . ." John looked down at B.J., ". . . Holy cow."

Ellen kissed me and said, "Wow, unbelievable! We've got to get into the hospitals even quicker now. Do you have reports of other cases?" she asked.

"Well, not yet," John said, "but I'm sure there are more. I've heard a few reports of spontaneous remissions, which now I'll look into more. Okay. What we'll have to do is go into the hospitals in the ten cities that have the biggest outbreaks. If we can continue getting the masses adjusted and then slow HADES in the hospitals where it's probably spreading the quickest, we can do it faster than I ever thought. Wow! Wow! Wow!" John jumped up and slapped the ceiling with his hand. "And you know what, not one chiropractor has come down with HADES. I forgot to tell you that. Not one chiropractor and not one chiropractic family member either. I just got a fax as I was driving here today."

"Oooh, faxes in cars! Aren't you special," I joked.

"It's good to be the king," John laughed, and then got serious. "You know, we may have to divert some of the students from the rural areas and prisons and have them concentrate on the areas with the highest outbreaks. We have to get inside the hospitals where they need it the most, and any inner city area where lots of people are living really close together."

"Hey, John, are we going to have any problems getting into hospitals? I mean, it is 'their' territory."

"I'm sure the few hospitals around that already have chiropractors on board won't mind, but being that 90% of them don't have any chiropractors on staff . . . Another battle."

"Maybe I should talk to the President?" I said. "He promised me six weeks. He didn't limit us on where we could or couldn't go."

"Okay. Excellent. Now, before I go I have one more bit of news," said John.

"Great. Shoot."

"Remember, those clones that went haywire and started all this? Guess why?"

"Guess why, what?" I asked.

"Jeez. Guess why they went haywire?" John said exasperatedly.

"Because man tried to play God?" Ellen answered.

"Well, yes. But more specifically . . ."

"Tell us, John, the suspense is too much," I said.

"Vaccines. A vaccine gone wild. At least that's what my snitches have uncovered. Plus, get this. Guess what the rocket scientists are using to try to formulate a vaccine against HADES?"

"I dread thinking what you are going to say," I interjected.

"That's right, Gary. The vaccine that they are testing is based on the vaccine that started all of this in the clones. Now, this isn't a hundred percent accurate fact yet, but my sources are pretty damn good."

Ellen and I shook our heads in unison. "No way," she said, "it can't be so. That's just too stupid."

"That's progress for you."

"Do you mean to tell me that they are right now developing a vaccine based on the vaccine that started all this? A vaccine to counteract a vaccine?"

"Yes. Brilliant, huh? The scientists are actually calling this an anti-vaccine behind closed doors. But wait, there's more. Remember a few years ago hearing about a vaccine under development that had 41 different viruses and bacterias in it. Well, the vaccine given to the clones had 150 different goodies in it because they wanted to protect the clones against every possible illness. Unfortunately, they didn't realize that it would completely blow out the clones' immune systems. I'll keep my people working on this and let you know of any new developments. Anyway, I've got to go."

"So, what's the game plan, John?"

"Well, obviously it changed tonight. So here's my thoughts; get teachers to go to hospitals in areas where there are the worst outbreaks of HADES, in the ten cities where the clones were. We may have to divert some from other places to concentrate on the worst case areas. We also have to look at the inner cities more closely and get the senior students only to those inner cities with the biggest risk. We may have to divert them from the rural areas for now to see if we can have the quickest impact possible against HADES. I'll also have to get some very quick research done to see if other HADES victims were turned around by chiropractic.

"Last, assuming that chiropractic does help boost the immune system of enough people who already have HADES, after we accomplish our goal of the major cities and the hospitals, we can redirect the teachers and senior students to the other cities and rural areas. That's the game plan for now. How does it sound?"

Before Ellen and I could say anything, B.J. said, "Superdeedooper."

"Well, it's approved," laughed John, and John and B.J. did a high five. "You are so cute! We have to make sure it's a better, healthier, chiropractically based, subluxation-free place for when you get older. That's why we're doing all this. Do you know that B.J.? You're dad, and I, and all the chiropractors want to make a whole new world and a whole better world for you and your kids. Okay?"

"Okay," B.J. said. "Bye bye."

"How did he know I was leaving?"

"He heard you say it. He understands everything, even if he can't say everything."

"Hmmm, interesting. Some people are just the opposite," said John. "They say everything even though they don't understand anything."

Chapter 15

The next few days flew by. Dr. John couldn't muster up TV air time, so he sent a letter in one of those bright red, white, and blue airmail envelopes that really stand out and you just have to open it immediately, to every chiropractor in the nation. The letter was short, one page, and hit every issue we had gone over with enormous positivity. It was extremely well written. He noted how the virus seemed to be unable to attack chiropractic patients, and commented that adjustments help boost the immune system of those already effected with HADES.

Patient volume shot up even higher after a press conference held by the President during prime time on Wednesday night. He mentioned that even he is giving chiropractic a chance. He also urged everybody in the nation to go for it, since this is the only chance we have to do something rather than wait for modern science.

Boy, that must have pissed the NMA off big time! And then the President said, in passing, that chiropractors would be rewarded for their efforts should this turn out to be the answer that the American public needed.

I thought we were flying before that, but then Thursday was a, "Hi," adjust, "Bye." "Hi," adjust, "Bye," day. More and more people were coming in every day.

Dr. John called me up Saturday night saying that his new stats for this week showed that an additional 20% of the U.S. population had started chiropractic care. Mostly, he said, because of the President's message.

"We're up to almost 75%," John said excitedly, "which means we only need 15% more before reaching everybody in the country except the hospitals, the inner cities, and rural areas."

He told me that Operation F-Troop was going to start next week. They somehow had coordinated all the teachers and senior students and actually chartered flights, where necessary, to get into the ten major cities that had been most effected. He was very impressed by the juniors who volunteered to teach the freshman and sophomore chiropractic classes in their teachers' absence. The

121

juniors also suggested that they take over the care of all the patients assigned to the senior students and the teachers while they were away.

"The ultimate in team spirit," he called it, and he said he was so proud that his son, John, Jr., was one of those junior students who had thought of the idea.

However, the long days were taking a toll on me and my colleagues. On Sunday, a patient told me about a TV program I should watch that night that was investigating chiropractic and its response to HADES. We tuned in as a family at 9 p.m. and the first question out of the anchor's mouth was, "Chiropractic said it could help reverse HADES, but people are still dying. Why?"

I yelled at the TV, "Because we need time to get everybody adjusted first, idiots!" and I started throwing my socks at the TV. The TV didn't seem to respond to that. Then they showed a segment of different chiropractic offices, all mobbed with people. Unfortunately, they interviewed the chiropractors and made them look bad, with all of them saying how wiped out they were and how they could barely keep up the pace. Several chiropractors down in the south said that people were forcing them to stay open at gun point until they adjusted their wives and kids. On a very positive note, they closed the segment with a clip from the President saying, "It is our duty as Americans to try whatever we can to stop this disease. So try chiropractic. I am. So should you."

The days seemed to blur together. Monday looked like any other day of the week now that I had been working seven days a week for almost three weeks. Another letter from Dr. John came in one of those bright airmail envelopes. He hand-wrote on mine that he was going to keep sending notes, trying to keep morale going until he could get the TV thing up and running. In the letter, Dr. John reminded us that if we really poured it on in the next few weeks, we could show the President that chiropractic could either level off or check the HADES death rate. Then, the vaccine would be unnecessary. He urged us to push harder than ever before so we could do this by September 18th, Chiropractic's birthday.

Monday night, as I walked in the door, Dr. John was on the phone again.

"Hey, great note today. I like the way you tied in September 18th and Chiropractic's birthday."

"Yeah, clever ain't it? Glad you liked it. But listen to this 'bulldinkle.' Operation F-Troop has hit a little road block. The inner

122

cities welcomed us, thank God, but guess what all, and I mean *all*, of the hospitals did?"

"Don't tell me they caused trouble?"

"Beyond causing trouble. The wouldn't even let us in. They said that without medical degrees they wouldn't let us touch anybody. Most of the hospitals said the same thing: 'Nurses are better trained than you are.' Yeah, maybe so in drugs and first aid, but nobody can adjust somebody except us. Damn it, those stupid sons of . . ."

"John, John, John, calm down. Let's think this through. What should we do?" I asked, trying to stop him from screaming. It didn't work, and for the next minute or so I held the phone away from my ear as he cursed away. "John? Earth to John. Come in John," I finally said.

"Okay, I'm done. Thank you, Gary. I love the way you placate me."

"Listen, while you were screaming, I thought of something. We've got to call the President again. We can't pussyfoot around with this one. We've got to get in fast and only he has the power to do that."

"Fine. Call him up right now."

"John, he didn't give me his personal line, you know. I'll have to call Senator Gallo and . . ."

"Hold on," he said and a Bruce Springsteen tune came on followed by a John Mellencamp tune. "Okay, here's the President's number," John said as he came back. "It's not direct, but it's the White House operator. Maybe if you are pushy enough, you can get him to call you back. Tell him it's an emergency and, well, you know what to say, you're a big boy now. Go to it, and call me back," and he hung up.

"Ellen," I yelled as I ran up the stairs. Ellen was giving B.J. a bath. "Ellen, I've got to call the President." I opened the gate at the top of the stairs and opened the bathroom door.

"Go ahead, Gary, call him. What's going on?" Ellen asked.

"John called and told me that the hospitals won't let the chiropractors go in and adjust anybody. Every hospital. It's completely ridiculous. Love you guys," and I closed the door, closed the gate and ran down the stairs and heard B.J. blow kisses at me.

"Mwah, dahdee, mwah, mwah, mwah."

"I love you," I yelled up as I grabbed the phone and dialed.

"White House operator, can I help you?"

"Yes, uh, um, this is Dr. Gary Adio. I wonder if you could possibly relay a message to the President that I called. It's most important that . . ."

"Did you say, Dr. Gary Adio, the chiropractor?"

"Yes, ma'am, I did."

"You were on TV a few weeks ago, weren't you?"

"Yes, ma'am."

"You were very inspirational, Doctor. I went to a chiropractor the very next day and took my husband and kids too."

"Oh, thank you. Glad you did. You'll be glad you did, too."

"As long as it works the way you said it will and we don't get HADES, we will. I'll tell the President that you called. Do you want to add anything?"

"Yes. Tell him that no hospital will let the chiropractors in. It's important that he let me know what I should do. If he or someone else calls me back, it would be really greatly appreciated. I mean, I don't want to trouble him, but it's, um, kind of, definitely, um, important."

"Don't worry," the operator laughed, "I'll give him the message. Stuttering and stammering included. You were much more eloquent on TV you know," she laughed again.

"Well, thank you. It's just not every day I have to call the President, so I, uh . . ."

"I know, just kidding. I'll get him the message. I think chiropractic makes common sense, especially the way you and the other doctors explained it."

"Thank you. Good night."

With that she hung up and I held the phone for a few seconds, wondering if the President gets messages like I do, only a bit more global in scale, on those little tear off sheets with yellow carbon copies?

We crashed from sheer exhaustion at 11:30 downstairs after watching "*Jungle Book*" and singing "Bare Necessities," a hundred times. My son's favorite movie song. It was so cute how B.J. was dancing. He's got good rhythm for a 2 year old.

We had all fallen asleep on the couch. With lights on and clothes on too, the phone woke me up around midnight. I got to the phone within four rings, right before the answering machine would have picked up.

"Dr. Adio, please."

"This is he," I answered, shaking my head and my arms to wake myself up a little.

"Please hold on for the President."

Wham! I was wide awake now. "Yes, ma'am."

I was put on hold for a few minutes as some very presidential sounding sort of music was playing.

"Gary?"

"Yes, sir, Mr. President, sir. Thank you for getting back to me so quickly, and for calling me yourself, sir."

"This is of national importance, son. I want the information directly from the source. My staff tells me you sounded as though my call woke you up."

"Oh, no sir. Well, uh, yes sir. I was sleeping, but, uh, I really was on the couch. So . . . we all were. Isn't it late for you, sir?"

"Do you think I can sleep with all this going on? Anyway, why wouldn't the hospitals let the chiropractors in?"

"I don't know, Mr. President, sir. The same reason as always, I presume. They don't trust us. Chiropractic isn't medicine, and anything that isn't medicine doesn't work, in their eyes."

"Yes, I see your point, son. Fine. I will issue an order to force them to open the hospitals up to you, even if only for the time being."

"Thank you, sir, Mr. President. I knew I could count on you."

"Look, son, first of all, I want this to work, and it makes much more sense to do this than to just wait. Second, if it does work, I will be a shoe-in for re-election, which you know is coming up next year. By the way, you did vote for me, didn't you?"

"Yes, sir, I did. You can count on my vote, and the chiropractic vote too. I'll make sure of it."

"I'll hold you to that, Gary. You know that."

"Yes, sir. I deliver what I say. You'll see."

"Good, son. So do I."

"That's why I voted for you, Mr. President. It seemed like you did."

"Good night, son. By the morning the orders will be at every hospital in the country."

"Thank you, sir. Good night."

"Good night. God bless you, and America."

My wife and son were still passed out on the couch. I picked up B.J. He stirred a little and mumbled, "Ka, Ka," the snake from

Jungle Book. He seems to always wake up with a character on his mind.

I tickled Ellen and whispered, "Let's go up to bed." She rubbed her eyes and stumbled along up the stairs behind me. The three of us dove into bed.

The next day was a cold, rainy day for August. It was the perfect kind of day for the news I got. Still working outside in the tents, Fred told me this week *for sure* we'd be back in, probably by the weekend.

During the midst of the usual chaos, Martha handed me the phone and said, "Dr. John needs to talk to you. Now, he said." I didn't know if it was morning or afternoon.

"Okay, no problem. Sorry, Joe, I'll be back in a minute," I said to the patient on the table.

"No hurry, Doc."

I released the hold button on my cordless phone.

"Damn it to hell! Even the President's orders did not work. Now they're in fist fights, violence, police stopping the chiropractors, and M.D.'s creating barricades. It's ridiculous. Can you believe this?" said Dr. John.

"Yes, I can. It's a shame that a President doesn't carry clout like he used to. I'll call him later."

"Call him now! You've got no choice but to call him now."

"John, I've got a hundred people waiting in the tent, dozens more in their cars, and people piling up every minute."

"Every minute you lose, someone dies of this stupid concocted thing."

"Okay! Okay! Okay! What's his number again?"

He gave me the number and hung up without saying good bye. How grumpy!

I called the President's special line again and spoke to the same nice young lady. This time getting her name, Alice. She told me the President was away all day, but she would personally tell his staff the news which, she explained, he probably knew anyway.

It was around 3:30 or so when Martha handed me the phone again. "My, aren't you important! It's the President."

"Oh, my. Excuse me, Bob. I have to take this call."

"No problem, Doc." I thought it was my wife again.

"Hello, Ellen! Got ya' this time!"

"Please hold for the President."

Whew, that's not Ellen. I didn't wait long after hearing John Phillip Sousa.

"Son, I'm sorry this didn't work. It used to in the good old days. Now being President and Commander in Chief of the Armed Forces doesn't have the same authority as when I was young. Why is it so important for you to be in the hospitals, anyway? I mean, once someone has HADES, it's a death sentence, isn't it?"

"Chiropractic can increase the functions of someone's immune system, with or without disease. We might as well give the people suffering with HADES a fighting chance. If they are strong enough, maybe they can bounce back. It's happened already in isolated cases. Imagine if we could save a few more lives! It's worth a shot, Mr. President. What can we do, sir?"

"Let me meet with my Cabinet and I'll get back to you shortly."

"Yes, sir. Thank you, sir."

And so the day went on. A cold, wet, rainy and windy day. Luckily the storm was short-lived and was about to blow over.

Chapter 16

I didn't hear from the President on Tuesday or even on Wednesday. Not Dr. John, either. As a matter of fact, I was getting suspicious about not hearing from them. I decided Wednesday night that I would call Dr. John to see what was up, but as karma would have it, the cosmic AT&T system had heard my request. No sooner did I walk in the door and give Ellen and B.J. a big kiss, then the phone rang. And it wasn't Dr. John. It was Captain Grapler of the "U-nited States Marines," as he put it.

"Is this Dr. Gary Adio, sir?" he asked, in a very official, military sounding tone of voice.

"Yes, sir. And to what do I owe this unusual pleasure, Captain?"

"You're presence is expected at 0500 hours, sir, at the Birkensack Medical Center for the official opening of that hospital and all other hospitals across the country to you brave chiropractors, sir!" he shouted.

"The official opening?" I asked, incredulously.

"Yes, sir! The President has asked the Marines to take over all hospitals in a list compiled by Dr. John McGrory, President of the Universal Chiropractic Association. We are to assure chiropractors have the opportunity to work on all patients in the hospitals, sir!"

"I guess the President still has clout, especially when he uses force."

"Yes, sir. And the U-nited States Marines will get the job done, and done right the first time, sir!"

"The President will like that. I'll be there."

"Excellent, sir. You'll be picked up by Sergeant Mosler at 0430 hours. Please be ready at that time, sir!"

"Oh, absolutely. I wouldn't miss this for the world."

"Yes, sir. Thank you, sir. See you tomorrow morning, sir. We will have the hospitals open across the U.S. by 0530 hours, sir." And with that, he hung up.

"That was different," I said to a perplexed Ellen.

"Whoever that was on the phone certainly talked loud," Ellen mentioned.

"Yes. It was a Captain in the Marines. He invited me to the official opening of the Birkensack Hospital tomorrow morning. I guess the President was tired of talk, and he sure doesn't want to waste any time."

"Do you mean the Marines are going to militarily force the hospitals to allow the chiropractors in?"

"Yes. There's no point in dilly dallying. And the best part—I'll have to get up at 3:30 A.M. to be picked up at 4:30 A.M.. Yes! No sleep, again!"

"Oh, you're going to love this, Gary. Who are you kidding? It's like the big kid in you."

"Might as well enjoy myself in the process, right? Process is more important than product."

"Yes, Zen master Gary. Now let's get you fed and off to bed," Ellen said with a kiss.

The next morning I was ready by 4:15 A.M.. At precisely, and I do mean precisely, 4:30 A.M. a large military jeep, much like a Hummer, pulled into our driveway and the adventure began.

As I approached the jeep, the Sergeant came out, introduced himself and said, "The Captain requested that you wear this jacket and hat, sir. A gift from the Marines to you for your service to your country."

A fatigue jacket with my name on it, and a fatigue cap, too. Always wanted the real thing. "Thank you, Sergeant," I said as I slipped on the jacket. It was the right size. I guess they knew everything about me.

My escort had been a long time chiropractic patient, he explained. We talked the whole way to the hospital about his experiences over the years with chiropractic and how his whole family has been under care, including his three kids. We arrived quickly at Birkensack Hospital, the 30 minute ride made quicker by good conversation and no traffic.

The sergeant parked the jeep about a block from the hospital and looked at his watch. I looked around and saw no sign of anything going on. "If this is what they mean by a military opening," I pondered inwardly, "we're in big trouble."

So I decided to ask. "So, Sergeant, where is everybody?"

He looked at his watch again. "Be patient, sir. You'll see the Marines work on exact time. Precision and discipline are what separate the Marines from everybody else. Now, please sit in silence, listen, and watch."

"Yes, sir," I said. I looked at my cap and noticed that the Marines had even embroidered my name on my cap, too. Then I heard something. My eyes turned to the right and then to the left. I heard something, but I didn't see anything. The noise got louder and louder. Leaves and dust started swirling around and the jeep started shaking slightly. Suddenly overhead, was this overpowering Boom! Boom! Boom! Boom! Helicopters! Four giant helicopters landed in unison in the parking lot in front of me. I turned to see the Sergeant smiling, pleased with the precision of his team. Four doors opened up on the helicopters and what looked like twenty men in battle fatigues with M-16 rifles ran out and formed two rows. Next, another loud rumble began behind us. I turned around to see sixteen armored vehicles, the ones with wheels and machine guns, come driving down around the jeep and come screeching to a halt in two rows of eight each.

Last came a large truck with flags flying from the fenders and a long green and black bus. The truck and bus stopped in between the two rows of armed vehicles. Stepping down from the truck was an older gentleman who looked like Norman Schwartzkoff. Tall, big framed, tough looking, lots of decorations on his chest.

"It's time," the Sergeant said, and we got out of the jeep. The sergeant ran toward the leader and I quickly followed.

"Lieutenant Colonel, sir! Sergeant Mosler reporting, sir! This is Dr. Gary Adio."

"At ease, Sergeant. Thank you."

The two saluted each other and I thought it was only proper that I salute the lieutenant colonel as well.

"Pleased to meet you, Dr. Adio. I'm Lieutenant Colonel Wexler of the United States Marines. Are you ready?"

"Uh, sure. I mean. Yes sir!"

"Good. Just sit back and watch for now while my boys do their work."

Just then, about a dozen police cars came screeching to a halt on the other side of the parking lot. Several officers in white uniforms came walking toward us and the oldest one asked, "What in the bejesus is going on here?"

"I'm Lieutenant Colonel Wexler of the United States Marines. We are here to open up the hospital to allow the chiropractors access by order of the President of the United States of America. There will be no shots fired. This is an exercise in teaching the hospitals that, when the President speaks, he speaks with the authority as the Commander in Chief of the Armed Forces. This is occurring, as we speak, in fifty hospitals across the nation. You boys are asked to keep your distance and let the Marines handle this. Understood, sir?"

"Well, yes, I guess. Yes, sir. What choice do we have? You guys got the big guns."

"Well done. Now, if you'll excuse me, gentlemen, we have an exercise to perform."

He blew a whistle and eighty Marines moved like clockwork, going through automatic doors with their boots sounding like marching drums. Sixteen armored vehicles all backed up in unison, blocking the entrance to the hospital as the last Marine went in. A small helicopter that I suppose was hovering overhead came down and began to circle the hospital with a bright floodlight blaring into the windows.

Just then I noticed ten people in plain clothes coming out of the bus. I recognized one as Dr. Ron, my philosophy teacher from chiropractic school.

They all came toward me and I said, "Impressive show, huh?"

"So this is the way we get into the hospitals. I guess the old way of asking never really worked," Dr. Ron joked as he came running toward me and hugged me.

"Great to see you, Dr. Ron."

"Even better to see you. By the way, you sure grew up from that punk that was in my class."

"Thanks to you. You helped grow the philosophy of chiropractic inside me."

We turned as we heard the clop, clop, clop, sounds of army boots. Three Marines approached me and one introduced himself.

"Sir, I'm Captain Grapler. We spoke last night. You may go in now. The hospital is secure. We have arranged for the chiropractors to be in one-half of the cafeteria. All the tables are moved. We will now bring in the chiropractic tables. Please follow us, sir."

I looked up to see another helicopter coming in for a landing. WBC News. I knew they couldn't be far off. The door was open and a camera was filming the scene as a reporter spoke quickly on a cordless mike. The helicopter landed and the crew ran over toward us.

"Dr. Adio, what's going on here?" asked the reporter.

"Oh, just another day at the office," I said.

132

The reporter looked stunned, as the other chiropractors laughed.

"Yeah, you know, just having the military open up a few hospitals. Typical, routine stuff," said Dr. Ron.

The reporter looked at us as if we had three heads. How dare we joke at a time like this, he probably was thinking.

"Listen, the hospitals wouldn't let the chiropractors in. The Marines came and opened them up. End of story. Come on, docs, we've got work to do."

We chiropractors ran past the reporters and cameramen in silence. Two rows of five spontaneously occurred, but looked planned. At the door were two big Marines. They turned around to lead the way in. Behind us ran twenty Marines, each pair holding a chiropractic table. There were Marines in every doorway and dozens of stunned doctors, nurses and other hospital support staff, as we all ran in two rows in almost perfect unison. Clop, clop, clop, clop, clop, clop.

We began to get cheers of, "Yes!" and "Go for it!." "I'm glad you're here!" from patients, and even some staff, as we ran deeper into the hospital. By the time we got to the cafeteria is seemed that the whole hospital was cheering. All except the doctor we encountered as we turned into the cafeteria.

"Who's in charge here? What kind of fiasco is this?" he asked. He was wearing a long white coat and a stethoscope hung around his neck.

A booming voice from the back yelled, "I'm in charge here. I am Lieutenant Colonel Wexler. The President's orders are to be carried out without any disturbance. Is that understood, doctor?"

"Do you realize the potential health hazard that you are all facing? This is the number one HADES hospital in the state of New Jersey."

"The Marines risk their lives every day, Doctor, as do you and all of your staff. That is not a problem," answered Wexler.

I liked that come back.

"Oh, well, do you know about the health hazard that chiropractors in a hospital can cause? These are sick people who need medical attention. Not chiropractic attention."

"Doctor, I presume you must hold an important role here. Do you realize this is an order by the President of the United States? I suggest you follow the plan. All patients and staff are to be brought here to be adjusted. No questions asked. Those quarantined with

133

HADES will be visited by the chiropractors individually in their rooms. This hospital shall conform until otherwise told so by myself. Understood?"

The doctor was turning all shades of red. It looked as though he were about to explode. "But, but, but, chiropractic is dangerous! It kills people! It permanently injures people. You can't just indiscriminately adjust every patient here without a thorough exam, diagnosis, and X-rays, and even then it's still risky for most people, especially patients in this or any other hospital. This is absolutely insane. I'm thinking about the welfare of my patients only."

The lieutenant colonel came to my side, "It's your turn now, son," he said as he patted my shoulder. "Please answer the man. I know it's right and so do you. Obviously he doesn't."

I sat there for a moment trying to think of what to say. Then I realized, the fact that he was a medical doctor did not change the chiropractic story for him. Tell the story the way you would tell any other father.

"I understand your fears, Doctor, because I was once in your shoes, not knowing what chiropractic was. Fearing for my life when the chiropractor was going to touch me. I was a patient first, before I became a chiropractor, and I was shaking like a leaf for two reasons. Number one, because I was so scared. Number two, because of all the asthma medication I had been on for years and years and years. You see, nothing had helped me in the twenty years previous to my first chiropractic adjustment. This was my last ditch effort to save my life. I had given up hope and I figured I'd just have to take pills and puff on inhalers for the rest of my life. I feared the day I'd forget my inhaler and die somewhere alone.

"This chiropractor that my mother dragged me to gave me hope. For the first time in my whole life, someone gave me hope. He said, 'Maybe we can help you.' He said, 'If the master communication system isn't working at a hundred percent, how could you?' He said if he reconnected me with the glorious healing power that is within me, that I could watch my life change before my eyes. He said, 'You can walk out of here and never come back and always wonder, what if, or you can give chiropractic a chance. If it works, if a miracle occurs, you could have a whole different life, a whole different destiny.'

"And, Doctor, I gave it a chance. He told me my lungs knew how to breathe but they were not getting a hundred percent of the message from my brain. He said anything less than a hundred percent is not enough for God's perfection. God wants us to be healthy, but we can't be healthy if we have interference with the master communication system.

"And lo and behold, my asthma began to disappear after three months of chiropractic adjustment. It's been fifteen years now since my last asthma attack, Doctor. Every breath I take is a good one, because I am living at a hundred percent due to chiropractic care. Nobody can take that away from me. I am no longer dependent on drugs, or inhalers, or anything. I am dependent on God within to heal me. And, Doctor, all I ask for is a chance to do the same thing with your patients and all the patients in all the hospitals.

"What have we got to lose? What happens if we don't adjust anyone here and they all die, including your whole staff, and you have never known the miracle that could have been? Don't live the what if. Live the now. It's time to go for it. Live the chance that this could be the time that we see the reconnection finally take place that the world has been praying for since this whole thing started. Please, Doctor, stand back and let's work together on this one for the better good of all humanity. I love and appreciate you and all the things you've said, but if you've never experienced a chiropractic adjustment, or experienced one that was not done with love as its major intent, let me be the first to offer you one. Okay, Doctor?"

He looked at me in a whole different light. He looked at me as if I were his grandson.

"Would you like to lie down here, Doctor?" I asked, pointing toward the table. Two Marines had set up a table next to me.

The doctor lay down, speechless. Guided by his inner light, I gave him the gentlest and warmest adjustment I could.

He smiled and said, "That's it?"

"Yes, Doctor, that is chiropractic."

He sat up on the table for a few minutes and it was so quiet the only thing you could hear was everybody breathing. He stared off into space for a few seconds and said, in a very soft voice, "I'm still totally against this because it is opposite to all the principles of medicine I know, but" he half-smiled at me, "I'm not going to stop you, either. Do what you have to do. We'll cooperate. Begrudgingly, but we will cooperate."

"You won't be sorry you did this, sir. I can promise you that."

The doctor turned around and walked out of the cafeteria.

"Well done, son, well done. Now how about my boys? Set up your tables and then give them adjustments," said Lieutenant Colonel Wexler.

"Yes, sir," I said, and everybody who had stood like statues during those tense few minutes began to move, creating an animated scene, coming to life. "I hope this victory is repeated 49 more times," I said to the Lieutenant Colonel.

"How about that adjustment?"

"I'd be glad to, Lieutenant Colonel, lie down."

After the adjustment, he got up, smiled, shook my hand, and then turned around and began helping set up the other tables with his men.

I said my goodbyes to the crew of chiropractors. Each one of them gave me a big hug, and Dr. Ron lifted me up in his arms and said, "It's awfully nice knowing that you were one of my students."

Sergeant Mosler tapped me on my shoulder. "It's 0530 hours. Right on schedule. Let's get you back."

As I was walking out of the hospital, escorted by Sergeant Mosler, we saw stationed at every double doorway and hallway, two to four Marines, with M-16 rifles. Some of them shook my hand or saluted us as we walked by.

"It's a shame we had to use such force to do this," I told the Sergeant as we walked on. "But I'm sure glad it was you guys, because you did an outstanding job. Quick, efficient and very impressive."

"Thank you, sir. You've seen the bumper stickers, haven't you? Semper fi! Death before dishonor. If we are told to do something, it's done right the first time. We knew every inch of this hospital before taking it over. It was a matter of executing the idea as precisely as possible, sir."

"You certainly did that. I thank you and want to tell the Lieutenant Colonel that not only do I thank the Marines, but the whole country will thank you when HADES is over. You'll see, chiropractic is the answer. We are not defenseless against HADES."

"I believe you, sir. What you said in there was something I've never heard before. Don't you wish everybody believed this way, sir?"

"The basis of chiropractic philosophy never died, and now we have a chance to show the world a secret that has been kept down for over a hundred years."

Just then we came to the hospital entrance where I could see the armored vehicles still blocking the doorways, especially from the press who were now camped out en masse.

"Oh, boy," I groaned and sighed heavily, "here we go again."

"Sir, do you want me to drive the jeep right up to the front so we can make this a quick exit?"

"Hmmm, yes. Thank you. If you don't mind."

"Okay, sir. No problem. See you in a minute, sir."

I walked behind him as he sprinted off. There was a long walk between these armored trucks and a horde of press awaiting me. I decided not to walk slowly but to run toward them, changing my mental state. As I neared them, you could see them getting themselves ready and I didn't give them much time by running.

"Dr. Adio! Dr. Adio! Dr. Adio!" the reporters erupted.

"No questions, please. I'll make a brief statement, then I must get back to my office. Chiropractic is here to stay. The President has said, after his investigation of chiropractic, that it is the thing to do right now, and the Marines made it possible for the chiropractors to enter the hospitals as well. Every man, woman, and child in this country should get adjusted by the end of next week. The chiropractors have organized such that areas that are not well-populated with chiropractors will have chiropractors sent to them. Hospitals, inner cities, rural areas, and prisons will see chiropractors flown in shortly from around the country. The President has given us the challenge of making a difference in the death rate of HADES within six weeks. Mark my words, you will see a drop in the HADES death rate, provided every man, woman, and child gets adjusted. This cannot work without you. If you are not getting adjusted, go. Please. For your sake, and for your country's sake.

"President Kennedy said, many years ago, 'Ask not what your country can do for you. Ask what you can do for your country.' The time is now. Make a stand. You cannot sit idly and wait for a miracle to occur, you must make the miracle occur one person at a time. You can make the difference. The only way we can stop this thing is if enough people get adjusted and turn on the life force to a hundred percent in this short period of time, so we can hit HADES head on.

"Chiropractic is an American original, discovered in Davenport, Iowa in 1895. It was said then, and I repeat now, chiropractic can change the world. But we can't do it without you. We can't stop it without you. Get adjusted. Get your life turned on by chiropractic. Let's beat this thing. Together we can. Thank you and thanks especially to the President and the United States Marines for an outstanding job. God bless you."

I walked to my right and hopped directly into Sergeant Mosler's waiting jeep. The jeep was surrounded by reporters and cameras as we slowly inched off.

"Do you think that all fifty hospitals across the country have been opened by now?" I asked Sergeant Mosler.

"Well, sir, you know this operation was a coordinated one at 0530 hours, but I'm sure some hospitals were less cooperative than others."

"You don't happen to have a radio in here do you, Sergeant?"

"No, sir. This is a Marine vehicle, no place for fun and dancing, sir."

"Oh, I didn't mean it that way. I thought we could catch the news on armed forces radio."

"No, sir. No disturbances, sir."

"Right, of course," I answered. I knew it wasn't possible that all fifty hospitals would have been opened without a problem. I hoped so, but I was also thinking in terms of reality. Actually, I wondered, is any of this reality? It seems more like a surreal dream. Oh, well, nothing we can do anyway but pray.

The sergeant dropped me off at 0600 hours, and I mean, 6:00 A.M. The sun was shining brightly on the tents and on the crowd of people already sitting and waiting. It was a sight to see in comparison to M-16 rifles and green, angry looking helicopters.

Fred had promised me that the office would definitely, absolutely, positively be done on Saturday. I didn't know exactly how he was going to pull this off in three days, and I was getting a little frustrated still being outside, but I had to be strong because I knew that whoever had set fire to this place wanted me to feel that way. I couldn't let it distract me from my mission. Thank God it was August.

The day blew by as usual, adjusting all day long, not home 'til 9:00 PM. I was actually getting used to seeing a tremendous volume of people. I had been feeling energized the previous few nights, rather than exhausted. On the drive home, I had a flashback to the time that I was in chiropractic school. The thought of adjusting a large number of people each day while still in school had two connotations. Number one: it's not fair to the patients. Number two: it's not fair to yourself. The implication was that you couldn't possibly provide a good service if you didn't spend time with each patient. As a matter of fact, the concept seemed to be: the more time you spend with each patient, the more they are getting "their money's worth." Now I realized that *quality* of time spent is the most important thing, not quantity. If you're intent is to love each person you adjust and you are able to transmit that love to each patient, even a relatively quick adjustment seems to last longer. "You must have singleness of purpose," is what Dr. Charles had taught. "Be truly one with that patient and that patient alone. They feel that concentration of energy solely on them and it's as if your intent can actually make time stand still."

All the chit-chat is a waste of time. The whole idea of the adjustment is to turn on that person's power and, at the same time, have your intent so strong that they can feel your love for them coming through your hands and your heart.

"It only takes a moment to turn on a light switch," I have often said when asked about this. "Anything else you do to the light switch doesn't help the light turn on any faster, does it?" So true, now more than ever.

I recognized two major distinctions. Number one, anything is possible. Number two, what's not fair is: *not reaching enough people*. And a dizzying process emerged; the busier my office got, the more time I had to adjust more people. In the earlier days, adjusting a low volume of people in a day wiped me out. But now, seeing large numbers of people a day had actually energized me (as I had grown used to it). I am less tired and more focused on the pure act of giving, loving, and serving humanity.

There was no time for thinking, and especially no time to give anything less than a perfect adjustment to each person. This is what they meant by being in the flow. When you are in the zone, you tend to perform your best, every time, all the time. People who think they are beating the system by doing the least amount of work possible are actually cheating themselves more than they are their employer. They are losing the opportunity of how good it feels to do it right, every time, every minute, every day. Wasting time is a crime because you can never get it back.

When this first began, I wasn't in a rhythm. I felt "discombobulated." In the preceding few days, I had fallen into a groove, and that felt good. In the beginning, I was panicking, running the old program in my head: it's not possible, it's not fair. Today, I feel I can see more people than ever before, and it's not only fair, it's the right thing to do. To see as many people as I possibly can. It is my duty, as a chiropractor, to make sure that everybody I *can* touch, I *do* touch. What's really interesting is, once you get to the point of saying, "I can handle more," God says, "Okay, here's more." He gives you only what you can handle. It's called the vacuum phenomenon. Create a vacuum anywhere in the universe, and the universe will do anything to fill it and fill it rapidly. Vacuums don't work slowly, do they? So any time you say to God, "I am ready," and you really are ready . . . Bam! in an instant, the vacuum is filled.

This applies to anything. Not just chiropractors and how many patients they can adjust. It's sort of a universal truth. There's another saying that's similar. "When the student is ready, the teacher will appear." I guess chiropractic, as a profession, was ready, because this would never have happened—chiropractic could not have stepped up to the bat if it hadn't been ready. If we are students, then this is a hell of a teacher, I thought, as I pulled into my driveway.

Jack's Harley Davidson was parked on the brick deck in its usual spot. "I feel so much more secure knowing he's here," I said to myself. And just then, he appeared out the side door and came running over.

"Doc, it's not like me to request extra hours, but I believe that you might want to keep me here longer," said Jack in his typical roundabout talk.

As I stepped out of the car, I gave him a sideways glance, and asked, "What's going on, Jack?"

"Well, you started getting the phone calls again, like you did when it all began. And I believe that the best way I can be of service to you is to be of service."

"Fine. Let me talk to Ellen, but I'm sure she'll agree."

"As a matter of fact," interrupted Jack, "the clown who called you warned specifically of tonight, so I thought, if you don't mind, I'd invite a few of my biker friends over. We can hang out for a while in your driveway, which would make an unpleasant sight for anyone approaching your place."

"Hmm, that sounds, um, different."

"And none of us drink, or smoke, or anything. I'm a member of the Clean & Sober Harley Davidson Club of New Jersey."

"Oh, catchy name. I like it. Come on inside, Jack, let's talk to Ellen."

So Ellen, Jack, and I talked it over and we agreed the next few nights we needed extra protection. We asked Jack to join us for dinner and watched in amazement as Jack turned into a kid lover. B.J. kept on playing with his beard and the two of them were hysterical laughing. After dinner, six of Jack's friends rolled up our driveway in a loud Harley-type thunder. We went outside to meet them with B.J. leading the way. I was unaccustomed to that decibel level of noise as they arranged their bikes on our driveway. B.J. thought it was hysterical and let go of my hand to run toward the loudest bike, handled by what appeared to be a World Wrestling Federation champion. I ran over to grab B.J. and introduced myself.

"Just another night out," said Bear, as he shook my hand. "We'll do anything for Jack, and if it means just sit there and look scary, we can do that just fine."

"I appreciate your help, Bear," I said, thinking that was an appropriate nickname. "Have you all been adjusted, by the way?"

"Oh, absolutely. A member of our club is a chiropractor. Ed Young, do you know him?"

"No, but tell him I said, 'Hi,' and thanks."

So there we all sat and talked. B.J. had the time of his life. All the bikers put him on their Harleys, and he tried on their helmets. He loved it. By the time we were done, B.J. was saying, "B.J.'s bike, B.J.'s bike, B.J.'s bike."

Of course, Ellen said, "Don't get any ideas, Gary. These bikes aren't moving and they're much safer when you sit on a parked driveway."

"Don't worry, Ellen, I have no interest in one at all," I said unconvincingly, since I was sitting on Jack's Harley with the chopper handlebars.

We all went to sleep late and Jack said they'd leave when the sun came up, except for him. He said he was on 24-hour watch for the following few days until this blew over.

I woke up early the next morning and the whole crew was already gone except Jack.

"Hey, Doc, I'm glad we were here last night. You might have had a visitor," he said, standing in the hallway as I walked into the kitchen from upstairs.

"A visitor?" I asked, surprised. I hadn't heard anything.

"Yes," Jack said, scratching his eyes—obviously he hadn't slept all night. "Around 4:00 AM we were all hanging out outside when a car turned down your driveway. Bear was already on his bike, so he kick started it and his headlights shone right into this big, brand new Lincoln. The guy slammed on his brakes and threw it into reverse. Bear asked, 'Should I go after him?' and I told him not to. The Lincoln screeched out of here like a bat out of hell. It gave us all a big laugh, but I suspect mischief. Someone's up to something, Doc."

"Wow! Damn!" I said, still groggy from sleep, "I'm glad you guys were here. Did you get the license plate number?"

"Of course. Bear has a photographic memory. He can fix any Harley because he's memorized all their insides," said Jack, handing me a piece of paper.

"Excellent," I said, as I wrote it down on a small pad of paper. "In case I lose it, you keep this copy in your wallet. Don't tell Ellen about this. I will tonight when I see her. Do you think the boys want to have a 'party' here again tonight?"

"I'm sure they won't mind. Might have to take shifts though. All of them are working boys, you know."

"No problem. Thank Bear profusely for me."

"Will do."

"Okay. Let me get moving. My rebuilt office will be ready by tomorrow and Fred told me he needs to talk to me early today so he can get the final touches done."

"Including an alarm system, I hope?"

"Yes, and sprinklers, too."

"You'll need security there too, Doc. Want me to ask a few of my friends to work for you?"

"Okay. Next thing you know, the Marines will be at my door."

Chapter 17

The Marines *were* at my door. I pulled up to my office, with its now typical line of people, and thought I was having a déjà vu experience. "Didn't I just say that before? I was just joking about the Marine thing . . . but I guess not," I said out loud as I pulled into the driveway staring wide eyed at the military presence around my office, including one of those lightly armored vehicles on the grass between the tents and my office door.

About thirty to forty Marines in khakis were standing in two lines. My patients had practically surrounded them, probably asking them lots of questions. As I walked towards them I recognized their faces as the ones that had opened up the hospital the day before.

The lieutenant colonel was standing at the front of the line (where else?). Each Marine shook my hand as I walked by, until I reached the chief.

"Good morning, Lieutenant Colonel Wexler." I saluted him.

"Good morning, Doctor." He saluted me and we shook hands. "The boys want to show their appreciation for all you've done in light of the latest breaking news. Plus, they all want to be adjusted. Your men in the hospitals are really busy and we don't want to take up their time right now. Can we barge in?"

"Oh, my pleasure. But let's back up to the latest breaking news thing. What was that?"

"Y'all don't watch TV now, do you?"

"No, sir. Not a speck."

"Probably better off. Well, forty-eight of the fifty hospitals went easy. Two had a problem, which is good odds, actually. But in Boston and L.A., we had some resistance. The Marines handled it with no casualties, but people really went out of control. Barricades, throwing glass. Lots of bad apples, I guess. Once the hospitals were open and the ones responsible for the disturbances apprehended, the M.D.'s at Boston promised retaliation by saying, 'We will fight them on their own turf.' So we suspect more wrongdoing in chiropractic offices just like a few weeks ago. And being that we saw your office burn up once, we decided that our little presence would be relatively threatening."

"Well, thank you, Lieutenant Colonel. How about your boys get first adjustments and I'll buy you all lunch?"

Just then, a big black Lincoln screeched around the corner and came to a dead halt in front of my office. The driver began revving the engine as if he was ready for a drag race. The lieutenant colonel blew his whistle and his men, armed with M-16's, began to run toward the street in perfect unison.

I yelled, "Get down everybody!" and we all fell to the ground. People began screaming. The black Lincoln rocked with anger as the engine raced louder and louder. By this time the Marines had lined up along the sidewalk, guns pointed, seemingly ready to fire. The lieutenant colonel unsheathed his 45 and pointed it at the driver's side window. The window rolled down and a large man with dark sunglasses yelled out, "You bastard!" He rolled the window up and peeled away.

"Don't shoot!" yelled Lieutenant Colonel Wexler.

I saw the license plate, DMCP357, as he turned right on the side street.

"All clear," he motioned for me and my patients to get up. Another whistle blew and his men filed back to form two lines in seconds.

"Do you know him, Doc?" the lieutenant colonel asked, puzzled.

"No, but he sure knows me. I think he's the one that came visiting last night at my house. I have the license number in my wallet." I pulled it out, and it was a match. "Thanks guys. You have my gratitude." I wrote the license plate number on a business card, putting the original back in my wallet.

"Can one of your men call the police and give them this plate number, Lieutenant Colonel?"

"Consider it done, Doc. Now get to work and I'll see to it that my boys stay for a few days."

So away we went. The day zoomed by. First adjusting all the Marines, and then God knows how many people, with a fifteen minute pizza break, since I had promised to buy lunch for the Marines.

Fred and I spoke briefly about the final touches for the office. He was close to 80 years old, but stood tall and strong and still had a full head of hair. I often told him that I hoped I had as much energy as he when I'm in my 70's. Fred explained how the alarm system worked with a direct line to the local police department. As he said the word, 'police,' who should pull up, but a patrol car with lights flashing.

Tony, your standard, young, good-looking and athletically built rookie police officer, opened the door of his police car and ran towards me saying, "They nabbed somebody and they have him in the county jail. They just faxed his picture. Is this him?" he asked. Then he stopped, looked at the armored vehicles and Marines and said, "Uh, nice tank, Doc. New decorations for the office?"

"No, this is temporary in light of all the wonderful new friends I'm making." Tony handed me the picture and I straightened it out and handed it to the lieutenant colonel. "What do you think, Lieutenant Colonel?"

"Could be. It was so quick, but there's definitely a resemblance."

"I agree. And if he was in that Lincoln last night and this morning, I'd like to ask him some questions myself."

"Well, we're going to book him and find out who he's working for. They told me he's a drug rep for one of the big pharmaceutical companies up here. They also told me he had some serious weapons in his possession. Including some weird stuff nobody's ever seen before."

"Bio-tech, I bet," said the lieutenant colonel.

"I don't know yet. Didn't see it myself. Anyway, can I get adjusted, Doc, before I run back?"

"Sure, Tony, hop on." So I adjusted Tony as Fred handed me the keys to my newly renovated office. Finally!

"We'll see how long this lasts," I thought to myself, looking around at the scene in front of me. It looked like a dream come true for a young boy playing, complete with police cars, lights flashing, a small tank and a bunch of toy soldiers. It was like playing G.I. Joe at headquarters for a top secret mission, and across the street the garden apartments suddenly transformed into the forces of evil, and I imagined a bunch of toy soldiers on the other side of the street, all in their pre-set frozen positions. Most vividly I recalled the two soldiers using a bazooka, one holding it and aiming this way, the other loading a shell into the back of it. Then there was, as always, that toy soldier leader whose machine gun was facing this way, but his head was turned to look behind him as his right arm

145

was in position over his head indicating, "Move forward. Follow me."

When I was in first grade, I remember I played with a youngster named Ford, and he and I would set up the entire living room filled with toy soldiers. Even though Korea had come and gone and Vietnam was going on as we grew up, we always played us against the Germans and the Japanese. I wondered what kids do today. Do they still play World War II, or do they play Desert Storm? Will yesterday be remembered in the history books as the day the Marines stormed the hospitals to get the chiropractors in? Or will that be removed from the history books like "double talk" in George Orwell's *1984*? I wondered how much "Big Brother" is involved in all this.

Chapter 18

Three weeks to the day that the office had burned down, I was back in. We kept the tents so that people could wait comfortably. We also left the receptionist's desk outside so she could hand out numbers and maintain some order. The waiting room inside became the on-deck circle, and on Friday, seven new chiropractic tables were delivered. We put three tables in each room which allowed me to go table-to-table without necessarily going into another room. We could accommodate 19 people at a time now; nine lying on tables and ten in the "on deck" waiting area. That kept things flowing very quickly. The multitude outside under the tents were listening to music via a speaker Fred had installed over the outside door.

As they had promised, the Marines left their cute little assault tank at my front door, complete with two Marines who rotated every eight hours in a 24-hour watch.

The day was going crazy as usual, although honestly, we were so accustomed to the al fresco adjusting that it felt weird to be inside. Martha interrupted me with a phone call from Patrolman Tony.

"Doc, you didn't here this from me, okay?"

"Didn't hear nothing, Tony. So what didn't I hear?"

"Well, the guy the county police nabbed yesterday? They were questioning him and the FBI calls up and says, 'Let him go.' But he was really sweating in that jail. I guess he's not used to that kind of lifestyle. And then he has a heart attack and he almost dies right there in the interrogation room, but they do CPR and save him. He starts talking about seeing the light and hearing God's voice, and seeing Jesus, and all that stuff, and then says, and I quote, because I've got it written down, 'Tell Dr. Adio I'm sorry and we must talk. It's the vaccine. We made it. It's the vaccine.' What the hell is he talking about?"

"I'm not sure, Tony, but that's sure telling me something. By the way, where is he? And what's his name? I've got to go see him, obviously."

147

"I can't tell you that he's in the hospital where the Marines are, and his name is not Jack Larson, and he's not in room 827."

"Right. No clue. No problem. Thanks, buddy. I owe you one."

I sat there in the X-ray room which I hadn't used since this all started. I was stunned. This drug rep had a near death experience, was 'embraced by the light,' so to speak, and suddenly wanted to tell me everything. "It's the vaccine?" Dr. John had mentioned something about vaccines a while before. Could it be that all this is the result of a vaccine going amuck? And what vaccine? Is it a standard one? A new one? An experimental one? Even though I could hear a multitude of patients outside, I called Ellen.

"Hey, babe, I've got to go to the hospital tonight. They arrested some drug rep who probably was the one who was threatening us, and he had a heart attack and is now babbling over with confessions. Especially about a vaccine as a causative factor. I've got to meet him before he is shut up."

"You better video tape this," said Ellen. "I'll come by and bring you a veggie sandwich and give you the camcorder."

"Great, I'll see you soon. You'll love the new office. The colors you picked out are awesome."

"Of course. See you soon."

And off I went, adjusting, adjusting, adjusting, until 9:00 P.M. strong. Ellen popped by with B.J. and I adjusted them both. B.J. was fascinated by the Marines and the tank and they took him inside for a tour. They even let B.J. hold a machine gun, which Ellen wasn't very pleased about since B.J. never had exposure to any guns before. The Marines said, "Say bang, bang!" so B.J. thought it was some big heavy thing that made a "bang, bang!" noise.

I adjusted a few more people and then ran to the rental car, armed with my camcorder and several freshly charged batteries, thanks to my beautiful and smart wife.

The Marines were still in full force at the hospital when I pulled up. Ellen had reminded me to put on my Marine jacket and cap so they could recognize me easily. Walking toward the entrance, I noticed that the Marines that were standing guard were not stopping anyone and questioning them, and I was a little relieved. I was hoping martial law was not in force there.

I was expecting guards but found none when I walked into Room 827. I was greeted by a man who was scribbling madly on a pad of paper and who had an open Bible draped over his stomach.

"Mr. Larson, I'm Gary Adio. I heard . . ."

"Oh, praise the Lord! My prayers are answered again! First I prayed that I not die and I didn't, and then I made a pact with God. I said, 'God, if I live through this, I will tell the truth. I'm tired of living a lie.' So here I am. I have a second chance. Then I prayed that you would come so I could tell you everything, and I mean everything. Do you have a few hours?"

"Yes, and a few hours of video tape, to boot. Are you up to this?" I asked, pointing towards the heart monitor as it stood beeping away.

"Oh, yeah, yeah, yeah. This is my life's mission now. Oh yes, indeed. I was spared a straight ticket to hell to be given a second chance. I was headed right down to hell, and saw St. Peter himself as I was in that horrible jail. I saw the light around him and the angels, and he said to me, 'You are not ready to leave, son. Become righteous and free yourself from your lies and live again. The next time I see you, you will be greeted with open arms.' So I'm ready. The sooner I do this, the lighter I will get."

"The lighter?" I questioned.

"Oh, yes. The heaviness I've felt over the years has been horrible, especially recently. Especially what they wanted me to do to you and your family. Thank God you were smart enough to protect yourself. Oh, the weapons I have developed! Oh, what I have seen and done myself! A brilliant scientist who wanted to help make the world a better place and then became corrupt with evil and filled with selfishness when his good ideas were used as instruments of death. Oh, Lord, forgive me for I have sinned. I was lured by the money, and the power, and the prestige. And I sold my soul in the process. Doc, forgive me and then hear me, and then tell others. You've got the mouth. I've got the knowledge. Will you forgive me, please?"

What was I to say? Just a few hours before he had tried to kill me and my family, and then he wanted my forgiveness. Well, in exchange for some invaluable information on how vaccines fit into all this, I asked Ellen in my mind, "Is this okay?" and I heard her say, "Yes, Gary. Give for the sake of giving. We love you."

"Okay. I forgive you, Mr. Larson. I . . ."

"Oh, thank you. Thank the Lord! Now turn on the video recorder. Sit down and listen to this."

For the next three hours I sat in awe at what he was telling me. I was so grateful that Ellen had packed extra batteries and tapes because nobody would have believed me if I had simply told them

149

this. He gave me names, dates, places, prices, everything. I shook my head in disbelief for the entire interview.

Larson told me that once scientists had cloned sheep, his team of researchers at a company called BTWS, Biotechnology Weapons Systems, had been called in, along with the military's cloning experts at a company called Replay Technologies. Their mission: Develop human clones at a breakneck pace for biological warfare purposes. The idea: We can send clones into countries like Iraq, and kill millions of people once these clones infiltrate the government and then let loose a disease that is highly communicable. At the same time, Replay Technologies was asked to do test runs on creating clones that could be used for espionage, both domestically and internationally, to infiltrate major companies, foreign military, and drug growing operations in South America and Asia. They were programmed to have all languages necessary to walk right into wherever their assignment was and fit in perfectly.

Larson was called in, along with his colleagues, to develop a vaccine against the biological weapons to be used with the first set of clones. Sort of an antidote. What would happen is, the country would be ravaged by the disease, and the U.S. would come in and pretend to save the world by heroically coming up with a vaccine that would counteract the disease. It would save the country after a certain percent of its population was decimated and we would be the heroes and take over the country, like the U.S. took over Japan after World War II. This was to prove especially useful for getting easy access to OPEC oil in the Middle East.

The problem occurred when the vaccine was developed for the biological weapon. The disease, which they called HADES, was so susceptible to mutation, that the inactivated virus in the vaccine could easily mutate back to an active and highly lethal biological weapon. Of course, they didn't know all this until a few months ago after the military intelligence and Replay Technologies vaccinated all their clones and sent ten of them out on what was supposed to be a four to seven day test run.

They had only tested the vaccine on mice, and the furry little animals did not have the same reactions (even though mice are supposedly similar to man's chemical makeup). The clones were equipped with body function and video transmitters in their left eye, so military intelligence was able to jump on their clones immediately when they malfunctioned. But they never expected to see HADES reactivate itself. This was the same problem with the AIDS vaccine research. They didn't think that HADES could mutate that fast, since they had studied the AIDS virus and had developed a recombined genetically altered virus that would self-destruct if it tried to reactivate itself. Unfortunately, the HADES recombination for self-destruction didn't work.

So the ten clones in ten cities developed HADES—the most highly communicable disease ever seen by man—after only a few days on the test run. And now the scientists were scrambling to create a new vaccine. The amazing thing that the scientists didn't count on, Larson said, was the intelligence of the virus itself. They had looked at the virus as being in a submissive position and one that would just perform the way they wanted it to. They didn't count on the inactivated virus, wanting, or having any desire to reactivate itself. They never thought that a virus is a living organism that has a strong desire to perform its normal life function and will do anything in its power to reactivate itself.

They had seen glimpses of this intelligence with all the other childhood vaccines and the adult vaccines, but they felt that any casualties were worth the benefits. The scientists had realized that the inactivated or killed vaccines all came back to life, one way or the other, whether as the actual virus itself, or as a mutated close or distant cousin. But the childhood diseases were minor and were not as genetically engineered as HADES and other more recent biological weapons were. Larson said that they had tried with this latest vaccine to take all this into account, which is why they had put in so many redundant backups.

"But life is too strong," he said, "too powerful for us to safely tamper with. We grossly underestimated the power of life, even in such a small unit like a virus, and grossly overestimated how smart we thought we were," he said, with a sad look on his face.

"We scientists and doctors thought that, once we could manipulate bacteria and viruses, we could change the course of history and create a planet without disease. One problem. It backfired. We created more disease, more cancer, more diabetes, more heart disease, and overall, worsened the quality of life on this planet. But the real sad thing is that it's too late, it's too late for us. We can't turn around now and say, 'Oops, we goofed, and we shouldn't have vaccinated all of you. We shouldn't have genetically engineered foods and animals.' We can't say that. We'll lose everything if we say that. These little damn viruses. How can they be so strong?

"Then," he said, "chiropractic comes into the picture. We never planned on that either. Never planned on chiropractic offering any solutions. It never even dawned on us. You pissed us off, because you know what? You are right. You are absolutely right. The virus is so damned intelligent that it can reactivate itself after we have killed it and all our fire power is useless. All the drugs in the world won't save us now. This virus eats drugs like candy. Drugs actually strengthen it. So what would work? If the body was so strong that the body itself became resistant. That's why all those ambulance personnel and nurses who survived the first case of HADES made it. It's a miracle that someone even noticed that the similarity among all the survivors was chiropractic.

"And then, the senator calls you in, and you start making all these damn speeches. We knew you were right, and we had to fight you." He went on for another 45 minutes. I was beginning to get dizzy with fatigue.

Suddenly he said, "Ding! Okay, that's all folks. Good thing this heart attack did not affect my brain," and he smiled and extended his hand.

I shook his hand and gave him a big hug. "Thank you, Mr. Larson, for this. I think I'm going to put these tapes in a fireproof safe and send a few copies to some choice TV news anchors."

"You know, Doc," said Larson, "when you see death look you in the face, your perspective changes. I look back at my life and how I ruined my marriage and alienated my children and my friends, and had no life except work. Until now. When I saw the light, and St. Peter standing there saying, 'You aren't ready. Go back and make a difference. Earn your right to come here with us. Try to undo what you have done.' And I think of all the people who are dying right now that could have been spared if I had just spoken out earlier. Even if I had spoken my thoughts as they were developing all this. I kept on thinking, 'This isn't right,' but I kept it quiet, because everyone would have thought me to be bonkers. You can't have a conscience when you do this stuff. I'm sure I'm not the only one who had these thoughts. Now, I'll be the only one opening my mouth."

"You did the right thing, Mr. Larson," I said and added sarcastically, "and thanks for not hurting me and my family."

"Hey, that's your smart planning, Doc. Motorcycle gangs and Marines were not expected to be guarding you."

"Believe me, I didn't expect any of this. I'm just a chiropractor."

"You *were* just a chiropractor. Now you're an evangelist. A crusader. A missionary. A visionary. How did you ever get involved in this anyway?"

"God knows."

"Yes, he does. Now go home to your family, Gary. Go to sleep, then get to work."

"Your whole life is different now that you're on our side," I said.

"Hey, speaking about your side. How about one of those adjustments you've been talking about on TV?"

So I adjusted him, and he smiled a happy smile and said, "This is what I've been fighting all these years? I must have been nuts!"

"No, you were in the dark ages. Now you've seen the light."

Chapter 19

Saw the light, all right. The last three weeks went by faster than the speed of light. I sent the video tapes of the Larson interview all over, but no major news station covered them.

Interestingly enough, Larson disappeared from the hospital a few days after I met him and has not been heard from since.

I'd been busy adjusting, and adjusting, and adjusting. Running from 7:00 A.M. until 9:00 P.M. practically non-stop, all day, every day. We chiros had all been pretty burned out since the previous Saturday when the latest death toll figures still were climbing as rapidly as ever. Thousands dead, possible millions with the disease. But my own patients told me, "Don't worry. Just keep your head down, keep adjusting, and you'll see the results."

Dr. John and I spoke often and he told me some good news about the fifty hospitals the chiropractors were in, about how the death rate from HADES was actually dropping there. The problem was that more and more people were coming in with HADES so they couldn't even keep up and had no idea when they could leave the fifty major hospitals. Another bit of news that week was that none, "And I mean zero," he said of the hospital staff in the fifty hospitals that got adjusted came down with HADES.

But then, five weeks after the challenge by the President and less than a week before chiropractic's birthday, the news came in. Headlines with bold, huge print. Every TV station and radio station interrupted with this broadcast:

"HADES death rate slows down."

Instead of the exponential increase that had happened every week for four weeks since I had spoken to the President, instead of every week hearing, not a doubling, but practically a squaring of how many people were dying, the death rate that week was only a small increase from the previous week! Of course, the NMA was saying that this could be the calm before the storm, or how it could be an aberration so don't get your hopes up yet, and some other such really positive remarks, followed by how the vaccine was almost ready.

That night, I turned on the TV for the first time since it all had started. On WBC News, Dave Davidson (the anchor who had interviewed us during our video conference a few weeks ago), said this, "From undisclosed sources we have found that HADES might be linked directly to covert government operations that have gone awry." Then he showed a brief clip of Larson with his face blurred intentionally and his voice changed, talking about how the vaccine had run amuck in the clones. They showed a map of the United States and showed the ten areas most affected by HADES. These ten cities were named by Larson as where the clones had been placed.

There was a buzz of excitement in our patients that day. "Did you hear the death rate is slowing down?" I was asked all day long. And in an interesting side note, they also asked, "Why wasn't chiropractic mentioned?"

"I don't know," was my answer to that one, "I couldn't tell you why." Except I knew there were still some powerful forces out there against chiropractic. However, they knew it was working and they were scared to admit it or let anyone else admit it.

Another common question I was asked was, "How is it possible for a vaccine to start all this?"

My answer would always be, "Vaccines are man-made poisons. You tamper too much with perfection and eventually it catches up with you."

I had to limit my answers to a sentence or two since I only spent a minute with each patient now, if that much. A little longer with new ones, although at this point, we weren't seeing many new patients because almost everybody in the country was getting adjusted.

Dr. John told me great news today in a brief phone call. He said, with the exception of the rural areas and some prisons, and smaller hospitals, practically the whole country was being adjusted! Over 90%! When the death rate drops, he said, they'll spread out to the rural areas and other places.

"Awesome stuff, isn't it?" he'd said excitedly.

"Yes sirree," I'd answer, but weirdly enough, not with the usual vim and vigor I normally possess. During the previous few days, I had been feeling a little tired and was worried that I was getting what the profession called, "Chiro overload cold." In other words, weeks of high stress, high volume of patients, long hours, and not enough sleep, eventually weakens your own immune system, no matter how many adjustments you get. It seemed that every chiropractor I knew was getting the problem now, and why should I be any different?

I finished up a big Saturday at six o'clock, and I knew I was in for it. I stopped at Dan's for an extra adjustment. He was sniffling, too.

"Jeez, I'm tired," he said. "I'm sure glad we got good news today, because I was getting a little frustrated at doing all this for nothing." Dan was my height but double the muscle and with a well-trimmed beard.

"Amen, Dan. I did feel like we were working in vain for awhile. Wait till next Saturday, you'll see the death rate will either plateau or even drop. I just know it. Right now, though, give me the best adjustment you've got."

"Every adjustment is my best adjustment, Gary."

"Good comeback. Now quit the self-confidence kick, and adjust me, will you?"

"Do any of your patients ask you why you don't take any drugs for symptoms like this? Sometimes I feel like they just don't get it."

"Yes, but you have to admit it's a hard concept to understand. It took a major catastrophe like this for the public to finally jump on the bandwagon of chiropractic. But I think having no choice than to wait for a vaccine or to go to the chiropractor made it a simple decision. Why wait and risk getting HADES?"

"Yet, if a patient of yours was to get a cold, they also have an immediate choice. Is that what you're saying?"

"Yes, Dan. The patient with a cold like mine or yours could say, 'Either I can take this pill and feel better immediately, or I can wait and get adjusted first and let my body do the work?' The patient with a better understanding and a little patience would chose the way of the adjustment. The others may not and pop a pill. But that's okay. At least if we've got them here in the office, we have a chance to educate them."

"Yeah?" laughed Dan, "When? We don't have much time to talk to anyone these days. Getting to know their names is a task in itself, let alone educating them."

"You know, you are right, Dan. You are so right." We had finished adjusting each other and were standing in his waiting room. "We need to teach our patients why this is all working and how chi-

157

ropractic is not a HADES cure, but a better way to live, a healthier way to live."

I sneezed loudly and ran for a tissue. Then Dan sneezed and I gave him a tissue as I sneezed again. "See now, the adjustments are really working," said Dan. "You need some rest, kid. Go home, eat some dinner and get some sleep."

"Yes, sir, Sergeant Dan. When do we get to go on leave, sir?" I asked in a military-like tone.

"In the middle of the invasion of Normandy, did the soldiers take vacation breaks?"

"Good point. Suck it up, soldier! Right, Sergeant?"

"You got it. Now get back to work and clean the mess hall."

"Gee, thanks, you're all heart. Remind me to sneeze on your head a few times."

"That's it, soldier. You're headed right for a court martial."

"Yeah, yeah, yeah. But first you've got to catch me. Bye, Sergeant Dan, thanks for the adjustment."

We hugged each other and laughed at the absurdity of it all.

"When all this is over," said Dan, "and we're back to normal times, let's go out for coffee or something?"

"Okay, I'll take the 'or something.' You've got a deal."

And he opened the door to his office and stood frozen, looking down the barrel of a shot gun.

Chapter 20

"You Dr. Dan?" asked a truly southern accent.

"Uh, yes. Can I help you?"

I was standing right next to the door at a point where I wasn't visible. I saw Dan motion with his eyes upward and I looked over my head and saw the alarm system control panel. I quietly lowered the little protective window and pressed the police button, as Dan and the southern stranger were exchanging pleasantries.

"I got the first signs of HADES. Sweating, shaking hands, all that crap. You know, 'cause you're a doctor, ain't ya?"

"I'm a chiropractor," said Dan. "Want an adjustment?"

"No, that shit don't work. That's a lie. I've been going to chiropractors all my life and I've still got this thing. It's gonna kill me, ain't it?"

"I don't know. When's the last time you were adjusted?" asked Dan.

"A couple of years ago. Shit feels good for a few minutes, then good is gone. Shit didn't work."

I heard him cock the gun.

"Well, uh, not if you do it that way. You've got to get adjusted regularly, especially now. What you did a few years ago is okay, but it's not going to help you during this crisis."

"Ah, bull. I'm living proof. Actually, I'm dying proof. Don't work for beans."

"Listen, put down the gun. I'll adjust you and we'll see what happens. Some people with HADES get better. You can too, especially since your catching this early."

"Y'all just want more money, don't 'cha?"

The man's voice was getting angrier and the shotgun barrel was shaking like a leaf. "I'm gonna blow all you chiro-liars away. All that I can find, 'till this HADES thing gets me. Serves y'all right."

Just then, the blinking police lights flashed in the driveway as two cars pulled quietly into Dan's parking lot. The man must have turned around to see what was happening, and Dan tackled him by jumping under his shotgun into his midsection. The gun went off and blew the door right off it's hinges. I dove to the floor and then

159

crawled to look outside. Dan had disarmed the man and turned him on his side as the officer was cuffing him. A second officer had his gun pulled and was reading the man his rights.

The officer pulled the guy up by his arms and Dan said, "Wait. Before you take him away, let me adjust him."

The officer looked at him cockeyed. "Okay, Doc. I wouldn't adjust this worthless scum, but go ahead."

"This adjustment might change your life, and certainly might save your life. And any life worth saving is worth adjusting." So Dan adjusted his neck and there was a scene I wish I'd had my camera for. A definite Pulitzer prize winning, Kodak moment. This guy who almost shot Dan is handcuffed, on the edge of his porch on his knees about 7:30 at night. Police lights are flashing and blinking in the background as a police truck pulls up. And there's Dan standing next to him on the stairs, with his hands around his neck, about to adjust him. The ultimate in giving for the sake of giving.

"That's what chiropractic's all about," I thought. "We take nothing away from the body, we put nothing into the body, except for love." Watching that adjustment, I was watching an act of pure love. Dan and his attacker almost in silhouette in front of the pulsating police lights of multiple colors. I know that Dan was thinking to himself, "That bullet could have been for me. It wasn't my time." And there almost appeared to be a halo of white light around Dan's head. Was it a reflection of the police spotlight or not? The adjustment was done in a second, and Dan just walked away, his job done. He came over to where I was sitting on the floor of his waiting room and sat down.

"Thanks, buddy. He could have killed me if it wasn't for you," he said, rubbing his hands through his hair and down his face.

"Heck, I didn't do anything but push a button."

"Exactly what chiropractic is, Gary. That's all you did, but that's all you needed to do to save me. It's the same with adjustments. Chiropractic is like pushing a button on the spine. That's all we need do to save lives. As B.J. says, 'It's as simple as that.'"

"Boy, Dan, that's pretty good. When did you get into reading B.J.?"

"I got scared when all this HADES stuff started to happen, so I said, 'Why don't I just go to the source and start studying?' Like the quote from Dr. Charles, 'Do what you're trained to do.' I just never expected to have a shotgun pointed at my face over this."

"I hear you, Dan. I never expected my office to get set on fire, my Jeep to blow up, or to have a bodyguard protecting my family. Chiropractic is rocking the system right now, Dan. Rocking it to the core. The medical and pharmaceutical establishment is breaking up and breaking down. And they don't know what to do about it, and some people are freaking out. The people have been led astray for so long that they don't know who or what to believe. Who knows? This guy might have been a solo lunatic or tied to the pharmaceutical industry, just like that guy Larson who tried to kill me and ended up being the vaccine informant."

A police officer in a white uniform came in and shook Dan's hand and said, "Is my chiropractor okay?"

"I'm fine, chief. Thanks. A little shook up, but fine. Chief Amato, this is Dr. Gary Adio."

"I thought you looked familiar. Nice work on TV there, Doc."

"Thank you, sir. A pleasure to meet you."

"Now I got to ask you boys a few questions, okay? Dan first."

I excused myself, called Ellen, and told her the latest episode.

"Being a chiropractor is not as safe as it used to be," she said.

"Yes," I agreed, "occupational hazards like this were not in the career pages of the school brochures." I told her I'd be a bit late because now I had to be questioned. She understood, as always.

We all retired into the house (Dan has a home office) and ate peanut butter and jelly sandwiches as we were asked about a jazillion questions.

Finally, close to midnight I was about to leave and I said to Dan, "Hey, my cold is gone! Adjustment or adrenaline?"

"Probably a little of both," answered Dan. "Thanks again for everything."

"That's what friends are for."

As I drove home, I thought about what a different society we lived in compared to the one in which the profession of chiropractic had started. Chiropractic began in 1895 during the height of the industrial revolution. I truly believe that it was given to the planet at the perfect time for four reasons. First, the concept of vitalism, or the idea that the whole body is greater than the sum of its parts, and that the body is governed by an intelligence greater than ourselves, was practically wiped out by 1895. Chiropractic was the only profession to grow large enough, at that time, to keep vitalism and any other vitalistic approach alive.

161

If it wasn't for chiropractic, I believe there would be no other health care choice in this country except medicine, because nothing else would have survived. I even feel that chiropractic is in some way responsible for the development of the environmental movement and the exercise and nutrition movements, because it paved the way for alternative thinking in America.

The second reason why chiropractic came at the perfect time is because this country, during the industrial revolution, was getting very sick. The sweat shops in the early 1900's were a breeding ground of sickness and many people's lives were spared from the 1918 flu epidemic because of chiropractic. Chiropractors were even offered, in certain states, medical licenses because they did so well in helping with the flu epidemics. But, of course, they turned them down.

Third, the industrial revolution was the transitional period between our culture being an agrarian culture and a mechanical culture. That switch caused major health problems because of several reasons. Most people, before the industrial revolution, walked all day and did hard physical labor. This kept men and women in relatively good shape. Plus, they ate relatively well, in terms of low intake of meat, dairy and sugar products (because either they couldn't afford it or the lack of refrigeration and slow rate of transportation prevented people from easily getting this kind of food). However, after the industrial revolution, most people sat or stood at work, thereby eliminating the constant physical exercise their bodies were accustomed to. Meat, dairy and sugar were more readily available to them since it started to be mass produced and refrigerated. This caused a major health shift in this country, as evidenced by a switch, in less than a hundred years, in the number one and number two killers in this country. Deaths due to infectious disease was the most common killer in 1900, as compared to deaths due to heart disease and cancer (both diet and lifestyle related) in the 1990's.

This switch from physical labor and healthy eating to a sedentary lifestyle with a poor quality diet actually affected the health of people's spines. Prior to the industrial revolution, people's spines were much stronger because they did much more physical labor and had so much better quality food with no chemicals, preservatives and antibiotics in them. After the industrial revolution, people's spines suffered from lack of movement, limited exercise, lack of good nutrition and increased stress that the industrialized, mechanistic, money-oriented society precipitated.

Another important health shift was the move away from rural living into urban living, which meant away from fresh air and the pure outdoors to apartment buildings and crowded row housing. This is obviously not a healthy way to live. Research has even shown that too many mice in a small area become less healthy and more violent.

Chiropractic came at a perfect time when all these health factors began to weigh heavily on the American people. Chiropractic began in the heartland of America, in Iowa. And it spread across the country and the world, like nerves emanating from a giant spine.

As I was turning into the driveway, I had the thought that chiropractic really helped the world twice; first from the industrial revolution and the near death of vitalism, and again, a hundred or so years later, from the disease that we now know was created by man to kill man, under the guise of a vaccine.

The next week was the planned introduction of the new vaccine and I was very thankful that the death rate had stopped its rapid climb, so by the next week, vaccine or no vaccine, the death rate should be level or slightly decreased.

I walked in the door and I looked at my beautiful two year old son as he lay sleeping in my wife's arms.

Why would anybody want to put a poison vaccine into such a perfect baby? Why introduce a disease into a baby that has none? I thought to myself as I kissed Ellen hello. I kissed B.J.'s little forehead as Ellen took him upstairs to bed.

Bad enough regular vaccines, I thought, but a HADES vaccine? A virus that mutates itself so quickly? What was that line in *Jurassic Park* by Jeff Goldbloom, when the scientist who created *Jurassic Park* said that the dinosaurs were all females so they couldn't reproduce Jeff Goldbloom said, "Oh, they'll find a way," or something like that?

You can try to stop Mother Nature with a vaccine. You can make it look like it worked by pointing out and saying, "Look, see, there's no more polio, so the vaccine worked." But that 'ain't science.' That's no proof that the vaccine did anything. That's like saying, "My friend sneezed on me when he was sick and I didn't get sick, therefore I'm immune to his cold." You're forgetting about a million other factors.

As a matter of fact, that's one of my biggest problems with vaccines. They are standardized for the average person, so every baby gets the same dose at the same time. That does not take into account that everybody is different. Nobody is the same as the average. Everybody, especially a newborn baby, is completely unique, and to give every baby the same dose of vaccines at the same time of life is outrageous.

Even when utilizing antibiotics (which should be limited to absolute emergencies), the doctor gives you a prescription that's hopefully right for you. But with a vaccine, there is seemingly no thought involved. Everybody gets the same dose whether the baby is boy or girl, just got over being sick or healthy, weighs ten pounds or fifteen, and so on, and so on . . .

Ellen came back downstairs after putting B.J. down to sleep. "Dr. John called at 10:00 PM. I told him what had happened to you and he said it's happening a lot, all over the country. People are not convinced yet. And get a load of this: He said Sunday's paper will read, 'Vaccine trials start tomorrow. One week test run in ten selected rural areas. *STAMP OUT HADES* officially begins the following Monday at all public and private schools.' What are we going to do now? The death rate isn't dropping yet and now the vaccine will look like it's the hero, not chiropractic."

"Hold everything," I said, giving Ellen a hug. "First off, the public has to go get the vaccines. Maybe this week's goal is to somehow get the word out not to vaccinate."

"By the way," said Ellen softly, "ask Dan to go to your place to get adjusted from now on, okay?"

Chapter 21

I woke up without the alarm on the Sunday of the vaccine announcement. Of course, as soon as I pulled up to the office every patient showed me today's front page of *The News-Herald* saying,

"VACCINE TRIALS START TOMORROW"

I was overrun with questions about the vaccine. "Couldn't chiropractic and the vaccine work together?" "Do you think I should get the vaccine?" and, "Are you going to get the vaccine?" and, "What about your son?"

It got to the point where the questions were really slowing me down, especially because I was answering the same question over, and over, and over.

Should I tell my patients flat out, "Don't vaccinate?" I pondered? As the day went on it came to me. The MD's are probably saying, "Don't go to chiropractors, it won't work." Chiropractors shouldn't say, "Don't get vaccinated, it won't work." That's falling into their game. I decided, then and there, to say to everybody, "I'm not getting vaccinated, and neither is my family. That's how I feel, and I know in my heart it's the right decision." I must have said that line a million times all day long, and all week long.

Many patients seemed to be hanging on to the medical model idea of vaccines ridding society of all the diseases. Like Dan said, I can't blame them. That's all everybody's known for years. The truth is that God put the diseases here, so only He can get rid of them. Diseases are here for a reason. Even HADES has a reason. I know, and I know that I know, that injecting this vaccine into everybody will cause massive problems.

Of course, all week every newspaper headline said that the trials in the ten rural areas were going wonderfully. 'Little or no adverse reactions, but it was too early to tell for sure'. It was reported that 100% of vaccinated people were not contracting HADES. Sounded too good to be true.

The senior chiropractor students and teachers did not get to the rural areas until the end of that week. The meds had come and gone by then, with everybody in the area being bussed, or shipped to central vaccination locations.

When the chiropractors finally arrived, they saw a whole different picture than the one in the newspapers. Dr. John declared to me in a Friday night phone call, that it was like a scene out of the *The Dawn of the Living Dead* movie. "Practically a hundred percent of this population was vaccinated in the three or four days before we got here," said Dr. John, who had personally gone into the Appalachian mountains with a group from his alma mater chiropractic college.

"It looks like something came out of the sky and destroyed everybody it touched without touching the buildings."

"But that's not what the newspapers and TV are telling us," I said. "They are announcing major victories and that they will start on the general population next week." I gasped at the thought.

"Okay, first off—Nobody's dying of HADES. So that fact is true. But they're dying. Dropping like swatted flies. Those that didn't die are zombies. Granted, not everybody is dying or dazed, but I'm talking lots—the majority—big amounts. You've got to get your buddy, Rick, whatever-his-name-is, to speak up about this. He needs to come here with me and see it for himself."

"Rick had been doing a great job until recently, hadn't he? Then he sort of dropped out of existence this past week. I'll call him tomorrow."

"Listen, Gary, this vaccine is killing people, just like all the other vaccines ever invented. Only this one is doing it quicker. Somebody's got to stop them. Call him now."

"I'll do it, John."

I called Rick at home, even though it was almost midnight and was probably waking him up. My first try didn't work. I let it ring twelve times before the answering machine picked it up. I just kept on hitting redial, redial, redial, until finally Rick answered the phone.

"This better be damn important," a groggy Rick barked loudly.

"Uh, yup, Rick, it's Gary, I need to talk to you."

"For Pete's sake, Gary, couldn't it wait until morning?"

"No, Rick, it can't."

"Okay, listen. I was pulled off the case. I mean the whole story. I was told by my boss that I was getting too emotionally attached to this story and they pulled me off it. They put some new kid on it who hasn't done a thing about it. I know you're pissed about it, but

I'm sorry. I don't own the paper and I'm not my own boss. But did you have to wake me up, for crying out loud?"

"I'm sorry, Rick, about waking you up. And actually it wasn't about your lack of writing I'm calling about, although I was wondering what was going on. The real reason I'm calling is this: The vaccine trials are killing people and the medical association is not admitting it, and no newspaper or TV station is telling the truth."

Silence. "Rick? Did you hear what I just said? The vaccine is killing people." Silence again.

"How is that possible," said Rick. "for the vaccine to be killing people and for nobody but you to know about it?"

"Okay, Rick, listen. I just got off the phone with the President of the Universal Chiropractic Association, Dr. John McCroy. He is in the Appalachian mountains, at a town aptly named Hope. He called me from his cell phone. He arrived a few days after the vaccine was administered and this is what he told me. People are dying left and right there, but not from HADES. From something completely different, he said. Either they're dying, or people are like walking zombies. He called it, *The Night of The Living Dead.*"

Silence again. "No shit?"

"Honestly, Rick. Will you help us, please?"

Silence. I didn't like this silence stuff. I knew it meant no.

"I want to, Gary. You know I do. But my hands are tied. They've got me covering some environmental issue in Nova Scotia. A gas company, who will remain nameless, seems to have had a few tankers hit each other and they want me to fly up there even though I've never done any environmental reporting."

"Well, tell them about all the people dying in the Appalachian Mountains from a hazardous chemical that was just dumped in there. And tell them that it's probably happening in nine other rural areas, all this week. Like some kind of conspiracy. Just don't tell them it's the vaccination."

"And who should I tell them is the source of this information leak? They don't send me on wild goose chases you know. They send out feelers first, before I get out there."

"I know, I know, I know. What can I tell you, Rick? Please. You're the only one I can count on. I don't know who else there is to turn to. Please, Rick. You've got to help us. Can you help us, please?"

"Oh, jeez. God, I hate that guilt stuff. You used to pull it on me all the time in college."

"Yeah, and it's still good, because it works."

I heard Rick breathe in and out very deeply and click his tongue a few times. "Okay, fine. I'll do it. Let me get some sleep and I'll figure it out myself and call you in the morning. You know, it will cost me my job if I'm wrong."

"I know, Rick, and I appreciate what you're saying. I won't let you down. You've been telling the truth since it all started. Thanks for not stopping now."

"God, Gary, you should have been a politician!"

"That's not nice to say, Rick."

"Oh, get some sleep will you? Don't you ever sleep?"

"Sleep? That's something I swore off when B.J. was born. Wait 'til you have kids."

"Too bad. You're fault for having kids. Good night. Don't call me, I'll call you, okay?"

"Thanks, Rick. You got it."

Chapter 22

VACCINE PRODUCTION POSTPONED.
COULD THIS BE A CHIROPRACTIC VICTORY?

VACCINE TRIALS CAUSE MORE HARM THAN GOOD.
"BACK TO THE DRAWING BOARD FOR MINOR
REVISIONS,"
SAYS THE NMA.

reported by Rick Lord of *The Washington Reporter.*

Just three days after its introduction into the mass population, the HADES vaccination was ordered to be postponed indefinitely. This came after the sweeping proclamation on Saturday: The death rate from HADES has dropped significantly. "We asked the President for six weeks, and he gave us six weeks. Show me the results, he said, and we have," said Dr. Gary Adio, Chairman of the HADES Committee of the UCA. "It's far from over, but this is the first step we've been waiting for and praying for." Dr. John McCroy, President of the UCA, says his statisticians predict six more months based on the new findings. "I'm inviting every man woman and child in the country to get chiropractic adjustments regularly. There are still areas where people aren't receiving chiropractic care, such as rural areas and certain hospitals and jails. Plus there are a small minority of people who are objecting, for one reason or another, to obtaining chiropractic services."

"There's nothing we can do about this," said Dr. Larry Spalding, President of the NACA. "We can't make them get adjusted, and we hope this doesn't create any lingering problems. We are reaching more than 95% of the population so, if one person in a hundred says, no, we move to the next person and go back to them later."

Stern warnings were issued by the NMA, the CDI and two drug companies, both of whom, incidentally, are the only manufacturers of the HADES vaccine. "Let's not jump to conclusions," said the warnings, "that great drop in one week doesn't mean that next week there won't be a sharp rise in deaths," said Dr. Block of the CDI. "The idea of chiropractic adjustments boosting people's immune systems to stop the worst epidemic in history is preposterous."

When asked if he was receiving chiropractic adjustments himself, Dr. Block said, "Yes, but I'm going for my neck and back pain."

Critics or not, it's obvious that something pretty powerful is happening. After uncovering the HADES vaccine coverup in the rural areas of our country in which over 10,000 people, including 2,500 children, died and countless others were marred by an unexpectedly lethal vaccine, and witnessing firsthand the pharmaceutical industry's attempt to keep this secret, I am grateful that our team of reporters infiltrated a heavily barricaded rural town in the Appalachian mountains appropriately named Hope.

It seemed like the plan was to vaccinate these people and then isolate the town. All roads in were blocked off by fallen trees and huge boulders. We had to walk several miles before finding the town of Hope, and as soon as we got there, we knew there was "no hope." It looked like a Wild West ghost town, complete with people dead in the streets, doors open and blowing in the wind, and cars abandoned in the middle of the road. It was then that we called the Associated Press and got them to send out reporters to all the rural areas that had vaccine trials to verify this sight. Each team came back with the same story and we met with the President on Monday. His decision was swift and final and we applaud him for his actions. Incidentally, there has not been one report of any person who is currently receiving chiropractic care who has contracted HADES. This comes from the White House, which said, even the President himself and his staff have been receiving chiropractic adjustments.

"Praise the Lord," I said, "the death rate has dropped! The vaccine was recalled, the vaccine scandal was revealed. Now we can get on with chiropractic," I said to Ellen ecstatically after a long Wednesday of adjusting.

"Everyone was flooding in with a newspaper in hand. This is a major victory, Ellen. I was very, very concerned about the public choosing between chiropractic and the vaccine."

"Or," corrected Ellen, "do both, which couldn't work either."

Just then the phone rang. "God, we get more phone calls around midnight than any other time, Gary. It's all your fault."

"Yeah, like I planned this, Ellen?" I picked up the phone. "Hello, late night at the Adio residence."

"Hello, this is Senator Gallo. I want to, well, semi-congratulate you on a job that is going very well."

"Oh, you're semi-welcome," I laughed.

The Senator chuckled, "Well, like it said in today's paper, it's not over yet. But it's a damn good start."

"Did it say 'damn,' Senator?"

"No, I added it for good measure. We were counting on your chiropractic profession, son. Chiropractic even proved itself worthy of the task in uncovering the vaccine trial situation. I am shocked and appalled that that kind of result was considered an acceptable risk by the vaccine makers. Thank you for helping to reveal that."

"Hey, it wasn't me. That was the Universal Chiropractic Association's rural chiropractic team who didn't get fooled by the knocked down trees and big boulders and 'Road Closed' signs. Good thing they had tremendous trust in the road maps that told them this was the only way into the Appalachian town of Hope."

"Yes, that's true. But now we need you again. Two vaccine manufacturers, BTWS and Replay Technologies, are claiming that they have made minor changes in the vaccine and it should be ready in a week's time. Plus, they claim that it wasn't the vaccine that caused all the death's in the rural areas." He paused. I hate these pauses. "They say it was chiropractic."

"What? That's not possible! Chiropractors didn't arrive until they had left."

"You know that, and I know that, but they are out to prove otherwise. They're going to use the fact that it was mostly students in these rural areas doing the adjusting, and not licensed chiropractors, and put the blame on their inexperience."

"Oh my God! This is an outrage! What do we have to do now?"

"Well, son, you have to come back to Washington next Thursday and testify again. You have to testify when the chiropractors walked into the rural areas, with specific dates, etc. and prove

171

where the chiropractic students were before, so we can show that they can't be in two places at once. Then you have to explain how the vaccine is dangerous and how the country should just stay the course with chiropractic and not let these barbarians poison our people again."

The Senator sounded much more emotional than I was used to hearing.

"Wow, Senator, I didn't realize you were so anti-vaccination."

"Honestly, Gary, I never was until now. You see, my future daughter-in-law's family comes from the rural areas in Arizona and they were practically wiped out by this supposed HADES miracle vaccine. My future daughter-in-law is an American Indian and her family and most of the people on the reservation where she grew up were killed in the worst devastation because of the vaccine in all the ten areas."

"Wow! I'm sorry. Okay, I'll fly in Wednesday night or Thursday morning."

"Don't do anything. There are a lot of people out to get you and Dr. John McCroy from the UCA. We're going to pick you up in a private limousine and fly you both in a military helicopter to Washington next Thursday morning. And don't run into any trouble, you hear? Hire yourself a bodyguard or something."

"Yes, sir. I already thought of that. One of my most loyal patients has been guarding my family around the clock. And I've had a Marine light armored truck parked in front of my office since the hospital situation a few weeks ago, including a couple of Marines for good measure. So I feel relatively well protected."

"Good, son, because now I'm madder than ever, and we've got to get to the bottom of this. So we really need you safe and sound. Until then, keep crackin' them backs."

"Uh, adjusting, Senator. Adjusting. Crack is a drug."

"You're right, sorry—adjusting."

Chapter 23

One week later, as I was about to go to Washington for the next round of debates, I walked to the news stand across from the train tracks and picked up a newspaper to read the headlines.

VACCINE BACK IN ACTION AS OF MONDAY.
THE QUESTION: STAY WITH CHIROPRACTIC OR
SWITCH TO VACCINE?

The smaller sidebar headline read, "Did Inexperienced Chiropractic Students Kill The Victims In The Rural Areas?"

"Amazing," I thought. "They really are going to try to pull this one off," I mused as I walked back home. The limousine was due here in a few minutes. It's just going to be plain embarrassing and humiliating when the UCA proves by airline tickets, daily roster lists and hospital sign-in sheets that the students were nowhere near the rural areas prior to the HADES vaccine introduction. I shook my head and exhaled loudly. "Why would they do this?" I asked.

No sooner did I walk in my front door than the limousine pulled up, complete with a police escort.

"God, this is so out of control," I said to Ellen as I walked in. She had gotten up after she heard me leave earlier than she expected.

"Where did you go? To the news stand?" I guess she saw me holding the paper in my hands. "This morning of all mornings? Are you crazy!"

"Hmmm," I mumbled. "I just wanted to be, ah, prepared?"

"Wrong. Don't do that again. Anyway, have a great trip. Knock 'em dead!"

"Knock 'em alive, you mean, " I smirked. We kissed and off I went into the limousine. At the Teatree Armory, a waiting military helicopter sat with its rotors spinning away.

With little conversation, I was buckled in next to several very tall and very heavily armored military personnel. It looked as if they anticipated a major land-to-air battle.

We took off so quickly that I lost my breath for a second. I closed my eyes as the helicopter banked to the left and I began to feel a little air sick. I tried to get my mind off my impending nausea. I guess the NMA made up their fables to undermine chiropractic's effectiveness, especially now that chiropractors are adjusting close to one hundred percent of the U.S. population. They're grasping at straws and trying to make us look bad in any way they can.

Dr. John told me the day before that some people actually believed the negative propaganda they've been reading in the last week and have stopped getting adjusted. "But," he said, "the report has shown that this is only a very small percentage of the population."

"What will they come up with today?" was my next thought, followed by, "I can open my eyes now. I don't feel queasy any more." I blinked a few times and meekly smiled at the men seated next to me. I couldn't talk with them if I wanted to since the noise from the helicopter was so deafening.

The NMA surely realized at that point it 'ain't gonna fly.' I had no doubt that they had prepared themselves, even though the day's headlines hadn't given me any clue.

I had asked Dr. John to arrange for Seth to come and cover my practice just for today. Seth is a former patient who is now a senior at Southern Chiropractic College. I had to beg Dr. John to fly Seth from a rural assignment in the deep south to help me.

"Hey," I yelled at Dr. John, "you are a seven chiropractor operation. I'm a one-man-show. The least you can do is get him up here. Besides, when this is all over, and he gets his license, I'm going to hire him as my associate."

"Hey, yourself," said Dr. John, "you should have thought of that before. See, not only am I the big cheese, but I've got the staff to prove it."

"Yeah, but I've been on TV more than you have. Ha, ha!" I said to him, like the little boy that I am.

"Oh, shut up. You're bothering me. Well, I've been married more times than you, so there!"

"Well, John, you've got me there. That's one category I'm glad you beat me in."

With that thought, I somehow managed to fall asleep in the bumpy green military helicopter. I woke up just as we were landing at an Air Force base near Washington, D.C. As I walked from the helicopter into a waiting black Town Car, Dr. John was seated inside with his maroon attaché case across his knees.

"Ha! Beat you this time! Are you ready for this one?"

"No," I said, a little groggily after my bouncy, sitting-up sleep. "What's up now?"

"They're going to drop all the accusations they made against the students."

"Really? That's great!"

Dr. John looked at me and shook his head with a very straight face. "You are so idealistic it's scary. Did I say I was done? That's the good news."

"Oh. What's the bad news?"

"Well, those God-damned sons-of-bitches came up with this memorandum issued yesterday by the CDI."

With that, he burst open his attaché case and flung a piece of paper at my head. I caught it just as it crashed into my hair.

"Wow, you are dangerous with paper! Good thing I didn't get a paper cut."

"Oooh, just read it," said an obviously very annoyed Dr. John.

"The CDC now has updated its report of the initial HADES incidents in the ten major cities and has determined that there were *no* survivors from the first contact. The idea that chiropractic patients who were ambulance and medical personnel that survived the first contact with HADES, was a deliberate ploy by the chiropractors to create a dramatic anti-medicine, pro-chiropractic campaign, designed solely by chiropractors for chiropractic financial and competitive advantages."

I sat there and bit my tongue and my breathing completely stopped. "No, way," I muttered, "no possible way. Has Senator Gallo heard this?"

"He's the one who told me about this in the first place. And you haven't even read the next page," said Dr. John, throwing the second page at my head again.

I read:

"Dr. Gary Adio, the chiropractic spokesperson, was the master mind behind this coverup. It was he who made the initial contact with Senator Gallo and the President, and convinced them of the supposed efficacy of chiropractic by arranging to falsify the records of a small number of deceased ambulance and medical personnel to make it appear that they survived. Coroner reports prove that there were no survivors and that all did perish in the first contact, and it was Dr. Adio's influence that created the beginning of the ascension of chiropractic. This was a calculated move on Dr. Adio's part, who was waiting for the right moment to pounce on a vulnerable population. It was alternative medicine's greatest accomplishment until the records were uncovered."

"What records?" I screamed. "I started all this? How do I have such connections to falsify records in ten cities? Besides which, the Senator called me. I was minding my own business when the Senator called me."

"Don't tell it to me, Gary. Save it for later. I just wanted to show you this so in ten minutes when you start getting filleted, you'll know where they're coming from."

"Filleted? What do you mean by that?"

"They're going to try to slice and dice you, Gary. We know that this is a lie. All I can tell you is this: We can't prove that it is. They've got documents and we don't. It's you against them. I wasn't prepared for this. I've got my boys on it right now, but these bastards have had a head start."

Dr. John wasn't looking at me. He was looking off into space with the most forlorn look on his face. He shook his head in silence and pursed his lips, blew a long breath out and said, "We thought everything else was the test and we passed it. Now we're back to square one." He shook his head and closed his eyes. "You better hope for some divine intervention, kiddo. I hope you're a believer."

"I am, John, but what's He going to do now for us? What more can He do? Hasn't He done enough already? How much more can I ask of Him?"

"Hmmm," Dr. John smirked, "one more, okay? Ask for one more."

We rode in silence from then on. I decided not to think about this and what I was going to say. I just flat-out prayed.

"God," I began silently, "you sent me to a chiropractor when I was 20 and my asthma and allergies were getting out of control. A miracle occurred and you healed me and showed me a whole new path to follow for my life. So I took the road you mapped out for me and I met Ellen and fell in love. Now I have two loves, my family and chiropractic. I struggled after I graduated, but you showed me the path again. Dr. Charles has guided me with his wisdom since chiropractic school and reopened my eyes when I was struggling in the early years. He helped me remember why I had become a chiropractor in the first place. The Chiropractic Beginning Weekend in New Jersey has transformed my life by giving me constant support of my strong beliefs in chiropractic, along with lasting friendships and camaraderie. Dr. Charles' path, and the Chiropractic Beginning Weekend helped form a new vision—a higher purpose for my life. With these two foundations in place, Ellen and I latched on to the GFC philosophy—God, Family and Chiropractic.

"Then this, all this. I never wanted to be here. I never asked for this. But You thought I was ready, and so, here I am. I thought that chiropractic did it. The whole country began to get adjusted. The death rate is going down, the vaccine has been stalled. What can I do now? I can't do this alone, God. I know I'm supposed to thank You in advance for that which I believe will occur, but I thought I already did that. This is approaching the final buzzer, God. We were neck-in-neck and pulling ahead. Inch-by-inch we were one stride, then two strides, then three strides ahead. But our momentum wasn't enough, was it? The race isn't over yet. We still have to run another lap before the finish line."

A tear came to each eye as I saw the Capitol building in the distance. I said the watchword of the Jewish faith, called the "Shema," which means, "Hear" or "Listen." And then, after saying, "Amen," I said with every ounce of strength and conviction I had, out loud, "Thank you, God, for helping the truth today be victorious. The truth. The truth has prevailed. You have sent us a sign and have caused the other side to back down. We are Your humble servants. Thank You for our eloquence today. Thank You for our victory, for chiropractic's victory, for the people's victory. Amen."

"I hope you are speaking the truth, Gary," said Dr. John, as we abruptly stopped a block from the Capitol.

"Why are we stopping here?" I asked the driver.

"Follow the Secret Service," the man in black glasses replied.

We stepped out of the limo and three very tall and broad men in black suits, mirrored sunglasses and microphone ear pieces, escorted us into Chen's Chinese Laundry Shop, which looked just like any other dry cleaners when we first walked in. But, when we went to the back behind the thousands of hung up garments in plastic bags, we saw a huge surveillance system set up and a door that led to the basement. Of course, this was no ordinary basement, but a long tunnel that we traveled through for about five minutes until we came to a stairway leading up. Nobody said a word. We just followed the big guys in dark suits.

The next thing I knew, we were in a hallway in the Capitol building that I vaguely remembered from my first visit. And voilá, here we are at the Senate chambers. And there's my buddy, Dr. Block. The memorandum from the CDI that I'd just read wasn't from him, but I knew he'd had a hand in it. The smirk on his face as he greeted me from his roost set the stage for the Senate's investigation committee.

After the initial mumbo jumbo and assorted Senatorial necessities were over, Dr. Block assumed his role and began to rip into me as though I had torn the head off his favorite Raggedy Andy doll.

"So, Dr. Adio, how do you feel now? About two months later with your chiropractic profession in the seeming 'catbird seat,' as James Thurber once said."

"I don't understand the question, Dr. Block," was my reply.

"Okay, let me put it more bluntly, Dr. Adio. You practically singlehandedly have created chiropractic to be the savior of the world, and now have most of the country going to get their bones cracked."

"Adjusted, Dr. Block. The word is 'adjusted.' Bones don't crack. Besides, crack is a drug, and we don't use any drugs in chiropractic."

"Right. So you have almost 90% of the country receiving chiropractic care and with this massive increase of patients you have, I dare say, a relatively substantial increase in income. Isn't that true?"

"Obviously, yes. There has been an increase in the financial realm. But only because there is an equal exchange of value-added services. Even though we are providing a life saving service, we are receiving only a modest fee per patient, since we are adjusting all people, regardless of financial ability or condition."

"Okay, so even if it's only a modest increase per patient, would you say that the numbers of patients have so dramatically increased that the total amount of increase is actually quite significant?"

"If you're implying, Dr. Block, that the reason this occurred is because we wanted more money for chiropractors, then you are out of your mind," piped in Dr. John.

Dr. Block smiled again. "And you are?"

"Dr. John McCroy, President of the UCA. You must be Chief Financial Officer of the CDI. Is that your title, doctor?"

"No. I am Dr. Block, Medical Chairman of the Senate Committee on Health and Human Welfare and the head of the CDI."

"Oh, sorry. You're concern about money had me thinking you were an actuary, or something," said Dr. John. He was in rare form today.

"Ah, yes, a comedian," Dr. Block said. He opened his briefcase, took out a large binder, slammed it down and opened it to the first few pages. "Yes, Dr. Adio, I have here in this notebook a complete listing of all the ambulance and medical personnel who had first contact with the clones who had contracted HADES. Do you know what kind of reports they are? Coroners' reports. And do you know what's interesting about them? There were no survivors who had initial contact with HADES. None. Zero. Zilch. Now, isn't that fascinating? Where did you get this fictitious story that the only survivors in each city were people under regular chiropractic care? Hmmm, Dr. Adio?"

"I think you have your facts wrong, Dr. Block. Why would top government officials tell me otherwise during the start of this whole thing? Or are you implying that I somehow had a hand in doing this?"

"First off, Dr. Adio, I don't have any facts wrong. I went to great expense to find out this information. How come we have never seen or heard from these fictitious survivors? Where did they go? Did they just vanish?"

"I haven't a clue, Dr. Block. I'd like to know what all this is leading to, because I have some questions for you."

"Oh, yes. I guess I should just hurry up now, shouldn't I. Wouldn't want to waste any of your precious time that could be earning you such copious amounts of money. This is all volunteer work right here, you know."

"Get to the point, Dr. Block. What are you insinuating? As if we don't already know" barked Dr. John. He was like a hungry dog seeing a piece of steak. Practically foaming at the mouth.

"Okay, here's the point. You, Dr. Adio, and you, Dr. John McCroy, deliberately falsified the records in order to create a huge advertising campaign for chiropractic. To take advantage of a very vulnerable American public during a tremendous crisis for the sole benefit of advancing chiropractic and especially for financial gain. You took advantage of a weakened public morale and created the most successful marketing campaign ever in history, where now almost every American has been forced to be subjected to unnecessary and dangerous chiropractic treatments. Just for your professional and financial gain."

Dr. Block yelled out this last sentence and it echoed over and over again in the chambers. Dr. John and I looked at each other.

"First off, Dr. Block, you know you're lying. I know you're lying. We all know you're lying," I began.

"I am not lying, and I take offense . . ." Dr. Block interrupted.

"Shut your mouth and sit down," I yelled in a voice that was not even my own. It came from some inner recess of knowing that I spoke the truth. "You listen to me and you've got ten seconds to act on it. Look at the American public. The death rate is going down. It is going down without a vaccine, but it's not going down by itself. It's going down because chiropractic is keeping this country alive. You know this to be true, and you can't take the truth. The fact is that you botched up and that your clones, and your clones' vaccines created all this. You are just trying to pass the buck.

"Who cares, even if what you said was true, which it is not. You started all this and then you have the gall to try to push a vaccine on the public that was made from the vaccine you already gave the clones. And you call this science? I call this treachery. I call this playing God. Chiropractic is working and you are not in control. You are shaking in your boots, and you will try anything to get us.

"You set fires at thousands of chiropractic offices. You tried to kill me by blowing up my Jeep and by having an assassin try to stalk me who eventually told me everything. And I have his word on tape to back me up. You tried to fool us into thinking that the vaccine trials were fine, when thousands of people either died or were rendered catatonic by the vaccine. You blamed the deaths and injuries on the chiropractic students, and then you rescind this and don't even have the decency to say, 'I'm sorry.' You dragged me and my colleague out of our offices, where we should be adjusting, to dump more lies on us? You've got ten seconds to back down or this video tape goes on and you and your profession go down in the history books, next to Richard Nixon going down with Watergate. One . . ."

"Dr. Adio, your methods are unprofessional and . . ."

"Two . . ."

"I will not tolerate this sort of behavior. You are a madman and . . ."

"Three . . . "

"Dr. Adio, the evidence I have here is incriminating beyond reasonable doubt . . ."

"Four," I stood up.

"It has your name, and your signature on document after document," said Dr. Block. He stood up again.

"Lies! Five."

All the Senators and other people were watching us and nobody wanted to stop us. Dr. Block walked from his position at the head of the table and pulled his microphone with him. He came face to face with me.

"Six," I glared at him.

"Dr. Adio, I have no choice but to do this, since obviously the evidence is incontrovertible proof of your guilt."

"Seven."

"Guards," yelled Dr. Block and, out of nowhere, came four armed police officers.

"What the hell do you think you're doing?" Dr. John jumped up and ran in between me and the police officers. "Nobody's going anywhere until they pass through me."

Dr. John, at 6' 4" was a formidable solid brick wall.

"Now hold on, gentlemen. This is the Senate chamber." Senator Gallo jumped into the middle of all this. "You must behave like professionals and this has gone too far. Everyone take your seats, including your rent-a-cops that you somehow conjured up from your outrageous budget. Now!" he yelled, and we all slowly returned to our seats. The police officers remained standing to my right.

"We are supposed to be conducting a hearing on the efficacy of chiropractic and the need or lack of need for the introduction of the vaccine. This display of hostility was a little overwhelming at first, but I thought I'd let it go to see how it played out. However, this behavior is uncalled for."

"Sir, with all due respect, I have overwhelming evidence here that Dr. Adio ordered these records and documents to be falsified in his own very unkempt and sloppy handwriting."

"What? Impossible! I never knew anything about this until I came down to Washington. It was here I first heard discussed the possibility of chiropractic saving the lives of ambulance and medical personnel who were in the original . . ."

"Bullshit, Dr. Adio! You were waiting for this moment to happen and then jumped on when it did. Chiropractic has been praying for this for years because otherwise medicine would have swallowed you up and diced you in two. This was the only way out and you knew it, and you took advantage of it. You and your Errol Flynn colleague next to you."

Senator Gallo pounded his hand on the table and I swear the whole room shook.

"Enough!" the Senator yelled. "This is enough. This committee is in recess until . . ."

"Until when? Until your little chiropractic underdogs can come up with another ploy to lie to you and the President? Who are you going to trust, Senator? The CDI, the most influential and important medical institution in the country, or these two quacks?"

Dr. John bolted out of his chair and jumped across the table. He picked up the desk that Dr. Block was sitting at and threw it across the room. The four police officers came charging toward Dr. John with their weapons pulled.

The Senator was banging his shoe, like Kruschev did years ago, screaming, "Order! Order! Order!" when suddenly a gun shot rang out and a light fixture in the far corner of the room blew out. We all turned around to see the President holding a smoking shotgun.

"Now that I have your attention," he said. We all just stared at him. About 20 Secret Service men in black suits surrounded him. "Oh, you don't have to stop just because I'm here," he chuckled to himself as he and his circle of bodyguards made their way down the stairs into the center of the room.

"Oh, and you boys down there with the guns? I suggest you put them away. I'm the only one allowed with a gun in this room, being the President and all," and with that he clicked the shotgun and a discharged shell fell clunking to the ground as another shell was ready to fire.

"I was a marksman in the Marines many years ago. Still got my skills, after all these years."

The policemen surrounding Dr. John had holstered their weapons and backed off as the President and his men came closer.

"Everybody take your seats. I have an important announcement to make. Several, actually. Oh, and guys, let the press in please."

I saw Dr. Block go white as he slumped back in his chair. The doors opened in the back and dozens of cameras, reporters and TV camcorders piled into the room, Rick included. The entire back and side of the room, within minutes, was lined with reporters and cameras armed and ready to write and film. The chambers were deadly silent. Frozen in a moment of time was the President, standing at the podium with his bodyguards still around him at the back of the room. In front of him were the doctors from the CDI and other dignitaries and a space which now contained the desk which Dr. Block had been sitting at, overturned with its contents strewn across the floor. Next was the short row of tables at which I sat next to Dr. John, Senator Gallo and some of the other Senators. Behind us were the committee members and practically the whole Senate filled the rest of the chairs in the room. And then all the news people.

The President stood at the podium and just gazed around the room, as if waiting for the right moment to come to start off his talk. The shotgun he had discharged was still smoking on the podium in front of him.

"Dear friends, Senators and fellow Americans. A diabolical plot has recently been uncovered and I am embarrassed, as an American citizen, to admit this could possibly happen in this great country of ours. I'll keep this short, sweet and to the point so we can all get on with our lives.

"HADES is a biological warfare creation that somehow became contaminated in a new, powerful vaccine that was being tested on human clones. All those responsible for creating HADES and the contamination have been arrested, and the two companies, one of which created the HADES virus and the other which created the vaccine, have been permanently closed down. Methods of destroying the contents of their buildings are being finalized. Unfortunately, thousands of Americans have perished over the last few months because of this dangerous playing with human chemistry. The creation of clones was under top secret orders to have no outside tampering. We just wanted to see how they could be used in a covert military setting. The vaccine was not part of the originally planned program. Once the clones had received the vaccine that was unknowingly contaminated with the HADES virus, it was just a matter of time before the virus spread.

"Dr. Block, you've been a good ally to my Presidency and even my senatorial campaigns for many years, and for that, you have my appreciation. However, we have reason to believe that you knowingly allowed the contaminated vaccine to be used because you wanted to keep to a deadline and have the first human clones working before any other country did. I believe you were not aware of the fact that the vaccine used for the clones was contaminated with the HADES virus, but nonetheless, instead of waiting for a clean vaccine, you decided a few months was not worth the wait in the military race for supremacy and hence, with your signature and stamp of approval, you let this happen. For that, I will strip you of your position at the CDI and recommend that you lose your medical licensure and charge you with treason of the highest degree.

"But, being that I am the President, and I have the power to do this, I hereby exercise my option to pardon you of the treason charges. I've always wanted to do that, and now I did.

"Now the good news. Chiropractic. Thank the Lord for chiropractic. I have to thank Senator Bart Gallo for putting one and one together and having the good sense to call Dr. Gary Adio after noticing the minutest detail of all the records that surrounded the initial HADES contact, the fact being that the only survivors of the first contact with the virus were chiropractic patients. For whatever reason, I heard that some people think there were no survivors, but that is not true and I'll prove it to you. Bring them in."

The back door opened again and one by one, thirty men and women walked toward the podium where the President was standing. One by one they went to the microphone, stated their names, the hospitals where they worked, and all of them said, "I was saved from HADES by being a chiropractic patient." After the last one spoke, the President continued.

"Thank you, my friends, for coming forward on this important day for your country." He began clapping, and the next thing you know the entire auditorium was clapping and cheering. After a few minutes of this, he motioned everyone to stop and sit down, so we all followed his orders. He really captivated his audience.

"Senator Bart Gallo, it is an honor to call you a friend, and I am proud to say that I am going to nominate you for the Congressional Medal of Honor for outstanding service to your country." The crowd erupted again in thunderous applause. He motioned the Senator to stand, which he did.

The Senator almost shyly nodded his head, waved his left hand, picked up a microphone and said, "God bless America. God bless you, Mr. President. And thank God for chiropractic." The applause heightened, and I couldn't believe how this many people sounded like a huge stadium. Finally the applause died down and the Senator took his seat.

"And the best news of all, ladies and gentlemen, is that, as of today we have seen an almost 50% decrease in the deaths from HADES and, unbelievably, over 50% decrease in new HADES cases. And we owe this all to chiropractic. Thank you, chiropractic." He once again started clapping, and the crowd cheered like crazy. The President motioned for Dr. John and I to stand, so we did and the applause went to almost deafening pitch. Finally the applause started to die down and John and I sat back down.

"It's not over yet, my fellow Americans. We must keep on getting chiropractic adjustments. At this point almost every man, woman and child in this country has received an adjustment. An 800 number will flash across your TV screen and will be in every major newspaper tomorrow morning for all those people who want to receive chiropractic adjustments but have not done so already. We've coordinated with Dr. John McCroy, President of the Universal Chiropractic Association, for teams of chiropractors to travel to areas of most need. We also now have chiro-mobiles, thanks to an idea from a chiropractor from New York, which will travel to nursing homes and private residences for people who are not able to get out of their house or nursing home.

"Television has created a new era in communication. Recent presidents have used TV to their advantage to help win presidential elections, and my new friend, Dr. Gary Adio, a chiropractor from New Jersey, is also tapping this medium to get his message across. I know we still have a long way to go, son, but it looks to me as if we are over the hump. My researchers say that HADES should be contained within three to four months. If and only if, we Americans, myself included, continue to receive chiropractic adjustments on a regular basis.

"My fellow Americans, three months ago when Bart and I first sat down for a briefing about HADES, I thought I was going to be known in the history books as the president who watched his entire country perish. Even though the losses have been staggering, especially in ten cities where the clones were first introduced, I see now that we have been very fortunate.

"Because of chiropractic, and only because of chiropractic, and a little help from its friends, Senator Gallo and I, the death toll has been minimized. Instead, I'll be known as the president who took the bold initiative. I'll be known as the president who made one of the hardest decisions of the 1990's, and that is to steer away from the tradition, away from the norm, away from what so many special interest groups were telling me, and chose the right path. Not just the correct path, but the right one. It would have been very easy to do what everybody else said I should do. Everybody said, 'Don't take a chance on chiropractic,' but I wondered, when all this first began, if chiropractic was only for back pain, how could it have survived this long? There must have been something more to it. If it was only for back pain, I truly believed chiropractic would have died years ago. It would have been taken over by the medical profession. But it's fought for over 100 years to stay separate, and now I know why.

"Chiropractic reminds me of America's humble beginnings. Imagine a tiny nation of a few scattered people, deciding to fight for its own independence against the strongest, most powerful nation in the world. Imagine Thomas Jefferson, and Ben Franklin, and John Hancock, and George Washington, and all the others sitting and saying, 'Yeah, I think we can beat them. We have no army, no navy, no organization, no training. They have the best equipped, best trained, most organized army and navy in the world. We can take them, because we have one thing that they don't have, and that's the will.' And, as one of those elder statesmen said, 'Either we will all hang together or we will surely hang separately.' As is obvious, they accomplished the impossible. Well, it seems, so has chiropractic.

"One thing you were right about, Dr. Block, is that chiropractic has been waiting for this moment, and they seized the opportunity, just as our ancestors did in the American Revolution. Against all odds, these chiropractors, for 100 years fought to stay independent and when HADES reared its ugly head, they set down their own Declaration of Independence and said, 'This is the way to safety and freedom.' Just like the American's Declaration in 1776. Yes, lots of lives were lost, then and now, but if it wasn't for chiropractic, who knows how many millions upon millions of lives would have been claimed.

"They singlehandedly, and I mean that literally as well as figuratively, have done the impossible. Yes, Dr. Block, chiropractic has won this battle. Now it's up to the chiropractic profession and the medical profession to work out a peaceful coexistence. It's obvious that chiropractic is far more valuable than most of us once thought.

But, and I stress this very highly, I expect a more amicable relationship between the two professions than what occurred after the American Revolution.

"What do I mean? Well, one mistake I believe was made by the early American pioneers was to destroy the American Indian population. We could easily have lived in peace with their beautiful nations, but instead we chose to conquer. Now I feel we are ushering in a new era as well as a new millennium. It is time for us to work on higher goals and aspirations of self service. It is time for us to transcend to a higher place of consciousness. To all work together for the common good of America. It is time to think about the best possible help for my country which ranks number 84 in overall health of the top 100 industrialized nations. My fellow Americans, we can and will be number one again, once chiropractic and medicine begin to work together and not separately, towards achieving the optimum health care for every citizen in this great country of ours.

"How do I know that we have to do this? Two quotes from Albert Einstein will tell the tale. 'We cannot solve higher problems with the same solution that got you to the present level.' And, 'Once a mind has been stretched, it can never return to its original form.' In other words, the thinking that got us into the present mess will not get us out of it. We need new, bold, higher thinking. And that's where chiropractic came in. Even more importantly, now that we have had a taste of the new thinking because of chiropractic, we can never go back to the old ways again.

"In conclusion, my fellow Americans, let us continue getting chiropractic adjustments, and let us start this new path today. Right now. This very moment. Within three to four months, HADES will be under control and if we keep up this pace we will have in our hands a new America. Come with me, America, on a new journey. On a journey towards new freedoms. On a journey where you and I and everyone around us can be healthier and happier than we've ever been. It is all in our hands. Thank you. God bless you. And God bless America."

Epilogue

It was four months after the President's speech which interrupted every single TV and radio station in existence. Just a few days ago, the President went on TV again announcing that HADES was now labeled by the NMA and the UCA as being contained. Notice I said the NMA and the UCA together. A new partnership had been forged.

There are still pockets of outbreaks here and there, mostly in inner cities and rural areas, but there was no real fear of spread. The entire country was now under chiropractic care on a once a week basis, and this safeguarded every adjusted person's immune system.

"As long as we keep on getting adjusted, we'll keep healthy," said the President in his speech.

It was truly a whole new world. Rick and I had just walked from the Capitol building where we had the final hearing in front of a joint session of Congress. We had secured a small grant for every practicing chiropractor. The session began with a call to follow the President's further recommendations to establish a committee on chiropractic and medical cooperation. Next was the announcement by Senator Gallo of the lowering of the status of HADES from epidemic to disease, which brought on a twenty-minute standing ovation. Finally, a call by the President to open fifteen more chiropractic schools was issued and a waiver of the state boards for all students who participated in Operation F-Troop was requested, so that these young chiropractors could come out and practice with the just slightly overwhelmed chiropractors in the field.

"It's nice to laugh again, Rick. I've got to tell you," I beamed as Rick and I sat eating lunch in a Washington, D.C. restaurant.

"It is, Gary. That it is. Those early days of this HADES thing really kicked my butt."

"You aren't kidding," I replied.

Rick looked at me for a moment in silence. "Fascinating how we've hooked up again after all these years."

"Sure is, Rick. If it wasn't for your constant push for the truth and push for the headlines, I don't know if we could have pulled this off."

"Hey, one good turn deserves another. You gave me evidence, I printed the truth. Now I'm up for a Pulitzer Prize for Excellence in Journalism. It was worth the leap of faith. But I've got to tell you something, Gary. I've been getting some puzzling phone calls lately."

"What do you mean, Rick?"

"Okay, well, it's like this. A few days ago an ex-hospital administrator calls me and says he was fired from his job because he began to notice that there were less surgeries being performed, less hospital admissions, less cancer, less heart attacks and strokes, and he was told to shut up and keep it all quiet. But he didn't. He said he felt that was all due to the new chiropractic department of the hospital adjusting every patient. He was looking at the ordering records and noticing that they didn't need as much new equipment and drugs per month. The hospital was performing less surgeries and having less severe health problems. So he spoke up and he was canned.

"Then there was an ex-jail warden from some high level prison who called me. He said he was fired after continually commenting on the excellent behavior of the inmates since they were getting regularly adjusted. He kept on suggesting to give the inmates less sedative drugs and allow them more freedoms, and he was fired too.

"Then I get a call from an ex-head of a major psychiatric hospital, who says he began noticing less admissions lately and an even less need for serious psychotropic and sedative drugs for his patients since they were getting regular adjustments. He was even noticing how some cases that used to take months to be relieved are now being relieved in a few weeks. And he noted all this occurring since chiropractors began to be on staff. But guess what—he was fired.

"And then," Rick continued excitedly, not letting me get a word in edgewise. "I've been getting all these calls from priests, ministers, rabbis and all kinds of clergy saying that people are coming to churches and temples in record numbers. Not just to give thanks for deliverance out of this mess, but actually becoming members. All over the country, every denomination possible, churches and temples are flooded with new praying, paying people. What do you make of all this?"

I sat there in utter joy. B.J. Palmer's words had come true. Empty the hospitals, jails and asylums. Fill the churches and temples. That's what he had dreamed about. If only the whole world would be adjusted and become free from subluxation. I just sat there and smiled.

Rick smiled back at me, cocked his head slightly to one side, and said, "Is all this possible because of chiropractic?"

My eyes widened as I grinned from ear to ear. I only wished that B.J. Palmer, the developer of chiropractic himself, were here to witness this. But then again, I guess he is.

B.J. Palmer had written so many books on chiropractic. Each one of them stood alone, but in a series, you couldn't help but notice the common theme running through each 300 to 600 page text: A better world is possible when you unite man with his infinite possibilities. He had predicted this, now it came to pass.

Rick and I had been staring off into space for a while, each of us thinking, pondering, wondering. He broke the silence.

"Hey, this would make a great book, don't you think?" he asked.

"Yes," I said, pensively, "yes, it would."

"Let's start it right now, together," Rick said. "What do you want to call it?"

"Hmmm? How about, *The Adjustment?*"

THE END

Chiropractic Resource Directory

For information on a referral to a chiropractor in your area, contact:

Chiropractic America
call toll-free 1-888-52-HEALTH
or visit their website at http://www.chirousa.com

For general information about chiropractic, contact:

International Chiropractors Association
1110 N. Glebe Road
Arlington, VA 22201
Voice: 1-800-423-4690
Fax: 703-528-5023

For more information on chiropractic seminars, contact:

1. New Beginnings for a New Future Philosophy Weekend
   c/o Jim Dubel, D.C.
   410 Pine Street
   Red Bank, NJ 07701
   Call 732-747-4646, or visit their website at
   http://www.newbeginningschiro.com

2. Dynamic Essentials Seminars
   1269 Barclay Circle
   Marietta, GA 30060
   Call 800-233-5409, or visit their website at http://www.
   lastingpurpose.com

For more information on chiropractic schools, contact:

1. Life University, School of Chiropractic
   1269 Barclay Circle
   Marietta, GA 30060
   Call 800-543-3398, or visit their website at
   http://www.life.edu

2.   Life Chiropractic College West
      2005 Via Barrett
      P.O. Box 367
      San Lorenzo, CA 94580
          Call 800-788-4476, or visit their website at
          http://www.lifewest.edu

3.   Sherman College of Straight Chiropractic
      2020 Springfield Road
      P.O. Box 1452
      Spartanburg, SC 29304
          Call 864-578-8770, or visit their website at
          http://www.shermancsc.org

For more information about vaccinations, contact:

National Vaccine Information Center
512 Maple Avenue West, Suite 206
Vienna, VA 22180
    Call 800-909-SHOT, or visit their website at
    http://www.909shot.com

An Invitation . . . . .

To share *The Adjustment* with others, you can order directly using our toll free number, fax number or e-mail. Discounts are available for quantity orders.

Call 1-877-3-ADJUST (toll-free)

e-mail: rubinchiro@aol.com

Fax the order form below to 201-569-5561

Visit our website at: theadjustment.com

Price List: Prices are per book for the following number of copies on the same order:

Number of Books	1	2—9	10 or more
Cover price	$19.95	$19.95	$19.95
Discount	0%	20%	40%
Price per book	$19.95	$15.96	$11.97

Call us for bulk dealer and distributor discounts

Shipping: Book rate: $3.20 for the first book (USA - priority shipping)
$0.75 for each additional book up to 10
call for price quote on 11 or more copies
(International shipping prices vary)

6% Sales tax: NY & NJ only

ORDER FORM

Name: _____

Address: _____

_____

Phone Number: _____ E-mail:_____

Fax Number: _____ # of Books: _____

Credit Card #: _____ Expiration Date_____

Signature: _____

195

Clip and FAX

An Invitation . . . . .

To share *The Adjustment* with others, you can order directly using our toll free number, fax number or e-mail. Discounts are available for quantity orders.

Call 1-877-3-ADJUST (toll-free)

e-mail: rubinchiro@aol.com

Fax the order form below to 201-569-5561

Visit our website at: theadjustment.com

Price List: Prices are per book for the following number of copies on the same order:

Number of Books	1	2—9	10 or more
Cover price	$19.95	$19.95	$19.95
Discount	0%	20%	40%
Price per book	$19.95	$15.96	$11.97

Call us for bulk dealer and distributor discounts

Shipping: Book rate: $3.20 for the first book (USA - priority shipping)
$0.75 for each additional book up to 10
call for price quote on 11 or more copies
(International shipping prices vary)

6% Sales tax: NY & NJ only

ORDER FORM

Name: _____

Address: _____

_____

Phone Number: _____   E-mail:_____

Fax Number: _____   # of Books: _____

Credit Card #: _____   Expiration Date_____

Signature: _____

Clip and FAX

About the Author

Drew Rubin is a chiropractor with a large family practice in Cresskill, New Jersey. He graduated from Life Chiropractic College in Marietta, Georgia in 1989. His wife, Lisa, and three-and-a-half-year-old son, Palmer, provide the source of his inspiration. This is the first in a series of three novels that deal with the emerging trends in health care for the new millennium. He is available for workshops in your area, (call 1-877-3-ADJUST).